SIBLING LOVE AND INCEST
IN JANE AUSTEN'S FICTION

Sibling Love and Incest in Jane Austen's Fiction

Glenda A. Hudson
Professor of English
California State University

palgrave
macmillan

Published in Great Britain by
MACMILLAN PRESS LTD
Houndmills, Basingstoke, Hampshire RG21 6XS and London
Companies and representatives throughout the world

A catalogue record for this book is available from the British Library.

ISBN-13: 978-0-333-75207-4 (paperback)

Published in the United States of America by
ST. MARTIN'S PRESS, INC.,
Scholarly and Reference Division,
175 Fifth Avenue, New York, N.Y. 10010

ISBN 978-0-312-23215-3 hardcover
ISBN 978-0-312-21113-4 paperback

Library of Congress has cataloged the hardcover edition as follows:
Hudson, Glenda A., 1959–
Sibling love and incest in Jane Austen's fiction / Glenda A.
Hudson.
p. cm.
Includes bibliographical references.
ISBN 978-0-312-23215-3
1. Austen, Jane, 1775–1817—Knowledge—Psychology.   2. Brothers
and sisters in literature.   3. Sex (Psychology) in literature.
4. Incest in literature.   5. Love in literature.   I. Title.
PR4038.P8H83   1992
823'.7—dc20   91–22292
                                               CIP

First edition 1992
Reprinted (with new preface) in paperback 1999

This book is printed on paper suitable for recycling and made from fully managed and
sustained forest sources. Logging, pulping and manufacturing processes are expected
to conform to the environmental regulations of the country of origin.

10   9   8   7   6   5   4   3   2   1
08 07 06 05 04 03 02 01 00 99

To my brother Gary
and
my husband Edwin

Contents

Acknowledgements

I owe more than I can express to John Halperin. Above all, I am grateful to him for his unremitting inspiration and advice, his *savoir-faire par excellence*, his immense generosity with his time, and his great tact and sense of humour. I am also very grateful to Edwin Barton, my best friend and critic, for his encouragement, moral support, and remarkable insights, as well as his liberal and painstaking help with all drafts of this book. Roy Gottfried, James Kilroy, Laura Mooneyham, Jack Prostko, Frederick Schneider, and James Stathis also provided invaluable comments on this project. Cliona Murphy, Janice Kirkland and Lorna Frost gave expert help and advice. Thanks to Vanderbilt University and California State University, Bakersfield, for supporting my research on and writing of this work. I also extend gratitude to the following publications for permission to reprint parts of this book which appeared as follows: '"Precious Remains of the Earliest Attachment": Sibling Love in Jane Austen's *Pride and Prejudice'*, *Persuasions*, 11 (December 1989) 125–132; 'Mansfield Revisited: Incestuous Sibling Relationships in Austen's *Mansfield Park'*, *Eighteenth-Century Fiction*, 3 (Fall 1991).

GLENDA A. HUDSON

References to Jane Austen's Works

References to Jane Austen's works are to:

The Novels of Jane Austen, ed. R. W. Chapman, 5 vols, 3rd edn (London: Oxford University Press, 1932–4).
Minor Works, ed. R. W. Chapman (London: Oxford University Press, 1954).
Jane Austen's Letters to Her Sister Cassandra and Others, ed. R. W. Chapman, 2nd edn (London: Oxford University Press, 1952).

List of Abbreviations

PP	*Pride and Prejudice*
SS	*Sense and Sensibility*
NA	*Northanger Abbey*
MP	*Mansfield Park*
E	*Emma*
P	*Persuasion*
MW	*Minor Works*
Letters	*Jane Austen's Letters to Her Sister Cassandra and Others*

Preface to the 1999 Reprint

Since the initial publication of this book, a tide of 'Austenmania' has swept over popular culture. Film versions, television series, internet sites, and new editions of Austen's works have proliferated. The surge of interest is fascinating to contemplate as a cultural phenomenon. Still, many wonder why should Austen's novels so flourish at the end of the twentieth century? Her works were well-established as part of the canon of English literature during the twentieth century, part of Leavis's 'great tradition'. Nonetheless, she was regarded by some commentators and readers, especially in the early part of the century, as a writer who was limited and even trivial in her range. Nowadays, the precise limitations and demarcations of her fictional world are exactly the qualities that pique the interest of the audience. From the standpoint of the amorphous, fluid society of the late twentieth century, contemporary readers and viewers look back with nostalgia or cynicism on the hierarchical definitions and distinctions of Austen's period. In particular, Austen's works draw attention to the function of the family and to gender roles at a time when the institution of the family and the culturally-constructed roles of men and women are in radical transition in our own society. Far from being trivial as some earlier commentators asserted, the depth, complexity, and expansiveness of Austen's work have been highlighted by the recent wave of popular curiosity.

In her novels, Austen responded to the fictional formulae of her time, adapting and ameliorating them as she saw fit. She dealt especially with the subject of family relations and the eighteenth-century fictional obsession with incest. In 'When We Dead Awaken: Writing as Re-vision,' Adrienne Rich comments, 'We know more than Jane Austen because our lives are more complex, more than Shakespeare because we know more about the lives of women – Jane Austen and Virginia Woolf included.'[1] In some senses, of course, Rich would seem to be right. But she perhaps fails to consider the extent to which we have sacrificed an awareness of the complex collateral ties of family and kinship so relevant to the lives of women *and* men in Austen's period. To ignore these dynamics, which have now become so attenuated that we sometimes seem barely capable of appreciating them at all, is to elide the possibility that in many ways we know far less than Jane Austen did. For Austen's variegated vision of the family in her fiction affects all her characters, issues, and themes in the texts. If, as Rich suggests, deconstructing gender and familial roles has enabled us to 're-vision' them, we may yet appreciate the subtleties of relations between men and women, siblings, cousins, parents, daughters, and sons that Austen reveals, not only with insight but also with humor, wit, and grace.

Allegations about Austen's own family relations have recently caused much controversy. Terry Castle's article entitled 'Sister–Sister' in the *London Review of Books* alleges that incestuous feelings existed between Jane and Cassandra. In her review of Deirdre Le Faye's edition of *Jane Austen's Letters*, Castle fueled a heated debate by alluding to what she termed Austen's erotic attraction to her sister Cassandra and 'homophilic fascination' for women in general in both her life and literature. Castle's article was highlighted on the cover of the journal with the title, 'Was Jane Austen Gay?' – an assertion that enraged many readers and commentators.[2]

To be fair, Castle's argument was blown out of proportion, even misinterpreted by numerous analysts. Whatever one may think of Castle's claims about the 'unconscious . . . homoerotic imperatives'[3] of Austen's letters and fiction, her article made a serious point and helped to reinforce arguments I had made in my book several years earlier. For example, Castle comments, 'It is a curious yet arresting phenomenon in the novels that so many of the final happy marriages seem designed not so much to bring about a union between hero and heroine as between the heroine and the heroine's sister.' Moreover, she notes that Austen's letters reveal 'the passionate nature of the sibling bond.'[4] These are exactly the focal points in this book, although I focus on brother-sister relations as much as sororal relations. Castle notes that 'Austen's heroes are often more like sisters than lovers in the conventional sense'; to be sure, her lovers are like sisters, but, more importantly, they are also like brothers. Moreover, the type of incest I refer to is different from the kind that intrigues Castle; the incestuous unions I analyze are not sensational unions but a series of reactions to popular works of the time. Austen undercuts clichéd formulae of best-selling works of her period by mitigating the melodrama of the incest motif in her work; however, at the same time, she refashions the motif to highlight the significance of family ties and to consolidate masculine and feminine values. Such innovations in Austen's work place her at the vanguard of fiction in her own time. These innovations concerning the province of the family and balanced gender roles are also partly responsible for the contemporary popularity of and interest in her novels.

Over the past five years, a number of critical works have renewed cultural attention to incest and to all manner of familial relationships, functional and dysfunctional, in British fiction, including Jane Austen's. In this preface, I highlight and expand briefly on my earlier arguments in light of recent research.[5] In particular, I focus on Austen's subtle handling of gender politics in her presentation of ideal egalitarian relationships based on fraternal qualities. In reassessing my own arguments, I have found Anne Mellor's *Romanticism and Gender* (1993) helpful. She argues that the idea of community in the writings of Wollstonecraft, Austen, Edgeworth, and Mary Shelley emphasizes cooperation and 'promote[s] a politics of gradual rather than violent social change, a social change that extends the values of domesticity into the public realm.'[6] For Mellor, Austen espouses a value system grounded in a belief in 'women's capacity for intellectual and moral growth, in the desirability of egalitarian marriages based on rational love and mutual esteem, and in the prototype of domestic affection and responsibility as the paradigm for national and international relations.'[7] I elaborate on Mellor's argument by demonstrating the ways in which Austen's sibling-like unions promote the concept of a relatively coequal and gender-free community, in which the sterling attributes of both men and women predominate, and women are valued as much as men.

Maaja Stewart's *Domestic Realities and Imperial Fictions: Jane Austen's Novels in Eighteenth-Century Contexts* (1993) offers another interpretation of the family in Austen's work. Stewart analyzes the struggle for mastery in Austen's novels of the eldest son and his younger brothers 'who return after a circuit in international trade . . . to contest the supremacy of their hitherto privileged brother.'[8] While Stewart's book offers some significant insights, its focus on political and economic realities tends to downplay Austen's aesthetic and moral vision. Stewart notes, for example, that women are affiliated in Austen's texts with younger brothers because they are both displaced by primogeniture; she goes on to argue that moral terms have 'gender-specific connotations,' and that 'female domesticity and virtue' are used to camouflage male belligerence in the texts.[9]

Such arguments, though persuasive politically, fail to take fully into account Austen's visionary quality in her depiction of unions between women and younger brothers, such as Fanny and Edmund and Emma and Mr. Knightley. For Austen, 'equality' is a historically specific term. In the absence of any political equality for women and a limited franchise for men, she posits a system of relations between individuals based on a hierarchy of moral values. For Austen, the ideal relations between men and women are relatively equal in terms of the available options. In short, these relations are the best that can be attained in her day, and they project a vision of a progressive utopian society.

Consolidating both masculine and feminine values, the organizations of brothers and sisters at the end of Austen's novels redefine and counter the conventional marriage prescription. While many passages seem to suggest that male values embrace stewardship and responsibility, and that female values encompass fidelity, gratitude, and compliance, Austen implies that both men and women need to possess all of these qualities. In Austen's novels, specific moral values are not segregated to a particular sex; males are not sole keepers of male values, nor women of women's. At the close of her novels, a new type of domestic configuration is presented that places paramount importance on cooperation and communal responsibility. For her part, Austen modulates the significance of sexual difference in her fiction and sets forth a type of gender equality that counteracts the notions of dissimilarity and disproportion. Moreover, for Austen, this type of egalitarian relationship between quasi-siblings suggests that only the family, not the state or public sphere, can solve the problems experienced by men and women.

In a sense, Austen's notion that only families can solve such problems inadvertently contributed to Victorian formulations of separate spheres and the 'angel in the house' constructs in which many have identified a lack of freedom for women. These relations were certainly not in effect in Austen's day, but it is both compelling and poignant to note that her novels proffer a vision of social redemption that ironically paved the way for Victorian domestic constrictions and constructions. Unlike Victorian successors, Austen argues that private virtues such as sympathy, tolerance, and magnanimity should guide all public action. Victorian literature may be seen as a regression from Austen's more enlightened stance. As Mellor notes, it was 'a backlash in which female intelligence, activity, and power was once again *restricted* to the arena of the domestic household.'[10] In viewing the writers of the Victorian period from the point of view of late twentieth-century feminism, Austen's forging of a new utopian community based on fraternal qualities seems even more revolutionary. Indeed, the recent popularity of Austen's works attests to a contemporary interest in a fictional world where separatism was not the aim, and where moral distinctions preponderated over arguments about difference between the sexes.

NOTES

1. Adrienne Rich, *On Lies, Secrets, and Silence: Selected Prose, 1966–1978* (New York: W.W. Norton, 1979), p. 176.
2. Terry Castle, 'Sister–Sister,' *London Review of Books* 17 (3 August 1995) 3–6.
3. Castle, p. 6. On this subject, see for example, Eve Kosofsky Sedgwick, 'Jane Austen and the Masturbating Girl,' *Critical Inquiry* 17 (Fall 1991) 818–837 and Misty G. Anderson, '"The Different Sorts of Friendship": Desire in *Mansfield Park*' in Devoney Looser (ed.), *Jane Austen and Discourses of Feminism* (New York: St Martin's; Basingstoke: Macmillan, 1995), pp. 167–183.
4. Castle, p. 3.
5. Portions of this preface have appeared previously in 'Consolidated Communities: Masculine and Feminine Values in Jane Austen's Fiction' in Looser (ed.), *Jane Austen and Discourses of Feminism*, pp. 101–114.
6. Anne K. Mellor, *Romanticism and Gender* (New York: Routledge, 1993), p. 3.
7. Mellor, p. 52.
8. Maaja Stewart, *Domestic Realities and Imperial Fictions: Jane Austen's Novels in Eighteenth-Century Contexts* (Athens: University of Georgia Press, 1993), p. 23.
9. Stewart, pp. 36, 74, 106.
10. Mellor, p. 212.

1
Introduction

Children of the same family, the same blood, with the same
first associations and habits, have some means of enjoyment in
their power, which no subsequent connections can supply; and
it must be by a long and unnatural estrangement, by a divorce
which no subsequent connection can justify, if such precious
remains of the earliest attachment are ever outlived. Too often,
alas! it is so. (*MP*, p. 235)

This proclamation, embedded halfway through Austen's fourth
novel, makes a direct assertion, remarkable in its candour, about
what seem to her the truly extraordinary qualities of fraternal love.
Austen insists that, above all, siblings have the ability to recollect
experiences common to both and to retrace each former pain and
pleasure together. Indeed, for Austen the common mythology and
instinctive understanding of siblings is a great 'strengthener of love,
in which even the conjugal tie is beneath the fraternal' (*MP*, p. 235).
And so we should not be surprised to find that in Austen's novels
married love often appears to lack the advantages and power of
fraternal or sororal love: that is, except when those who marry
bring to their union these same qualities of sibling love that Austen
ratifies.

Although all of her works conclude with one or more marriages,
every Austen novel, as well as some of her Juvenilia, explores
the bonds of brothers and sisters, both exemplary and worthless
siblings, for their own sake. Indeed, each novel highlights the
magnitude of sibling ties as much as or more than marital ties,
and, in several cases, these seemingly distinct characteristics of
love prove to be wholly related. To be sure, the pivotal conflict in
each work is that between the hero and heroine. But, in half of the
novels, *Mansfield Park*, *Emma* and *Sense and Sensibility*, the leading
couple possess family ties and treat each other throughout most

1

of the novel more like siblings than lovers. Austen focuses on the operations and stratagems of kindred – the balance of their relations with each other, the joint and conflicting values and interests within the family, and the responsibility (in some cases abdicated) for each other's moral welfare – with a very particular purpose in mind. For her complex manipulation of the domestic arena throws light on much broader social and cultural contexts.

While it has become commonplace to assert Austen's deeprooted 'conservatism', critics have not yet done justice to the dynamic way Austen employs sibling relationships to negotiate within and to critique the complex ideology presented in her fiction. Austen endorses the qualities of endurance and effectiveness and condemns irresponsibility, abeyance of guardianship, and frivolity. Her ideal community is therefore a kind of meritocracy, founded on the values of competency, charity, and usefulness.[1] Individuals from both the gentry and the professional classes (such as naval officers) may gain admission to this ideal group, providing that they have the kind of qualities designated by the author as desirable. More importantly, Austen embodies her moral vision by presenting a reenergized and vindicated family circle at the end of each of her novels. And she portrays this family circle as an innovative social and moral power-base that closely resembles a fraternity or community of brothers and sisters, constituted either by actual blood relatives or by individuals having relationships that closely imitate those of blood relatives.

These sibships, as we may call them, embody a literary as well as a social innovation. Based on mutual respect, individual worth, and shared beliefs and concerns, they herald a new dimension in the English novel to the extent that they are relatively egalitarian societies. Members cherish and serve their confederacies, endeavouring to be useful and vigorous, assisting each other to the best of their ability. In *Pride and Prejudice*, for instance, Darcy even helps the unworthy Wickham to rise in his profession for the sake of Elizabeth and Lydia; Elizabeth reciprocates by acting as mentor to Darcy's sister, Georgiana, who resides with the newly married couple. In *Sense and Sensibility*, Colonel Brandon and Marianne, in their positions as master and mistress of Delaford, are able to promote the interest of their sister and brother, Elinor and Edward, at the parsonage on their estate. And how fitting it seems that Marianne should have the means and influence to benefit the sister who so generously watched over and counselled her. In *Northanger Abbey*,

Eleanor Tilney cajoles her father into consenting to the marriage of her beloved brother Henry and good friend Catherine. At the conclusion of *Mansfield Park*, Sir Thomas acknowledges the power of the group of siblings and cousins at Mansfield, particularly as it is constituted by successful, sensible members, 'all assisting to advance each other' (*MP*, p. 473). *Emma* closes with an idyllic vision of 'a small band of true friends' (*E*, p. 484); two brothers, George and John Knightley, marry two sisters, Emma and Isabella, consolidating sibling attachments 'which would have led . . . them, if requisite, to do every thing for the good of the other' (*E*, p. 100). Even *Persuasion* is no exception to this rule. Anne attaches herself to Wentworth's brothers and sisters as well as to the fraternity of the navy; however, she regrets that she imports no valued siblings of her own into these fraternal communities.

Each of the novels, therefore, concludes with the promise of a domestic circle which supports and defends the sanctity of home. Liberated or distanced from inferior family members and purged of irredeemable interlopers, the rejuvenated fraternal institution is a superior mechanism, one that may even seem farfetched. And yet Austen's endings are by no means conventional mythical resolutions; the dream-like triumph of the sibship has been hardwon and stands in striking opposition to the cynical depiction of the self-serving machinations of discreditable family members earlier on in the novels. The metamorphosed community of brothers and sisters epitomizes the values Austen would have us affirm – values she implies that must be applied to achieve progress in the future.

By the early 1800s, what Lawrence Stone terms 'the closed domesticated family circle' had been progressively formed. In middle- and upper-class English society of the late eighteenth and early nineteenth centuries, sibling relationships – brother-sister, sister-sister, and brother-brother – were generally stronger, more lasting, and more insulated than those of succeeding eras.[2] Such distinctive relationships originated because even in close families, parents were apart from their offspring for long periods during the day, leaving the children in care of servants, nurses, governesses, and tutors. Among the upper echelons of society, some parents handed over their children's upbringing almost entirely to other people in order to attend to politics or business or to do the rounds of fashionable society. Distanced from their parents physically and also psychologically because of the generational gap, siblings came to depend on each other for amusement and companionship. Moreover, since families were larger and parental love distributed between numerous offspring, siblings had another reason to seek attention and affection from each other, even in some cases to act *in loco parentis*. Whereas childrearing habits were generally authoritarian and disciplinary in the seventeenth century, they became more child-oriented, affective, and lenient during the eighteenth century among the upper and middle classes. These more permissive modes evolved owing to the popularity of a flourishing cult of sentiment and feeling as well as the spread of Enlightenment ideas, particularly the curb imposed on man's brutal or violent treatment of other human beings. But, towards the end of the century, certain families of the landed and professional classes, especially in the provinces, returned to stricter methods of childrearing because of the growth of Evangelicalism. Believing in the innate evil of human beings, some parents subjected their offspring to corporal and psychological hardships in order to break their will and to inculcate in them the necessity of self-discipline and humility. These hardships took the form, for example, of daily immersion in freezing water or threats to lock up a child for hours or days if he or she was naughty. In such a repressive household, children banded together with their siblings in search of consolation.

Special relationships between siblings also evolved because family members lived in close proximity to each other during a greater portion of their lives. It was not unusual for devoted sisters to share bedrooms, even the same bed, as children and as adults; Jane and Cassandra Austen, for example, shared the same bedroom all of their lives, even when there were plenty of bedrooms at their disposal (as at the house at Chawton). Likewise, brothers were sometimes the closest of friends, despite the rivalries created by the exigencies of patrimony. Transportation was slow, and people travelled less. If families or individual members left home it was usually to visit relatives or to go to a major town, unless they were very rich, in which case for the most part only the sons went abroad. People's horizons were limited not only geographically but also socially. They were expected to confine their socializing to members of their own class. Middle-class parents often warned their children not to mix with working-class children for fear that they might learn vulgar habits or catch diseases. Likewise, they were told not to play with upper-class children lest they become idle or lax in morals. The social and geographical insularity of the home especially in country families frequently meant that a child's friends and playmates consisted solely of siblings and cousins. As a result of isolation from the outside world and contingency to each other, siblings often developed intense bonds, which were not merely biological or legal contracts but powerful and developing ties siblings were expected to honour and cherish throughout their lives, and Austen documents this in her novels.

In her concern with the family and her depiction of the home as, ideally, the haven of domestic bliss, Austen anticipates Victorian attitudes. For middle-class Victorians, home was the last bastion of morals, a refuge from the debasement of the changing world and from war and revolution; it was regarded as a sacred place, a safe mooring resisting the buffeting and upheaval of external terrors.[3] The mid-century writings of such authors as Dickens, Trollope, Eliot and Ruskin reveal the primacy of this belief in much Victorian thought. But while Austen presents a domestic haven in the shape of the harmonious sibship at the end of her novels, she also exposes the discordant elements of home: the jealousies and rivalries, indolence and irresponsibility, cruelties and uncharitableness, backbiting and avarice of siblings. Intimacy and contingency, after all, also have the potential to breed rivalry and hatred. As Austen points out in *Mansfield Park*, the love between siblings, 'sometimes almost every thing, is at others, worse than nothing' (*MP*, p. 235). Brothers of Austen's class often competed for money and property, as Francis and Charles Austen did in the Navy. And sisters were sometimes bitter rivals for suitors. Indeed, vicious sibling rivalry materializes in every Austen novel, disrupting familial and social circles, even creating scandal. In Austen's novels, loyalty and affection between brothers and sisters become crucial to the advancement and immunity of the family. Rivalrous sibling relationships cripple the natural order of the family and may debilitate the siblings' capacity to accomplish their proper roles in the community. Austen regards conflicts between brothers and sisters as hazardous, since they threaten the order of family life, which she sees as analogous to the stability and harmony of society.

The final synthesis toward which Austen moves in her presentation of siblings emerges from a recognition of the positive and negative forces at work within such relationships. Mary Evans has claimed that Austen is no idealist, that she 'resists the ideological temptation of presenting the family as a "haven in a heartless world"'.[4] In some cases, Evans's argument certainly applies: we need only think of the chaos of the Price household, the stingy selfishness chez the John Dashwoods, the iciness of the home of the Elliots, and the intense sexual rivalry of Maria and Julia Bertram. But Evans overlooks Austen's creation at the close of all her novels of ideal family communities, built of core groups of sibling mentors and students of moral fibre, who, the author implies, will coexist harmoniously and guide each other through life, and who represent spiritual and moral hope for the future. Indeed, Austen's juxtaposition of the harsh realities of family life and the visionary quality of the sibships is crucial because it greatly enriches her art. Out of this tension between the idealistic and more nearly realistic depictions of the family, Austen creates complex textual intricacies. Moreover, by offering the family circle as a microcosm of broader concerns, she expands her vision to offer deft criticisms of the political and social scene.

Combative and quiescent sibling relationships elucidate Austen's view of contemporary affairs. Austen surveyed the shifting world around her with a gimlet eye. Indeed, V. S. Pritchett has meetly described her as 'a war novelist, formed very much by the Napoleonic Wars, knowing directly of prize money, the shortage of men, the economic crisis, and change in the value of capital'.[5] Two of Austen's brothers were officers in the Royal Navy; she had family connections with Warren Hastings; and her cousin Eliza de Feuillide's husband was guillotined during the French Revolution.[6] At the end of the eighteenth century, Englishmen, including members of the Austen family who were frantic Francophobes, reacted with terror to the devastating upheaval wreaked in France by the Revolution. French radicalism invaded England in the form of Jacobinism and led to widespread xenophobia and fear of rebellion. During the Napoleonic Wars, England struggled to maintain the balance of power and to arrest France's waxing military power on the continent. France repeatedly threatened to invade England and encroached upon her holdings in the West Indies. Given these conditions, home was fiercely guarded as a sanctuary of peace and security, a retreat from the contamination of strife and disorder.

For those who have learned to find in great novels a concise history of an age, Austen supplies economic insights as well. Most English people in the early 1800s still worked the land, but over the next thirty years more than half became involved in industry. In parts of England, enclosure had made agriculture more productive, but as a result a great deal of the countryside now belonged to affluent individuals who let the land to tenant farmers; subsequently, many of the old smallholders became landless agricultural laborers. A less duty-bound class of gentry arose in some cases, which gained its profits from trade and finance. Commercial and manufacturing interests disrupted the rural peace and structured feudal society of an earlier age. New attitudes were prevalent in England – ambitious, self-serving, acquisitive, cynical, irreverent, and, above all, critical of the traditional rural way of life.[7]

Austen's presentation of sibling loyalty, sibling rivalry, and the incestuous unions with which some of the novels end reveal her concern with preserving the sacred inviolability of the home in a time of upheaval and social change. Her narrative devices embody her ideology. A centripetal movement develops in most of Austen's novels, emphasizing her protectiveness *vis-à-vis* corruptive outside influences, a tightening of familial ties in an attempt to maintain traditional values in a rapidly changing *fin de siècle* world. Several of the works conclude with relationships that can be called incestuous in that they are kept within the family. In many cases, dangerous outsiders are expunged or excluded, and marriages take place between in-laws and first cousins who have fraternal bonds. These marriages are meant to protect and fortify the home and consolidate the family residing in it. There is no suggestion in Austen's novels that the pool of eligible spouses be expanded or broadened. Hers was a conservative temperament.

A major structural device in the novels is the campaign to promote, secure, or engender sibling ties. Moreover, the fates of siblings are often connected. For example, in *Pride and Prejudice* the relationships between Jane and Bingley and Elizabeth and Darcy dovetail, and the novel ends with a double marriage. *Sense and Sensibility* also concludes with a double marriage, and Marianne's husband closely resembles Elinor in attitude and temperament. Even more important for Austen is the idea that conjugal love should be patterned after fraternal love, that the perfect marriage should be like the ideal sibling relationship with its shared trust and understanding, love and esteem, high regard and loyalty, and that the partners should come not only from the same social circle but also, if possible, from the same family.

If the sibling relationships dictate the dramatic structure of Austen's works, so too the structure subtly reveals Austen's attitude toward the precedence of brotherly and sisterly relationships and her vision of the role of the family in society. Fraternal rather than sexual love preponderates in Austen's fiction, and, in many regards, the romantic scenes are domestic scenes. Charlotte Brontë evidently disregarded Austen's depiction of sibling love when she made her famous pronouncement, 'the Passions are perfectly unknown to her'.[8] To be sure, Austen omits details of lovers' tender encounters, usually providing a brief summary of the couple's declarations of love and agreement to marry. But in scenes describing the love of siblings, she provides direct access to the rapturous thoughts and passionate, heartfelt feelings of the characters. Moreover, Austen demonstrates repeatedly that the moral and intellectual instruction among siblings defines their moral progress as individuals, especially during their formative years as children and adolescents.

By focusing on Austen's presentation of siblings, one may begin to read her novels in a new way, and to see her endeavours in them to express her vision of an ideal society. If her stories sometimes resemble fairy tales, the reason may be precisely this: they are based on the actual world as she knew it, but they reach toward the world as she envisioned it. And yet, Austen's works are by no means merely the products of fancy. Without exception, she grounded them in the reality she knew and the practical wisdom she understood so well. Indeed, in the area of sibling relationships, which is our focus, the seeming fantasies of incestuous love and marriage are intended to provoke moral awareness rather than elicit immoral daydreams. And Austen's moral vision must enter into our examination; for, above all, her fiction asserts that relationships, sibling as well as romantic, should be taken seriously.

2
Antecedents and Successors

Three of Austen's novels end with marriages that have incestuous overtones. In *Mansfield Park*, Fanny and Edmund are first cousins; moreover, they have been brought up as brother and sister in the same household. In *Emma*, the heroine marries her brother-in-law, Mr. Knightley, who throughout much of the novel shares a fraternal relationship with her. In *Sense and Sensibility*, Elinor, like Emma, marries her brother-in-law, Edward Ferrars. And in the same novel, Colonel Brandon tells Elinor the story of his desire to marry Eliza Williams, a sister-in-law brought up as his sister.

In presenting such endogamous relationships, Austen was following a pattern well-established in English novels of the eighteenth century. The literary legacy passed down to Austen was laden with undercurrents and instances of brother/sister incest – incest evaded, suggested, or committed. Moreover, the obsession with such forbidden love was not limited to particular subgenres of the novel or to specific ideologies; it crossed boundaries, emerging in reactionary and radical works, in gothic, sentimental, parodic, conventional, and innovative novels. Indeed, the incest motif crops up in so much of the literature of Austen's period (especially in English Romantic poetry of the early decades of the nineteenth century) that it becomes almost a formula, even a code. Although Austen scorned and endeavoured to avoid the conventional methods of a great deal of popular literature, she exploited the fashionable topic of incest, the hallmark of numerous contemporary works, and challenged, metamorphosed, and transcended the subject. Instead of generating an entropic vision of society, or creating a sense of fear and chilled fascination in the reader, Austen's incestuous unions are, for the most part, positive and therapeutic. The marriages of consanguineal relatives such as cousins and of close affines are metonymic; that is, they stand for Austen's carefully wrought system of moral and intellectual discrimination.

In order to define the nature of incest in Austen's novels, it is

9

necessary to consider the powerful fraternal relationships between her characters and society's conception of the relationships. In *Totem and Taboo*, Freud comments on the prohibition of incest in ancient tribes:

> . . . exogamy linked with the totem effects more (and therefore *aims* at more) than the prevention of incest with a man's mother and sisters. It makes sexual intercourse impossible for a man with all the women of his own clan (that is to say with a number of women who are not his blood-relatives) by treating them all as though they *were* his blood-relatives. It is difficult at first sight to see the psychological justification for this very extensive restriction, which goes far beyond anything comparable among civilised peoples. It may be gathered from this, however, that the part played by the totem as common ancestor is taken very seriously. All those who are descended from the totem are blood-relations. They form a single family, and within that family even the most distant degree of kinship is regarded as an absolute hindrance to sexual intercourse.[1]

Freud stresses the great sensitivity of the tribe to incest, and how it replaces blood-relationships with 'totem kinship'. He goes on to suggest that the linguistic usage in totemic communities is also relevant to a consideration of incest, since the terms used by members of a tribe to refer to each other do not imply so much a relation between two individuals as a relation between an individual and a *group*. Thus, a man might use the word 'sister' not only for his blood sister but also for all the other women who may be considered his sisters according to tribal law. In this way, the kinship terms used by tribal members do not necessarily indicate any consanguinity but instead represent social rather than blood relationships.[2]

Although, as Freud points out, such extensive taboos do not exist in civilized society, it is nonetheless clear that in Austen's time some of these prohibitions, whether conscious or unconscious, existed in an attenuated form. In eighteenth-century England, marriage between first cousins, though authorized, was often discouraged. Middle-class and aristocratic families were aware of the taboo at least to some extent. In Austen's novels, the lingering and attenuated taboo surfaces, for example, when Mrs. Norris says near the beginning of *Mansfield Park* that it is 'morally impossible' (*MP*,

p. 6) for Fanny to marry Edmund.[3] Furthermore, marriage between close affines, such as in-laws and step-siblings, was also discouraged and even disapproved of by Austen's society since the individuals involved had previously treated each other as consanguineal relatives.[4] In particular, society regarded marriage to a brother's widow or deceased wife's sister as incestuous. Stories of men desiring a brother's wife thrilled the drawing rooms, especially of London, in the late eighteenth and nineteenth centuries; those belonging to polite society were scandalized by the incestuous implications of such relationships.[5] If Austen is the novelist we depend on to inform us about life in England at the beginning of the nineteenth century, it is worth noting her interpretation of and social attitude toward such endogamous relationships. *Sense and Sensibility* provides a case in point. For instead of being thrilled or horrified by Colonel Brandon's revelation about his attempted elopement with Eliza, the wise and morally responsible Elinor (a character who would seem to represent Austen's ethical standards) is sympathetic; indeed, she condones the incestuous nature of the relationship between Brandon and his adopted sister, who is also his sister-in-law.

If the taboos associated with ancient tribes were less apparent in eighteenth-century England, the notions of kinship in Austen's time were, in some ways, remarkably similar to those of totemic communities. When two families, such as the Dashwoods and Ferrars in *Sense and Sensibility*, or the Woodhouses and Knightleys in *Emma*, were joined by marriage, collateral relationships involving moral and emotional obligations were established as a result between other members of the families. It is precisely this notion of kinship that justifies the use of the terms 'brother-in-law' and 'sister-in-law' in the case of Edward Ferrars and Elinor, and Mr. Knightley and Emma.[6] Furthermore, in all of Austen's works, sibling relationships seem to include brothers-in-law and sisters-in-law who are often referred to simply as brothers and sisters. For example, when John Knightley warns Emma about her encouragement of Mr. Elton's affections, Emma ponders: 'Can it really be as my brother imagined?' (*E*, p. 118). Freud himself remarks that similar use of kinship terms is still evident in the twentieth century, for example, when children are encouraged to refer to their parents' friends as 'Uncle' or 'Aunt'.[7] At the very least, it would seem that the collateral ties of kinship, which were considered equally as important as blood ties in ancient tribes, were retained, in a diluted but still potent form, in Austen's time.

In many regards, the family system in Austen's *Mansfield Park* resembles an elementary kinship system. Paula Marantz Cohen notes that the introduction of Fanny into the Bertram household, which is the initial transaction between the estranged Bertrams and Prices, bears comparison to an ancient marriage transaction described by Lévi-Strauss, in which the exchange of women established a structured relationship between families and opened each family to a broader community.[8] When Fanny arrives at Mansfield as a young girl she is immediately placed on a footing of sister and daughter. Cousins Fanny and Edmund possess intense emotional and spiritual bonds of kinship. Indeed, Austen remarked in a letter to Cassandra: 'I like first Cousins to be first cousins, & interested about each other. They are but one remove from Br & Sr [Brother and Sister]' (*Letters*, pp. 414–15). Since, in Austen's novels, taboos do not figure in any overtly sexual sense as a thematic dynamic, there is no note of prurience in her presentation of these cousins' feelings; rather, she highlights their shared childhood and mutual associations. These joint experiences, Austen shows, create a potent and sympathetic love, a commingling of fraternal and erotic feelings, which, although the emphasis is very much on the former, we must recognize as a kind of incestuous love.

THE CULT OF BROTHER/SISTER LOVE

Incest between brother and sister is a persistent theme in English literature, particularly in the eighteenth and early nineteenth centuries. In fact, incest becomes almost a *sine qua non* in eighteenth-century fiction, adding a *frisson* of shock to titillate the reading public. In Defoe's *Moll Flanders* (1722), Moll describes herself as 'the most unhappy of all women in the world' when she learns that her third husband is her own brother; such are Redriff's unhappiness and guilt that he tries to commit suicide twice and sinks into a long, lingering consumption of which he eventually dies. In Richardson's *Clarissa* (1747–8), Lovelace fantasizes that Clarissa and Anna Howe will both bear him a child; in his prurient dream, Clarissa's son marries Anna'a daughter, for, as the narrator points out, 'dreams [have no] regard to consanguinity'. And in Fielding's *Joseph Andrews* (1742), Joseph and Fanny are horrified when they are led to believe that they are siblings (later their fears are allayed when it turns out this is not the case). In the gothic novel, actual or possible incest becomes a provocative subject. It increases dread and aversion and creates ghastly scenes, such as in Lewis's *The Monk* (1796), where Ambrosio violates and murders his sister Antonia.[9]

Historical reasons make it clear as to why there is such acute awareness of incest in eighteenth-century literature.[10] In the cloistered, insular familial world of the English upper and middle classes, intensely intimate ties between blood relations were forged. Moreover, restrictions governing heterosexual relations with individuals outside the family meant that unconscious sexual feelings were frequently enclosed within the family circle. The closest familial relationships usually formed were those between siblings and cousins; relationships with parents, aunts, and uncles did not possess the same freedom because of generational distance.[11] A brother or sister often functioned as the pivot of an individual's world. Women sometimes had to rely on the protection, guardianship, and economic munificence of their brothers and male cousins. It was not uncommon for a woman to end a relationship if her brother or kinsman took a dislike to, or was jealous of the attentions of, a suitor. Moreover, a woman sometimes delayed the date of her wedding so that her brother could make a settlement on her when he came of age. And sisters were important influences in their brothers' lives.[12] Indeed, ardent familial ties, especially those between brother and sister, were encouraged and exalted; the cult of sibling intimacy was closely bound up with the eighteenth-century cult of sensibility and delicacy. Unconditional love between immediate family members generated a great deal of sentimentality. Readers shed tears at and venerated the self-sacrificing tenderness, the rapturous bliss of devoted familial members depicted in literature. Novels were particularly heartrending if a sinning brother achieved salvation and redemption through the goodness and purity of his sister, who took on the attributes of an angel administering grace. Such is the case, for example, in Frances Burney's *Evelina* (1778), where the heroine saves her brother, Mr. Macartney, from self-destruction and morbid depression by her courage and kindness.

Brother and sister seemed to be ideal companions since they were so similar, even to the extent of being extensions of each other; such a relationship boded unity and harmony rather than antagonism of the sexes. Moreover, fraternal relationships were glorified because the siblings were equals; their love, founded on like-mindedness, the instinct of cooperation, and the cherishing of individual merit, was regarded as a model for marriage. When the time came to marry, siblings sought spouses who resembled their favourite brother or sister. Society generally regarded fraternal ties as being uncontaminated by libidinous feelings because they originated in childhood. But since the distinctions between *agape*, or brotherly love, and *eros*, or earthly love, could become blurred, people in real life and in fiction fantasized about the traversal of the boundaries between sexual innocence and experience and, particularly, the sealing of spiritual, emotional ties with sexual ones in relationships between individuals and their siblings and adopted siblings. Indeed, incest became a 'poetical circumstance',[13] as Shelley describes it, rich in psychological configurations and complexities, brimming with ambivalence and the potential for morbidity and tragedy. Authors explored the love of forbidden partners with trepidation but also with sympathy and even empathy, as in *Joseph Andrews*, where Joseph and Fanny's close brush with incest is viewed by the narrator with as much compassion as horror. Fielding implies that such a sin deserves pity rather than condemnation, since it reveals our human frailty and not our capacity for cruelty. As Jean H. Hagstrum has pointed out, the ingredient of delicate sensibility and the concomitant interest in the thrilling topic of incest figure in Fielding, who clearly comprehended the attraction of similars.[14]

Other factors led to the deep consciousness of incest during the eighteenth century. The incest taboo applied as much to familial members related by marriage as to blood relatives. Forbidden degrees of marriage were rooted in the laws of Chapters 18 and 20 in the Old Testament Book of Leviticus. During the Reformation, the secular courts reduced the number of previous incest taboos from cousins in the sixteenth degree to close blood relatives according to the Levitical degrees (which excluded first cousins). But, at the same time, the courts added the prohibition (believed to be implied by Leviticus) that a man could not marry his deceased wife's sister. To complicate further the situation, in 1603 the Church of England adopted a Table of Kindred and Affinity which extended the incest taboo to relatives related by marriage.[15] Thus, the network of kinship and affinity was much broader in the eighteenth century than it is today, since affines were treated like consanguineal relatives. Every Sunday, people were reminded when they attended church of the sixty forbidden degrees of marriage (including brother's wife, husband's brother, and sister's husband) as listed in the Table of Kindred and Affinity, which hung from the wall in every parish church and was also printed in the back of *The Book of Common Prayer*.

Such was the extent of the kinship network that people might even acknowledge that a relationship existed between an individual and his or her cousin's wife or husband. For example, in Frances Sheridan's *Memoirs of Miss Sidney Bidulph* (1761), Lady V—— tells Sidney that she had 'flattered [her]self with the hopes of being related'[16] to her when Sidney became engaged to Lady V's cousin Orlando Faulkland. Furthermore, strict observance of mourning for in-laws and individuals closely connected by marriage reinforced the network of kinship and affinity.[17] And so it was that, at a time when sexual relations between affinal relatives were often regarded to be as incestuous as intercourse between blood relations, incest presented itself as a major concern in the lives of people living in close contingency with blood relatives and in-laws with little chance for geographical or social mobility. Indeed, the incest theme prevailed in literature of the period precisely because this ultimate taboo affected an entire constellation of relatives. The fearful but alluring subject of forbidden degrees of marriage between affinal relations (who was permitted to have sex and who was not) therefore held a perennial fascination and impressed itself consciously or otherwise in people's minds.

Several critics have offered explanations for the frequency of incest motifs in eighteenth-century literature. Margaret Doody explains in her biography of Frances Burney: 'the incest-fixated eighteenth century found in incest a complex symbolism for sexuality outside conventional social structures, and free of the hierarchies and estrangements of customary heterosexuality.'[18] Manners and customs regarding heterosexual love and courtship were so rigid, so clearly defined, so demarcated in the eighteenth century, that it is not astonishing that contemporary writers sublimated their deepest feelings in the description of sibling love. The rapture of sibling love could be expressed without fear of repercussions, sexual guilt, or social stigma (unless, of course, the siblings overstepped boundaries and actually indulged in a physical relationship). Moreover, the patriarchal order of love conventions, which was delimiting for the female, meant that sibling love was a way for the female to manifest love without the fear of being viewed as forward or unladylike. It was also a way for her to assert relative equality with a male, by setting forth her individual worth intellectually and morally without having to submit to being a sexual object. Fraternal love gave both participants a type of freedom, especially the female; it also put them on equal footing and allowed them great indulgence in that there was no need for the female to be chaperoned, to display false modesty or coyness in order to attract the male, or for the male to put on a show of artificial gallantry. The attachment of the siblings was ideally one of spontaneity, confidence, and warmth without reserve or inhibition. They saw each other in all of their varying moods and built up a spiritual or mystical communion, in which they were able to anticipate and comprehend each other's thoughts and feelings as if they were their own. Since siblings had fewer restrictions socially and emotionally, writers found it easy to dream about the erotic possibilities of such propinquity, such intimacy in their work.

Frances Burney's relatively complex treatment of the theme of incest may well have influenced Austen. In *Evelina*, for example, the incest motif operates in a number of ways. Near the beginning of the novel, Macartney confesses to Evelina the reasons for his suicidal depression. He is deeply in love with a woman whom his mother has discovered to be his sister. To add to his plight, Macartney also finds out that since he fought with the woman's father, who insulted him after discovering their love affair, he has, in fact, come to blows with his own father. Happily for Macartney, incest is avoided since he discovers later on in the novel that the woman is not his sister. But, in the meantime, he appears to be on the brink of falling in love with another woman who turns out to be his real sister – Evelina. This double incest plot nicely illustrates the eighteenth-century fixation with the topic.

Macartney is confused and elated in Evelina's presence, especially after she prevents him from committing suicide. He regards her as a deity and kisses the hem of her dress. Indeed, his admiration comes to the notice of others. Mr. Branghton laughs at the idea of Macartney falling in love with Evelina. Lord Orville becomes jealous of Macartney's influence on Evelina. And people construe their meetings in the garden as lovers' trysts. Macartney also composes an anonymous poem in praise of Evelina's beauty and her power over men. When Evelina discovers that Macartney is her brother, she weeps with happiness; no mention is made of her revulsion at the thought of her brother's incestuous love for her, but then Evelina (in the tradition of the sentimental heroine) is always amazingly ignorant and bovinely naive, so her reaction comes as no surprise. To remove any suspicion of incestuous longing on the heroine's part, Burney includes the following speech in which Evelina cries in rapture: 'we are not merely bound by the ties of friendship, but by those of blood. I feel for you, already, all the affection of a sister, – I felt it, indeed, before I knew I was one.'[19] No imputation of incest is laid at the feet of Macartney; the narrator stresses his joy and astonishment but alludes to no repugnance or shame, except for his embarrassment at being a 'wretched adventurer' and an 'outcast', unworthy of being honored by the title of Evelina's brother.

Like a number of other eighteenth-century novels, the thrust of *Evelina* is the quest for and recovery of lost family ties. More than ample space is given to the sentimental shedding of tears generated by family reunions and the redemption and contrition of family members (Macartney and Sir John Belmont) who are brought back to the family fold by the agency of the angelic Evelina. Not only does Evelina discover that she has a brother, she also comes to claim a sister (Polly Green, who was exchanged for Evelina at birth by a washer woman and who therefore grew up as John Belmont's daughter). Evelina treats her generously, referring to her as her sister – 'for so I must always call, and always consider her' (p. 356). Eventually the displaced Miss Belmont marries Macartney; thus, the woman whom Macartney formerly believed to be his sister becomes his wife and Evelina's sister-in-law. And to augment the family circle, Lord Orville's snobbish sister, who previously treated Evelina with coldness and disdain, appears to be reconciled to the idea of the union of her brother and Evelina, for she attends their wedding 'at her own particular desire' (p. 377). Finally, the incest motif operates in another, quite different, way in *Evelina*. Lord Orville bestows on Evelina the 'affectionate title' (p. 323) of sibling, calling her his 'new-adopted sister' (p. 306). While such a title is merely honorary, it still bolsters the incest fantasy present in so many eighteenth-century works of fiction; it also exposes the blurred distinctions between fraternal and conjugal love which contemporary readers found so thrilling.

Even more pervasive than in *Evelina*, the incest motif surfaces again in Burney's *The Wanderer* (1814), published in the same year as Austen's *Mansfield Park*. The recovery of lost family ties is again a central issue in this work. Juliet claims a half-brother and half-sister in Lord Melbury and Lady Aurora; however, for a time, she must suffer the sexual advances of her half-brother, who is ignorant about their familial connection. Others also notice his attraction: Elinor even refers to the possibility of Ellis (the name by which Juliet is called at this stage in the novel) and Lord Melbury going off to

Gretna Green together; and Mrs. Howel observes Ellis and Lord Melbury closely, considering that 'as he was younger than herself, though her beauty was in its prime, his safety might depend, more rationally, upon her own views, or her own honour, than upon his prudence or indifference'.[20] Lord Melbury calls Juliet his 'Queen of the Night' (p. 90) and devotes his attention to her for entire evenings like a besotted lover. And while Juliet appears to have no sexual feelings for Lord Melbury, he loses control of his. Before taking leave of Juliet, Lord Melbury addresses her in a tone of gallantry. He asks her to settle a time when they shall surreptitiously meet again, requests a lock of her hair, tries to force a ring on her finger, and even prevents her from leaving him. When he confesses his love, 'Ellis now turned pale and cold; horrour [sic] thrilled through her veins, and almost made her heart cease to beat . . . .she turned from him, with an air so severe of soul-felt repugnance, that, starting with surprise and alarm, he forbore the attempt' (p. 127). Her reaction echoes Fanny's disgust at the quasi-incestuous elopement of Henry and Maria in *Mansfield Park*. Not only is Juliet repelled that Lord Melbury should insult her by asking her to become his mistress, but, more important than that, she is revolted by her brother's incestuous feelings, even though they seem to give her a thrill. Near the end of the novel, when Juliet claims consanguinity with Lady Aurora and Lord Melbury, her brother shows no regret for his earlier conduct. His attentions to her, though mixed with fraternal affection, are still those of an ardent lover. He has travelled all night to lay a scheme before her, and calls her his 'treasure' and 'loveliest Miss Ellis' (pp. 812–13). As in *Evelina*, the blurring of fraternal and conjugal feelings and boundaries is very much in evidence.

Both *Evelina* and *The Wanderer* tease (and even confuse) the reader with such a tangled web of consanguineal ties. Doody claims that, at the profounder psychological level, Macartney manifests in *Evelina* his need to reassert his ascendance and superiority over Evelina, who acted as his saviour. He achieves this by writing a poem for her, in which he extols her beauty but overlooks her bravery and responsibility. In this way, he diminishes, as well as embarrasses, her. The novel can then be read, in this critic's phrase, as 'an antimasculinist satire'.[21] However, *pace* Doody, Burney's satire seems to aim even more directly at the treatment of incest in contemporary novels. In other eighteenth-century works, authors bludgeon the reader with the dire possibility of an incestuous relationship. Burney was evidently familiar with contemporary works which exploited the incest theme for lurid purposes. Summing up her own attitude toward the sexualization of familial relationships, Burney expressed scathing criticisms of Horace Walpole's *The Mysterious Mother* (1768), in which Edmund unwittingly commits incest with his mother and later on marries Adeliza, the woman who is both his daughter and his sister. For Burney, this drama was ' . . . truly dreadful! A story of so much horror, from atrocious and voluntary guilt'. Moreover, she felt 'indignant aversion . . . against the wilful author of a story so horrible'.[22] In her first novel, *Evelina*, Burney's attitude seems dual-edged; she elects to reduce the incest theme to absurdity while retaining, in obeisance to popular demands of the day, the fearful possibility of its occurring. While incest is handled with some element of mockery in *Evelina*, in *The Wanderer*, published almost forty years later, the danger is much more serious. Such a transformation in Burney's attitude seems to reflect alterations in the handling of the motif in contemporary literature (especially in the work of the Romantic poets), as well as changes in Burney's own life.

In a muted way, the fantasy and fulfillment of incestuous dreams became a reality among Burney's coterie of friends and between her own siblings. Burney's close friend Hester Lynch Thrale and Hester's stepdaughter Queeney Thrale were both attracted to men believed to be their half-brothers. In the early 1780s, the Thrale family became anxious when Jeremiah Crutchley revealed his affections for Queeney, since Hester believed that Crutchley was the illegitimate son of Mr. Thrale. Such was Hester's fear that she endeavoured unsuccessfully to promote a match between Frances Burney and Crutchley to circumvent the incestuous union. Fortunately for the Thrales, no union ever took place between Queeney and Crutchley. Yet, despite her fears for Queeney, Hester herself engaged in a purportedly incestuous relationship. After her husband, Mr. Thrale, died in 1781, she soon began openly confessing her love for Gabriel Piozzi, whom she believed to be the illegitimate son of her father. Much to Burney's chagrin, Hester eventually married Piozzi. Still more significant, in 1798, Burney's own brother James eloped with their younger half-sister, Sarah Harriet, to the consternation of the entire Burney family.[23] Ironically enough, Sarah had described a quasi-incestuous relationship in her first novel, *Clarentine* (1796), in which the protagonist falls for her sailor guardian.

In all likelihood, Austen knew of these scandalous happenings in the Burney household in spite of the family's frantic attempts to conceal them. Austen regularly visited and corresponded with her cousins, the Cookes of Great Bookham in Surrey. The Reverend Samuel Cooke, Vicar of Great Bookham, was married to one of Mrs. Austen's cousins – her namesake, Cassandra Leigh, daughter of the Master of Balliol.[24] The Cookes were neighbours of Fanny Burney and her husband – by this time Burney was referred to as Madame D'Arblay – between 1793 and 1797. The D'Arblays apparently canvassed for subscriptions to Madame D'Arblay's new novel, *Camilla*, while Austen was staying with her cousins, for her name appears on the list of subscribers. We may assume that the Cookes heard of events in the lives of Madame D'Arblay and her family; and such information would doubtless have been of interest to the aspiring novelist, Jane Austen. Austen read Burney's works avidly and with admiration; some of her letters fairly teem with allusions to *Evelina* and to *Camilla*.[25] Austen also read Sarah Burney's *Clarentine*, although this novel inspired little more than a disparaging reference in her correspondence to its foolishness and lack of merit; in her opinion, the work was 'full of unnatural conduct and forced difficulties' (*Letters*, p. 180). Evidently, the influence on Jane Austen of contemporary writers, particularly Frances Burney, extends to the treatment of the topical subject of incest in a sense that has hitherto gone unnoticed.

Critics have endeavoured over the last twenty years to prove that Austen was involved in the literary debates of her time, that she was exposed to contemporary currents which she then responded to and disseminated in her own fiction.[26] Many have sought to argue that Austen took particular interest in the works of contemporary female novelists. And the most recent essay on Austen's reading (by Margaret Doody) briefly analyzes the possible influence of such writers as Frances Sheridan and Agnes Maria Bennett on Austen's work.[27] Sheridan's *Memoirs of Miss Sidney Bidulph* (1767) contains a germ which Austen may have used for *Mansfield Park*, published half a century later. In Sheridan's novel, Sidney brings a child (orphaned Orlando Faulkland) into her household and raises him with her daughters. Like Mrs. Norris and Sir Thomas in *Mansfield Park*, Sidney mistakenly and ill-advisedly believes that individuals raised in the same household rarely become enamored of each other. Doody speculates that Austen also read Bennett's *Agnes De-Courci* (1789), in which Edward Harley marries his beloved Agnes only to discover soon after the wedding that they are siblings. As a result of this discovery, Edward commits suicide, and the heroine goes into a terrible fit. Doody conjectures that these incidents in Bennett's novel inspired Austen in the writing of parts of 'Love and Freindship', in particular, the grotesque deaths of Edward and Augustus, and Laura's hysteria at the death of her husband. And yet, even if we accept this critic's conjectures, it would seem nearer to the truth to say that Austen used Bennett's work not only for the purpose of satire but as well as for presenting and reinforcing her own conceptions of familial, especially sibling, relationships in fiction.

Austen also had access to the novels of Charlotte Smith, Sophia Lee, and Mary Robinson. In Smith's *Emmeline* (1788), Delamere's passion for his cousin and father's ward, Emmeline, savours of incest. The narrator's hints that Emmeline and Delamere may be siblings are underscored by the uncanny resemblance of Emmeline and Delamere's sister Augusta, and by Lord Montreville's implacable opposition to the marriage of the cousins. Even though Delamere relentlessly pursues Emmeline, she refuses to marry him on the grounds that such an alliance would cause disruption in his family. While Austen appears only to be challenging the pattern of Smith's *Emmeline* in her depiction of the successful union of two cousins brought up as brother and sister, she appears to jeer at the machinations and maunderings of Smith's *Celestina* (1791). In this work, Willoughby suspects that his love for the heroine is incestuous. The novel dwells on Willoughby's unravelling of the mystery of Celestina's birth, and his fortuitous discovery that she is not his sister. Austen also seems to ridicule the absurd contrivances of the incest motif in the fiction of Lee and Robinson. In Lee's *The Recess* (1783–5), the illegitimate Mrs. Marlow retires to a secret place because she married a man whom she discovered shortly after the wedding to be her brother. And in Robinson's *Vancenza* (1792), Elvira discovers from a secret document that the father of her fiancé is also her own parent. As a result of this revelation, Elvira sickens and dies.

Austen clearly wanted to write a best seller.[29] However, she intended her bestselling work for an audience of intelligent, discriminating readers, more like members of her own circle of family and friends. Austen drew on, in some cases excoriated, and modified such popular works as those of Burney, Sheridan, Bennett, Smith, Lee and Robinson in an attempt to accomplish this goal. And part of the successful formula of late eighteenth-century novels involved the integration of the incest or quasi-incest issue. That is to say, Austen's pointed interest in endogamous unions or domestic passion was by no means idiosyncratic. Her inclusion of the issue of in-family marriage reveals merely the tip of the literary iceberg, since this was a prevalent theme in literature of her time. In *Mansfield Park*, Austen draws on the formula of the 'orphan' girl (who lives in the same household with, and either loves, or is loved by, a male relative) found in the sentimental and gothic fiction of Charlotte Smith and Ann Radcliffe.[30] Likewise, the two-brother, two-sister prescription in *Emma* was a familiar plot in novels of education in the late eighteenth century.[31] In the gothic novel, such a plot had potential for creating incestuous configurations. For example, Charles Brockden Brown's *Wieland* (1798) is the story of incestuous impulses activated in the relationships of Theodore and his sister Clara and Theodore's wife Catherine and her brother Henry.[32] But while Austen's employs typical incest-generating frameworks, her handling of incestuous relationships is unique. To wit, Austen's treatment not only satirizes the handling of the issue of in-family marriage in other eighteenth- and early nineteenth-century works but also turns it into a significant, highly serious, even an imperative component of her aesthetic and moral vision.

When we examine the presentation of sibling incest in the eighteenth-century English novel, a pattern emerges. In many cases, the incestuous or near incestuous incident is a titillating accident; the siblings are generally unwitting victims of an error rather than conscious rebels. The incest motif serves the purpose of creating suspense or mood; of manifesting evil; of reinforcing the hero or heroine's despondency; or of emphasizing the necessity of renunciation and penitance. Generally speaking, the real relation of the man and woman is not discovered until after their liaison begins; they are attracted to each other not by a shared childhood and associations but by instinct.[33] The attraction of similars held a fascination which deepened as the eighteenth century progressed and which reached a climax during the Romantic period. The Romantics eagerly read eighteenth-century novels dealing with the subject of incest.[34] But, for the Romantics, particularly Byron and Shelley, the incest motif operates in a different sense from eighteenth-century novels. In their work, the siblings are aware of their blood ties *before* their involvements start; their intense love results from their childhood memories and experiences. Daily association has not dulled but rather stimulated the potential for erotic feelings between the siblings. Moreover, the incest motif often unfolds a mirror-imaging of the self, or a solipsistic weaving of selves.[35] Passionate love, in English Romanticism, is often an extension of love of one's own self, or one's elevated self. The Romantic protagonist seeks a lover whose soul reflects his own. If the lovers are consanguineal relatives, this extension becomes even more plausible; indeed, such a love appears to be the most intimate and delectable of relationships, the most complete experience of the erotic. But the narcissistic attraction between family members is ambivalent: the sibling evokes the other's love because he or she is a double of the other; at the same time, he or she evokes the other's fear and hatred because the other is a double with a difference. James B. Twitchell claims that almost every preromantic treatment of incest is 'reflexively condemnatory'.[36] But Romantic poets such as Byron and Shelley sometimes glamorise and often express sympathy for characters who participate in incestuous family liaisons.

There is, of course, a clear-cut distinction in these works between sibling and parental incest; while the Romantics and the Gothic novelists are intrigued by the idea of brother/sister incest, parent/child incest is evil and sadistic because of the horror of child abuse and betrayal of trust. The difference seems to be that in a brother/sister relationship, unlike a parent/child relationship, the siblings love and understand each other because they have the same parentage. They are attracted to one another because they are similar in personality and appearance; they are two parts of one self.

Byron's infamous relationship with his half-sister Augusta Leigh tantalized and outraged the society of his time. Several of Byron's works – *The Bride of Abydos* (1813), *Manfred* (1817), and *Cain* (1821) – deal extensively with the theme of sibling incest and are parallel with his situation in real life. The tormented hero invokes the Witch of the Alps and confesses his incestuous love for his sister Astarte in the poetic drama *Manfred*. From this tragic love, Manfred's only escape is to die. Sibling incest is also an important theme in Byron's *The Bride of Abydos*, as expressed in the relationship of Selim and his half-sister Zuleika (in the revised published version Selim and Zuleika are cousins). Zuleika serves as the Byronic hero's complement or female half. Such a relationship is in many respects an act of self-love, as Selim is enamored of seeing himself in Zuleika. But their incestuous love ends in death; Selim is killed as he attempts to elope with his lover. In *Cain*, while Byron portrays the protagonist's love for his sister Adah as necessary for the race to continue, he also emphasizes that their incestuous love will always be renounced by their offspring. Thus, Byron neither advocates nor fully censures incest, but rather creates tragic, despairing victims of taboo.

Both Byron and Shelley used incest to break accepted social norms and to explore new boundaries; for them, incest was the symbol for expressing rebellion on a broader scale. But Shelley is more affirmative in his attitude towards sibling incest in his works. The poet, himself, was worshipped by his four younger sisters; moreover, the Shelley children became especially close because of the domination and antagonism of their father and the indifference of their mother. Shelley shared a particularly intimate relationship with his sister Elizabeth; there is tentative evidence that Shelley's love for his sister had pseudosexual overtones.[37] But, unlike Byron, Shelley did not apparently have a physical relationship with his sister. In 'Epipsychidion' (1821), Shelley amorously addresses his epipsyche as 'Spouse! Sister! Angel!' In *Laon and Cythna* (1817), the template of *The Revolt of Islam* (1818), siblings Laon and Cythna consummate their relationship and have a daughter. However, for Shelley, such a perfect relationship cannot last. At the end of the poem, the family is burnt one by one at the stake, and the daughter of the brother/sister union guides the spirits of her parents to heaven where they will live and love together for eternity. Despite Shelley's sympathetic portrayal, his tragic protagonists, like those of Byron, must always suffer and die. 'Incest may be, as Shelley proposed in the Preface [to *Laon and Cythna*], the result of "all sympathies harmoniously blended," but one should add that such are the harmonies of the heavenly spheres, not those of humankind,' claims Twitchell.[38] Both Byron and Shelley understood the importance of limits in their depiction of incestuous relationships. Byron's sibling lovers are wretched – as Byron himself often was in his relationship with Augusta – and ill-fated; Shelley's siblings celebrate their love only in a realm far removed from reality.

Although Austen satirized the gothic novel and poked fun at her contemporary Byron (in a letter to Cassandra she wrote 'I have read the *Corsair*, mended my petticoat, & have nothing else to do'),[39] and although her novels of domestic realism differ vastly from the works of her literary predecessors and contemporaries, the fantasy of incest is still present in her fiction, as it was in the drawing rooms of her time. However, the type of incest introduced by Austen did not involve blood siblings, but rather foster-siblings, first cousins and in-laws, individuals bound by strong familial obligations, whose affections have been formed within the domestic circle, and whose relationships are viewed by other members of society as fraternal. In Austen's opinion, shared experiences and familial associations are as important as mutual parentage; in her fiction, the relations between foster-siblings raised as siblings, or a man and woman who treat each other as siblings, hold the same obligations and ramifications as those between blood siblings. It is important to note, however, that the sexual aspect of the incestuous unions is consistently downplayed in Austen's novels. In contrast to the gothic novelists, she eschewed any overt appeals to titillation or prurience in her presentation of sibling attraction.

Twitchell's claim that no artist has embraced the palliative powers of incest with Shelley's enthusiasm needs qualifying.[40] Shelley condones incest, but such relationships are for him impossible in this world. In Austen's novels, incest between cousins and between in-laws, who act towards each other like blood brother and sister, seems to be purposive and is promoted as a way of fortifying the family. Unlike the Romantics, she affirmed strict moral and social codes; indeed, her concern was not with the individual but with society. And unlike other literary works of the time, where incest increases horror or creates moral chaos and violence, Austen's novels present incestuous alliances that preserve order and reestablish domestic harmony. In Austen's fiction, moreover, these alliances are attuned to a comic rather than a tragic genre; and they seek not a transcendent, but an earthly love and sanction.

Austen does not appear to be breaking any taboo or taking a rebellious or scandalous stand in her depiction of endogamous unions; rather, she seems to be concerned with desensationalizing the fixation with incest. Her concerns are wholly antipathetic to those of Byron and Shelley in their portrayals of incestuous liaisons. In fact, Austen finds positive reasons for members of the same family unit to marry, providing, of course, that they are not actually siblings. In her novels, the in-family marriages between the cousins and in-laws are successful because they do not grow out of sexual longing but are rooted in a deeper, more abiding domestic love which merges spiritual, intellectual, and physical affinities. Moreover, such unions form a new chapter in the fictional depiction of male/female relationships in that the participants are temperamentally equal; their union is relatively free from what Susan Morgan refers to as the 'politics of dominance and submission that we have been so carefully taught to confuse with a natural passion'.[41] Instead of being based on a pattern of female passivity and male domination, Austen's couples are cast in the same mould and are largely on the same par with each other. There are, of course, certain characters in Austen's novels who are either opposed to the unions between such close relatives or strongly believe that they are unlikely to happen; for example, Sir Thomas's initial objection to Fanny's coming to Mansfield is that she may marry either Tom or Edmund, and Mrs. Weston is incredulous when Emma tells her she is going to marry Mr. Knightley. But the mind-sets of these characters are described in a context of irony; their directions of thought come in direct conflict with the attitudes of the protagonists as well as those of the author herself, who seems to view the eventual marriages as natural and desirable outcomes. These undercurrents and conflicting perspectives create dramatic tension throughout the novels.

COUSIN LOVE

Cousin marriage in Austen's fiction merits special attention. The prohibition against the marriage of cousins has varied widely in scope according to region, class, and faith. Protestant areas have permitted the marriage of cousins since 1540 (although such marriages have been and still are, in many cases, discouraged, and in certain parts of the USA remain illegal). Catholic areas now prohibit only first cousins from marrying (in 1918 Catholics allowed third cousins to marry but not first). But the Orthodox Church still forbids such unions.[42] In any case, the recurrence of cousin marriage in Austen's novels may seem extraordinary to the modern reader. Fanny marries Edmund in *Mansfield Park*. Henrietta marries her cousin Charles Hayter in *Persuasion*. In the same novel, William Elliot pursues his cousin Anne. And in Austen's own family, her brother Henry became the second husband of their cousin Eliza de Feuillide.

The typical marriage of cousins in Austen's time occurred when a woman married her father's nephew, in order to keep her estate in her father's name – such is Elizabeth Elliot's ambition in her desire to marry William Elliot, the heir presumptive to Sir Walter's estate in *Persuasion*. Almost half of the marriages of cousins in eighteenth-century upper-class society were of this kind.[43] In *Pride and Prejudice*, Lady Catherine de Bourgh arranges for her daughter to marry her nephew Fitzwilliam Darcy in order to preserve 'the noble line' and to prevent the family fortune from being redistributed. And since the Bennet house is entailed in default of male heirs on a distant relation, Mrs. Bennet encourages several of her daughters to marry their cousin Mr. Collins in order to keep Longbourn in the family. This type of cousin marriage was well-established and mainly carried out for economic purposes. But, in the case of the marriage of cousins Fanny and Edmund in *Mansfield Park*, the economic function is subordinated to moral and emotional purposes. It is worth noting here that Austen approves of endogamous, and, in the special sense we have defined, incestuous unions only when such marriages unite individuals of strong moral character and like sensibilities. For this reason, Austen does not allow Darcy to marry Miss De Bourgh, Mr. Collins to marry Elizabeth, or Mr. Elliot to marry Anne.

During the eighteenth century and well into the nineteenth, the marriage of cousins was common practice in England, not only on account of of economic imperatives, but also because people's movements were restricted, and their social circle often confined to family and neighbours of the same class, especially in the country. In an early piece called 'Frederic and Elfrida', the young Austen observes that since the two cousins were 'both born in one day and both brought up at one school, it was not wonderfull [sic] that they should look on each other with something more than bare politeness' (*MW*, p. 4). In *Emma*, the heroine ponders the lack of geographical mobility of Harriet, Mr. Elton, and herself:

> Their being fixed, so absolutely fixed in the same place, was bad for all three. Not one of them had the power of removal, or of affecting any material change of society. They must encounter each other and make the best of it. (*E*, p. 143)

Until the spread of railways in the 1840s, travel was expensive and even then mobility in provincial society caught on at a far more sluggish rate than in urban areas. In Hardy's *The Well Beloved* (1897), which is set over a period of forty years in the second half of the nineteenth century, the isolated island community continues its old traditions of endogamous marriages and ratifying a betrothal by sexual relations. Such practices underscored the unwillingness of many rural communities to accept progress during the nineteenth century.

Some consideration of the tendencies of Victorian novelists in dealing with in-family love may help to define Austen's view of and motives on the subject. Marriages between first cousins persisted into the nineteenth century, as numerous Victorian novelists testify. In Collins's *The Moonstone* (1868), Rachel Verinder and Franklin Blake are first cousins who eventually marry. A number of Trollope's novels refer to the marriage of cousins: Lizzie Eustace attempts to ensnare her cousin Frank Greystock in *The Eustace Diamonds* (1873); Alice Vavasor jilts John Grey at the beginning of *Can You Forgive Her?* (1864–5) in favour of her reckless cousin George Vavasor; and Emily Hotspur wants to marry her cousin George in *Sir Harry Hotspur of Humblethwaite* (1870). In Hardy's *The Return of the Native* (1878), Mrs. Yeobright's ardent wish is that her son Clym will marry her niece Thomasin. At the end of the novel, Clym is about to propose to his cousin when she tells him she is going to marry Diggory Venn. And in Hardy's later novel *Jude the Obscure* (1896), the hero marries his cousin Sue Bridehead. However, while marriages between cousins were commonplace enough,[44] Victorian fiction attests to the ambivalent attitude of people toward such unions. The status of cousins was complex; they were related to each other but not forbidden to marry. Even so, although they were marriageable, some believed that the incest taboo applied to cousins as much as or even more than to affines. For example, in Trollope's *The Eustace Diamonds*, after observing Lizzie embracing her cousin Frank, Andy Gowran exclaims, 'Coosins!' on several occasions, and impertinently tells the lovers, 'Ye're mair couthie than coosinly', implying that they are acting in a manner more befitting unrelated friends than cousins. In other words, Gowran believes that the relationship between cousins should be free of amatory feelings. Literature also testifies that people sometimes exploited society's view of the asexual nature of cousinly ties. In the eighteenth-century work *Memoirs of Miss Sidney Bidulph*, Mrs. Gerrade tries to conceal the real nature of the relationship with her servant and lover, Mr. Pinnick, by referring to him as her kinsman: 'she called him cousin, the better to skreen [sic] a more particular connection' (p. 222). And in Hardy's *Jude the Obscure*, the young women at the school attended by Sue Bridehead gossip about a pupil who claimed she was meeting her cousin in order to conceal her real intention of gaining a rendezvous with her lover.

One of the most explicit of all Victorian novels on the themes of cousin marriage and incest is Hardy's *The Well Beloved*. Early in the novel, Jocelyn Pierston becomes engaged to his cousin Avice;

twenty years later he falls in love with Avice's daughter, Ann Avice; and after another twenty years he becomes engaged to Avice's granddaughter, who is also called Avice. So in-bred is the tiny island they inhabit that there are but half-a-dozen Christian names and surnames in the area. Jocelyn's 'genealogical passion'[45] for his three kinswomen is based on a racial instinct. These women possess 'a mysterious ingredient sucked from the island' (p. 84), which he finds appealing, and which he misses in women who are not of the island race. Although Pierston never consummates any of his relationships with the Avices, his love for all three causes suffering and disappointment; for 'though he might never love a woman of the island race for lack in her of the desired refinement, he could not love long a kimberlin – a woman other than of the island race, for her lack of groundwork of character' (p. 84).

The Well Beloved offers a parallel to a situation in Hardy's own life, much as Byron's poetry offers a parallel to a situation in his life. Hardy felt a strong impulse toward his three Sparks cousins – Rebecca, Martha, and Tryphena – at different times in his life. The Sparks sisters were widely set apart in age; in this respect, they appear to have been the inspiration for the three generations of Avices in *The Well Beloved*. Hardy made advances towards his eldest cousin Rebecca when he was an adolescent but was rebuffed. He wanted to marry Martha, but his aunt Maria refused the match and claimed that it was 'against the law of the church' for cousins to marry. In 1867, Hardy fell in love with Tryphena Sparks, a woman young enough to have been his niece.[46]

It is appropriate that a work such as Hardy's novel, which stresses the narcissistic quality of a man's love, should have as its epigraph, 'one shape of many names', a quotation from Shelley's famous poem about incest *The Revolt of Islam*.[47] Throughout *The Well-Beloved*, Hardy points to the results of intermarriage, remarking how features are 'uniform from parent to child through generations', and how, such is the extent of the inbreeding, that to 'have seen one native man and woman was to have seen the whole population of that isolated rock, so nearly cut off from the mainland' (p. 150). Pierston's affinity to women of the island who are 'scions of a common stock in this island of intermarriages' (p. 134) is comforting to him; however, at the same time, he stresses the restrictions these ties impose on his relationships with women who are not his kinswomen. In the third part of the novel, Pierston remarks on his shared childhood associations with the third Avice. Jocelyn feels closer to her because she inhabits the same house, even the same bedroom, where he spent his childhood. Moreover, this Avice shares his surname, a coincidence that calls our attention to the centripetal forces at work on the peninsula, where 'everyone' (p. 89) marries his or her cousin. Whereas Austen regards the shared childhood associations of Fanny and Edmund and the centripetal forces operating in *Mansfield Park* as propitious, in Hardy's *The Well-Beloved* similar associations and forces are viewed in a potentially tragic light.

Hardy appears to have been inspired to some extent in his depiction of endogamous relationships in *The Well-Beloved* (and in *Jude the Obscure*) by the contemporary debate and anxiety in late Victorian England over the dangers of inbreeding and cousin marriage.[48] We may assume that Hardy was influenced by his reading of Darwin and by the disputation over consanguineous marriage which spread not only through scientific and medical journals but also the popular periodical press.[49] Hardy even seemed to take a side. In *Jude the Obscure*, Jude attempts to quell his incipient sexual feelings for his cousin Sue by reminding himself that 'it was not well for cousins to fall in love even when circumstances seemed to favour the passion'.[50] And indeed, tragic events in this novel bear out this belief; the 'bad blood' of the family has been concentrated in this union, reinforcing in fiction Darwin's argument that inbreeding was harmful because it intensified genetic traits that could, in turn, lead to degeneracy. In later years, Darwin modified his position, mostly in light of the work done by his son George Darwin, who was himself the offspring of a cousin marriage. Scientists, sociologists, and anthropologists on both sides of the issue entered the fray; however, the general feeling about cousin marriage became increasingly negative because society had been disturbed by the controversy over the risk of dire genetic consequences. Even though little evidence was discovered by scientists, alarm and fear prevailed among people. The number of these marriages therefore decreased significantly.

At the conclusion of *The Well Beloved*, Hardy's attitude towards endogamous relationships is symbolized in his reference to Jocelyn's architectural schemes. Water from outside sources will be pumped into the townlet on the island to replace contaminated water in the old wells. In this way, Hardy seems to suggest that new blood should also be encouraged on the island to revitalise it. Endogamous unions, such as those of Jocelyn and the three Avices and of Hardy and the Sparks sisters, are inert and doomed to unhappiness. The old custom of in-marriage is an outmoded island tradition that should be abandoned. If, as it would seem, Hardy's equivocal attitude forms a marked contrast to Austen's view of the advantageous, practical nature of cousin marriage, the reason is that the *Weltanschauung* of Hardy's world with regard to the family was vastly different to that of Austen's. The family circle was no longer so confined, smaller families were on the increase, and fewer restrictions were imposed on extra-familial relationships. Moreover, people travelled more and stayed at home less. As a literary motif, cousin marriage in Hardy's *The Well-Beloved* and *Jude the Obscure* (although not in the earlier novel *The Return of the Native*) produces inertia and calamity. To redress the potentially dire consequences of endogamous marriages, Hardy advocates the opening of the family to a wider community.

In Austen's time, first cousins were permitted to marry by law and the church, but feeling against this practice, though certainly not as prevalent as in the late nineteenth century, was discernible. Eighteenth-century discussions of the marriage of cousins some- times discouraged the practice because of the general belief that cousins 'never live happily and prosperously together'.[51] Francis Hutcheson, for example, argued in *A System of Moral Philosophy* (1755) that close kin marriages, especially between cousins, would restrict families and prevent them from mixing with others; he stressed that 'by this means the sacred bond of affection would be too much confined, each family would be a little system by itself, detached from others'.[52] For centuries, it was a common opinion that children of the marriage of first cousins were likely to be insane or to have physical or mental defects – an opinion still held by many people. Nowadays we know that the marriage of cousins does not necessarily have any genetic consequences, although in some cases it can have serious effects.[53]

In *Mansfield Park*, when Mary Crawford shows some concern about the declarations of love in the scene in *Lovers' Vows* involving herself and Edmund, she says to Fanny: 'There, look at *that* speech, and *that*, and *that*. How am I ever to look him in the face and say such things? Could you do it? But then he is your cousin, which makes all the difference . . . . You *have* a look of *his* some- times' (*MP*, pp. 168–9). Mary's comment highlights her belief that cousins cannot fall in love. The society of Austen's time generally conceived the ties between cousins as fraternal and asexual rather than conjugal and romantic. But Austen's own belief in the salutary nature of cousins in love overrides that of the morally reprehensible Mary. Indeed, as we shall see, Mary Crawford is but one of several of Austen's characters whose objections to endogamous unions are rendered invalid, either by their unworthy ulterior motives or their lack of sense and moral vision.

3

Incestuous Sibling Relationships: *Mansfield Park, Emma* and *Sense and Sensibility*

Jane Austen's sister Cassandra attempted to persuade her to change the dénouement of *Mansfield Park*. According to Cassandra, Austen's failure to allow Henry Crawford to marry Fanny, and Fanny's cousin Edmund to marry Mary Crawford, constituted a major flaw in the work.[1] *Mansfield Park* concludes with the heroine happily securing a place as a member of the family at Mansfield and with the removal of the immoral, unprincipled Crawfords. However, Cassandra Austen's assessment, like that of many critics, overlooks or fails to appreciate the significance of the incestuous marriage of cousins Fanny and Edmund.

The issue of incest may also be considered as relevant in the case of Emma and Mr. Knightley. No literal tie of kinship forms a barrier between them, although it has sometimes proved otherwise between a man's brother and his wife's sister in Christian societies.[2] But it is significant that they act more like siblings rather than lovers, at least until the end of the novel. The sibling-like nature of their marriage betokens an exclusive, inward movement into the family; Mr. Knightley is Emma's brother-in-law and a close neighbour and friend of the Woodhouses. And like an elder brother or guardian, Mr. Knightley has helped to educate Emma. Their later love relationship may be seen as incestuous in that it grew out of a fraternal bond; they themselves emphasize that they are like siblings. That is to say, although they ultimately become involved romantically, their relationship begins as a domestic attachment, originating in and fostered by the intimacy of the home and the family.

33

In *Sense and Sensibility*, Elinor and Edward, like Mr. Knightley and Emma, are sister-in-law and brother-in-law. Although there are no blood ties between them, Edward 'looks upon [Elinor] and the other Miss Dashwoods quite as his own sisters' (*SS*, p. 130); indeed, there are frequent references to their fraternal regard for one another throughout the novel. As in the case of Emma and Mr. Knightley, they are close affines, whose love may be characterised as domestic in that it is stimulated by the familial matrix. In the same work, the relationship between Colonel Brandon and Eliza, although it is unconsummated, is doubly incestuous, as well as adulterous. They have been brought up together like siblings; moreover, their intended marriage is forbidden since Eliza is married to Colonel Brandon's elder brother.

Despite the evidence, commentators in the main have ignored the importance of the incestuous marriages in Austen's fiction. Only a few have discussed the subject. R. F. Brissenden points out the incestuous significance of the relationship of Fanny and Edmund in *Mansfield Park* and comments that this is what gives the union its underlying power. 'The [moral] values represented by Fanny and Edmund are under attack . . . . The mood of *Mansfield Park* is nostalgic and elegiac,' argues Brissenden.[3] Julia Prewitt Brown remarks that in *Mansfield Park* and *Emma* 'time and history are arrested. The sense of stasis . . . is partially explained by the incestuous marriages with which they end . . . . This is the darker side of the theme of cooperation in Jane Austen. In *Mansfield Park*, cooperation is a kind of inertia.'[4] Claudia L. Johnson declares that 'the concluding assertion of familiality [in *Mansfield Park*] . . . is really only a retrenchment, not an alternative'.[5] And Johanna H. Smith attempts to demonstrate the 'crippling effects' of the relationship of Fanny and Edmund in *Mansfield Park*.[6] The tendency on the part of otherwise astute critics to view these incestuous marriages as static and debilitating is rather curious.

Brissenden and Brown claim that *Mansfield Park* is an 'elegiac' and 'enervating' work, which 'exacerbates and finally exhausts us'. Johnson feels that the close of the novel is 'unsettling' and does not offer the satisfaction usually provided by a happy ending. Smith's argument is that the marriage of Fanny and Edmund symbolizes 'a paralyzed retreat within the family' and anticipates 'the nineteenth-century inescapable family'.[7] But Austen's works reveal nothing of the sort. Indeed, there is no evidence that she intended the end of *Mansfield Park* to be 'enervating', 'unsettling', or 'paralyzed' any more than she intended the conclusion of *Emma* to be dark or static. On the contrary, for Austen, the incestuous marriages of Fanny and Edmund, Emma and Mr. Knightley, and Elinor and Edward Ferrars are therapeutic and restorative; the endogamous unions safeguard the family circle and its values. Far from being 'elegiac', *Mansfield Park, Emma,* and *Sense and Sensibility* conclude optimistically with the expulsion or removal of menacing intruders and with the preservation and revivification of the home and family. Incest in Austen's novels creates a loving and enclosed family circle; by drawing in the bonds of the family tighter and tighter, the household is strengthened and reconsecrated.

MANSFIELD PARK

Not only are Fanny and Edmund first cousins in *Mansfield Park*, attached by matrilineal, consanguineal ties which Mary Crawford emphasizes in her reference to their similarity in appearance, but, more important, they have been raised as brother and sister under the same roof. Despite contemporary criticism of marriage between close consanguineal relations (even though it was legal) and the prohibition of marriage between close affines, Austen approves of the marriage of cousins Fanny and Edmund. Indeed, there is every reason to believe at the end of the novel that the two cousins will live happily and prosperously together. The endogamous union preserves the inviolability of Mansfield and excludes the risks attendant on marriage outside the family – to the Crawfords, for example. The marriage is more than just a conventional happy ending; it is symbolic of Austen's sceptical attitude towards a new age, moral transvaluations, and radical change.[8]

Sir Thomas's joyful consent to the marriage of cousins Fanny and Edmund forms a remarkable contrast to his earlier thoughts on the subject at the beginning of the novel. As he considers adopting Fanny, the very thought of cousins in love creates uneasiness within him, which is dispelled by Mrs. Norris:

'You are thinking of your sons – but do you not know that of all things upon earth *that* is the least likely to happen; brought up, as they would be, always together like brothers and sisters. It is *morally impossible* . . . . It is in fact the only sure way of providing against the connection . . . breed her up with them from this

time, and suppose her to have the beauty of an angel, and she
will never be more to either than a sister.' (*MP*, pp. 6–7, italics
added)

Thus the incestuous character of the relationship of Fanny and
Edmund is foreshadowed in the opening chapter. Later on in the
novel, the baronet apprehensively observes Fanny and Edmund
dancing together at the ball at Mansfield; however, his fears are
allayed by 'their sober tranquillity . . . [which] might satisfy any
looker-on that Sir Thomas had been bringing up no wife for his
younger son' (*MP*, p. 279). And when Sir Thomas anxiously ques-
tions Fanny about Edmund's matrimonial plans, Fanny removes his
alarm, and her uncle 'was easy on the score of the cousins' (*MP*,
p. 317).

Moral objections are raised by Sir Thomas and Mrs. Norris to
the possible connection between the cousins. But Austen distinctly
regards the incestuous relationship of Fanny and Edmund as natural
and highly beneficial and not, in any way, 'morally impossible'. Like
Mary Crawford, Mrs. Norris proves an inadequate judge in this
matter. And so too does Sir Thomas – until he becomes enlightened
about the strengths of such a marriage. Rather than trapping and
constricting the cousins within a narcissistic sibling relationship,
as one critic suggests, Austen authorizes and blesses the union
of Fanny and Edmund.[9] Any potential objections on the part of
other characters in the novel to the union are surmounted by the
domestic happiness of the married cousins and the invigoration of
the Mansfield family and estate. Austen challenges the handling of
the incest theme in contemporary works with her implied criticism
of the judgement of negligent or ill-advised parental figures. Other
eighteenth-century sentimental and didactic works moralize about
the significance of filial obedience. For this reason, authors sometimes make disobedience, in the form of a clandestine or forbidden
marriage on the part of young lovers, produce an incestuous union
between siblings or half-siblings. For example, the heroine of the
anonymous *Helena* (1788) becomes engaged to her guardian's son
without seeking the advice of her elders. She later discovers that
her betrothed is her brother. But, in Austen's *Mansfield Park*, Fanny
defies her surrogate parents by allowing herself to fall in love with
her brotherly cousin and by adamantly refusing to marry Henry
Crawford. Indeed, Austen underscores her objection to parental
despots in the ironic finale of *Northanger Abbey*: 'I leave it to be

settled by whomever it may concern, whether the tendency of this work be altogether to recommend parental tyranny or reward filial disobedience' (*NA*, p. 252). In Austen's works, as in Trollope's later on, worthy members of the younger generation, with a renewed sense of tradition and familial duty, eventually prevail over the tyranny or remissness of the older order.

Fanny's heart is divided between her real brother William and her cousin Edmund, with whom she also has a sibling relationship. Fanny and Edmund are of the same stock and are similar in appearance; they instinctively understand one another and share the same views and assumptions because of their common mythology and upbringing. They are close, both as children and as adolescents. To some extent, Fanny and Edmund's love seems narcissistic in that they love each other because they resemble each other. Yet, narcissism in the classic sense develops from a superficial attraction. That is to say, the narcissist appreciates and is moved by physical beauty. But the love between Austen's protagonists is based on inner beauty: moral character and good sense. As always, Austen's concept of love is grounded more significantly in domestic rather than sexual instincts.

From the beginning of *Mansfield Park*, Edmund acknowledges Fanny's good sense, sweet temper, and grateful heart. 'I do not know any better qualifications for a friend and companion' (*MP*, p. 26), he comments. Moreover, he is uncomfortable without his cousin's approbation of his actions. This need for approval works both ways, as tends to be the case in most ideal brother/sister relationships. As Fanny's champion and comforter, the narrator tells us, Edmund 'had supported her cause, or explained her meaning, he had told her not to cry, or had given her some proof of affection which made her tears delightful' (*MP*, p. 152). In return, Fanny's feelings about Edmund 'were compounded of all that was respectful, grateful, confiding, and tender' (*MP*, p. 37). Their mutual love and affection suggest an abiding, deeply sympathetic relationship between siblings.

Fanny falls in love with and later marries Edmund as a surrogate for her beloved brother William toward whom she feels an intense attachment. Throughout their long period of separation, Fanny and William relish their schemes to live their lives together in a comfortable little cottage. One critic has even gone so far as to say that William would make an ideal husband for Fanny.[10] When Fanny and William are reunited as young adults after ten years, the narrator pays tribute to the 'unchecked, equal, fearless intercourse' (p. 234) of the siblings. Indeed, Austen takes great pains in her description of their 'exquisite feeling' and 'agitating happiness'; when Fanny, for example, first sees her beloved brother in his naval uniform, she gazes at him for a moment in 'speechless admiration, and then threw her arms round his neck to sob out her various emotions of pain and pleasure' (*MP*, p. 384). Henry Crawford is aroused by their tender intimacy; Fanny's attractions for him double when he notices 'the glow of [her] cheek, the brightness of her eye, the deep interest, the absorbed attention, while her brother was describing any of the imminent hazards, or terrific scenes, which such a period, at sea, must supply' (*MP*, p. 235). Delighting in Fanny's fraternal affection, Henry exclaims to Mary, 'To see her with her brother! What could more delightfully prove that the warmth of her heart was equal to its gentleness?' (*MP*, p. 294). Fanny's adoration of William clearly encourages men who have her in mind as a sexual partner. Henry would like Fanny to kiss him as rapturously as she kisses her brother. But Fanny, as is appropriate for her, chooses not a stranger but a family member on whom to bestow her affection. Fanny's love for Edmund is a convenient displacement of her love for William. While Anderson argues that this displacement of love for a brother to love for a cousin was an established pattern of marriage in the nineteenth century, what is distinctive about Fanny and Edmund's relationship is that Fanny is removed at an early age from the household of the brother to that of the cousin who actually becomes her brother.[11]

To be sure, Fanny and Edmund's love is stimulated by their shared childhood experience and associations. And yet, it would be wrong to discount the effect of their more mature roles and duties as brother and sister. When Fanny and Edmund are both engaged in sending a letter to William, Fanny becomes an 'interesting object' (*MP*, p. 16) in her cousin's eyes. Furthermore, Edmund helps to educate Fanny, encouraging her taste and correcting her judgement. Such relations require an emotional investment. It is hardly surprising then that these fraternal obligations should encourage, in some cases, an affection that goes well beyond what is merely expected of brothers and sisters. And so, in the course of *Mansfield Park*, Fanny's love becomes more passionate than sororal. She grows jealous of the unworthy Mary Crawford and is enraptured by Edmund's compliments on her own face and figure and his regard for her. Her love deepens throughout the novel. After reading the letter in which

Edmund expresses doubts about his relationship with Mary, Fanny cries distractedly, 'Oh! Write, write. Finish it at once. Let there be an end of this suspense. Fix, commit, condemn yourself' (*MP*, p. 424).

For his part, Edmund attempts to differentiate between his fraternal love for Fanny and his conjugal love for Mary. These two, he claims, are 'the . . . dearest objects I have on this earth' (*MP*, p. 264). He seems to regard Fanny as his 'sister', his 'friend and companion' (*MP*, p. 26), whereas Mary is his lover and intended wife. But, even early on in the novel, Austen provides hints that his unconscious feelings for his cousin rival and even exceed those for his intended spouse. In his letter to Fanny, he proclaims that he cannot give up Mary because 'she is the only woman in the world whom I could ever think of as a wife'. But shortly afterwards he tells Fanny that 'I miss you more than I can express' (*MP*, pp. 421–3). It is perhaps his social conscience, governed by the unconscious taboo of incest, that makes his thoughts inexpressible. To articulate them would raise them to the preconscious or conscious level. Nevertheless, we learn that Edmund believes Fanny was born to be 'the perfect model of a woman' (*MP*, p. 347), and Mary reminds Henry that '[Fanny's] cousin Edmund never forgets her' (*MP*, p. 297). Before the Mansfield ball, Edmund shows his 'grateful affection' (*MP*, p. 270) for his cousin with his gift of a gold chain for William's cross, 'a token of the love of one of your oldest friends' (*MP*, p. 261).[12] During a conversation with Fanny at the ball, Edmund presses his cousin's hand to his lips 'with almost as much warmth as if it had been Miss Crawford's' (*MP*, p. 269).

That Austen stresses Edmund's brotherly affection until the end of the novel is of special import. When Fanny decks herself out in her finery to go to dinner at the Grants, Edmund looks at her 'with the kind smile of an affectionate brother' (*MP*, p. 222). As Fanny leaves for Portsmouth, her cousin gives her 'the affectionate farewell of a brother' (*MP*, p. 374). Apparently unaware of Fanny's love for him, Edmund tries to be of service to his cousin by his encouragement of Henry Crawford's suit, despite Fanny's vehement protest: 'Oh! never, never, never; he will never succeed with me' (*MP*, p. 347). After attempting to persuade Fanny to marry Henry, Edmund adds insult to injury by ushering his cousin 'with the kind authority of a privileged guardian into the house' (*MP*, p. 355). Following the scandal involving Maria Rushworth and Henry Crawford in London, Edmund arrives in Portsmouth to claim his cousin; pressing her to his heart, he barely articulates, 'My Fanny – my only sister – my only comfort now' (*MP*, p. 444). And after the disappointment and suffering in Edmund's relationship with Mary, 'Fanny's friendship was all that he had to cling to' (*MP*, p. 460).

Edmund's love for Fanny seems to be of a different quality from hers for him. She is in love with him throughout most of the novel in the way of a sister *and* a lover, whereas Edmund's conjugal love for her is not apparent until the end of *Mansfield Park*. He has to see first that an 'outsider' is *not* for him after all. In *Persuasion*, Anne Elliot claims that woman's love is different from man's:

'We certainly do not forget you, as soon as you forget us. It is, perhaps, our fate rather than our merit. We cannot help ourselves. We live at home, quiet, confined, and our feelings prey upon us. You are forced upon exertion. You have always a profession, pursuits, business of some sort or other, to take you back into the world immediately, and continual occupation and change soon weaken impression . . . . Your feelings may be the strongest . . . . ours are the most tender . . . All the privilege I claim for my own sex . . . is that of loving longest, when existence or when hope is gone.' (*P*, pp. 232–5)

In much the same way, Fanny has been deeply attached to her cousin since she was a child. Her tender feelings toward Edmund intensify as she matures; her love has always been more than sisterly or cousinly regard. But Edmund's brotherly affection changes to conjugal love only when his relationship with Mary fails; it dawns on him that his beloved 'sister' would make an excellent wife, and that going outside the home has its dangers – the dangers that attend to those who are too much unknown and easily misunderstood.

Not until the end of the novel is the fraternal affection of Fanny and Edmund fully transformed into conjugal love. But they find that their relationship has been strengthened by their early associations and instinctive understanding, Edmund's guiding and protection of Fanny, and their mutual love and esteem for one another's goodness and virtues. The author's emphasis, as always, is not on the sexual, but on the fraternal, spiritual quality of their relationship. In this respect, the union of the cousins is consecrated, freed from sin, and serves to verify and reinforce Austen's view of the sacredness of the home, which remains untainted in this 'world of changes' (*MP*, p. 374).

In its attitude towards the radical changes of the time and the sacredness of the home, *Mansfield Park* is often regarded as the most 'Victorian' of Austen's novels. At the end of the book, Fanny re-enters the world of the family at Mansfield for the satisfaction she finds impossible outside. *Mansfield Park* stresses the bonds of family love, the sanctity of the ideal home and family life, and the need for moral and religious reform in order to maintain stability. Austen uses the incest motif to investigate the evolving social and moral climate of her time. Her own ideology is affirmed and supported by the narrative structure of *Mansfield Park*; the centripetal progression in the novel is undergirded by the incest motif. The inward movement of the novel accelerates after Sir Thomas returns from abroad. Like a Victorian father, Sir Thomas emphasizes the necessity and desirability of domestic peace and tranquillity which 'shuts out noisy pleasures' (*MP*, p. 186). After his long absence and dangerous transatlantic journey, the baronet finds Mansfield in an uproar and Mr. Yates 'hallooing' in his private rooms. Not only is Yates wearisome because of his behaviour, but, as the friend of Tom and suitor of Julia, he becomes an offensive intruder. Sir Thomas' first decision is to dissolve the disruptive levity of the theatricals, which threaten to undermine the principles of the household, to overturn the control of 'outsiders', and to see off Yates, 'the worst object connected with the scheme' (*MP*, p. 194). It is telling that Fanny concurs with her uncle in his views of the play and of the sanctity of the home. In Portsmouth, when Fanny is sent away from her uncle's house, Mansfield becomes an absent ideal, and she thinks of the 'elegance, propriety, regularity, harmony – and perhaps, above all, the peace and tranquillity of Mansfield' (*MP*, p. 391).

Mansfield becomes a symbol of serenity and security during her exile, even though this was certainly not the case when she was there. For Fanny, 'To be in the centre of such a circle, loved by so many, to feel affection without fear or restraint, to feel herself the equal of those who surrounded her, to be at peace from all mention of the Crawfords, safe from every look which could be fancied a reproach on their account' (*MP*, p. 370) is a blissful prospect. Such a vision of Mansfield seems pure fantasy, especially at this stage in the novel; but, by the end of *Mansfield Park*, Fanny steps into and graces this dream-like landscape, in which the married cousins form the main focal point.

By way of suggesting the threat posed by a changing familial and social order, the author makes certain that evidence of the debasement of traditional ways is plentiful in *Mansfield Park*. Austen portrays a world in moral confusion. Secular values have replaced religion, symbolized by the distance of the church from the house and the chapel's disuse at Sotherton, the irresponsibility of absentee clergymen, and the indolence and self-indulgence of Dr. Grant. Moreover, marriage is often regarded as a commercial venture, a means of self-aggrandizement, as in the case of Maria Bertram's alliance to the affluent but foolish Mr. Rushworth. A fear of subversion pervades *Mansfield Park*; time-honored ethical principles of stability, endurance, reason, and *noblesse oblige* are abandoned and replaced by new, entrepreneurial ideas. Mr. Rushworth disclaims the old responsibility of the landowner toward the poor; he neglects the disgraceful and 'ugly' (*MP*, p. 82) cottages of the village and, instead, idly seeks to 'improve' the Sotherton estate. Likewise, Henry Crawford is a negligent landlord and spends little time at Everingham; the poor suffer while Henry selfishly indulges himself, visiting Mansfield, and, more particularly, London, an exciting centre of fashion and society, the influence of which is 'very much at war with all respectable attachments' (*MP*, p. 433).

It is significant that Fanny marries Edmund, a staunch paternalist (like his father), who will reside at his parish in Thornton Lacey, and who refuses Henry's solicitous proposals for the 'improvement' of it. Austen reveals her distaste and concern for the centrifugal or outward tendency of the community – the wider class divisions and exploitation of the poor, the selfish individualism of many of the characters in *Mansfield Park* – in her references to Henry and Mr. Rushworth's neglect of their duties as landowners as well as in Maria's indifference to her role as the mistress of Sotherton.[13] The marriage of Fanny and Edmund exemplifies Austen's defence of the traditional system. The union creates a centripetal or inward movement, a tightening of familial ties; their residence at Thornton Lacey and later at Mansfield will protect them and their parish from corruptive external influences. For Austen, as for the Victorians, the exemplary home is a haven from outside anxieties and commercialism threatening to adulterate society; it is a bulwark against the upheavals of a new age.

Henry and Mary Crawford are outsiders, modern, urban representatives of that age, who threaten to contaminate the sanctuary of Mansfield Park. The opening decades of the nineteenth century were characterized by the license and levity of the dandy and the epicure, self-indulgence and disregard for domesticity. A significant number of landowners were eager to profit by revolutionary schemes in both industry and agriculture; as a result, they paid less attention to the plight of the lower classes, and the division between rich and poor increased. In London, the court and the landed aristocracy pursued a life of pleasure. The profligacy of the court of the Prince Regent, who was notorious for his disruption of and disregard for domestic ties, was bruited throughout Europe.[14] In *Mansfield Park*, Mary and Henry emulate the manners and mores of the aristocracy. Recently, one critic has argued that the Crawfords 'are by no means a serious threat to the Mansfield Park order', that they merely manifest 'playful indulgence, a spiritual luxury of privileged people'.[15] But, on the contrary, Austen demonstrates that their self-indulgence is hazardous, that privileged people should be responsible and humanitarian rather than dissolute, indolent, and venal.

Rich, witty, and talented, but egocentric, insincere, and irreverent, the interlopers from London lack principles and, in this way, typify the hollow men and women of the age. Even more important, Henry is critical of tradition, and selfishly disrupts the family peace at Mansfield by flirting with both of the Bertram sisters and, ultimately, eloping with Maria. He is a capital improver, but his ideas presage harm. On the subject of alterations at Thornton Lacey, Crawford claims that 'the farm-yard must be cleared away entirely, and planted up to shut out the blacksmith's shop. The house must be turned to face the east instead of the north . . . . Then the stream – something must be done with the stream' (*MP*, p. 242). In his desire to make the parsonage fit for a gentleman, Henry resolves to 'shut out' the village and clear away the past. As Alistair M. Duckworth has pointed out, Austen distrusted 'improvements' of the kind favoured by Henry, for she believed they only widened the gulf between upper and lower classes and challenged cultural heritage by their radical nature.[16] Henry extends his desire for 'improvements' to the house at Mansfield by turning it into a theatre. In his reading of drama there is 'variety of excellence'; such is his love of reading aloud that he desires to preach, but only to a fashionable, educated London audience, and only 'now and then . . . but not for a constancy' (*MP*, p. 341). Henry's capriciousness and lack of principles imperil the propriety of Mansfield and compromise the respectability of Maria and Julia.

Austen's uneasiness about the new age and its moral transvaluations is revealed by the play-acting episode. The German source and revolutionary sentiments of *Lovers' Vows* (1798) mark it as suspicious and objectionable material, especially in light of Austen's critical attitude toward the Prince Regent and the immoral court of the Saxe-Cobourgs, and the general fear of France following the Revolution and the devastating Napoleonic wars. The foreign drama threatens to cause chaos at Mansfield.[17] Arguments break out between the siblings, and, as Edmund suggests, 'Family squabling [sic] is the greatest evil of all' (*MP*, p. 128). One objection to the play is that it is so close to the actual condition of the personages then at Mansfield that no one in it is really 'acting'. Maria plays the part of a woman about to be illicitly seduced. Rushworth is an asinine admirer. Mary is cast as the forward, immodest Amelia; Yates as a supporter of elopement; and Edmund as a clergyman in love with Amelia. All of the characters are playing exaggerated versions of themselves.[18] In addition, Fanny is shocked by the choice of the play because it deals with illegitimacy, seduction, and adultery, and therefore is 'totally improper for home representation' and 'unfit to be expressed by any woman of modesty' (*MP*, p. 137).

Ironically, *Lovers' Vows* reflects Austen's novels to some extent in that the organizing principle is the quest to recover lost family ties, particularly the fraternal ties of Amelia and Frederick, who are finally reunited at the end of the novel. Moreover, family ties are also the organizing principle of another notorious play by Kotzebue, *Adelaide Von Wulfingen* (1801). In this play, which Austen may well have seen since it was performed on the London stage during her time, the heroine marries her brother and bears him children; they live happily until a malevolent priest reveals the truth about their relationship. It is my contention that Austen drew on the themes of familial bonding in *Lovers' Vows* and incest in *Adelaide Von Wulfingen* and modified them for her own purposes in *Mansfield Park*.[19]

Not only are the circumstances of the theatricals untoward, owing to Sir Thomas' absence, Maria's betrothal, and the play's general inappropriateness and subversive content, but, in addition, the inviolability of the household is threatened by the proposed intrusion of an outsider from the town, engaged to perform the spare part, who is scarcely known to any of them. Such is Edmund's horror at the idea of the engagement of an outsider that he agrees to act – in order, he claims, to avoid 'the mischief that *may* . . . the unpleasantness that *must*, arise from a young man's being received in this manner – domesticated among us – authorised to come at all hours – and placed suddenly on a footing which must do away with all restraints. To think only of the licence which every rehearsal must tend to create. It is all very bad' (*MP*, p. 154). But his siblings find it difficult to conceal their smiles when the besotted Edmund descends from his moral elevation in order to act opposite Mary. Still, Fanny is alarmed: Mary's pernicious influence over Edmund robs him of his moral scruples and judgement concerning the acting scheme. The drama promotes license, and Fanny, chagrined by Edmund's inconsistency, cares no longer if she herself is finally obliged to participate in the play by the selfish inclinations of her cousins: for Fanny, 'no matter – it was all misery now' (*MP*, p. 160).

The outsiders Henry and Mary attempt, in effect, to corrupt Edmund and Fanny. Edmund errs, captivated by the inviting smiles and beauty of the temptress. Mary Crawford possesses wit and grace; her vivacity and talents at playing the harp and riding bedazzle Edmund. It is only at the end of the novel that the charm is broken, and Edmund acknowledges her 'faults of principle . . . blunted delicacy and . . . corrupted, vitiated mind' (*MP*, p. 456) – when Mary criticizes the detection and not the offence of her brother's elopement with Maria. Fanny fears Henry's lack of moral scruples but admits the apparent improvement in his character, his increasing kindness and consideration as he woos her. She seems about to relent in her refusal of him; however, her suspicions are confirmed when he elopes with Mrs. Rushworth. As Austen suggests, marriage to an outsider, such as Henry or Mary Crawford, would be dangerous for Fanny or Edmund. Elsewhere in the novel, the consequences are disastrous when a Bertram goes outside the family, as in the case of Maria's marriage to Mr. Rushworth, and Julia's elopement with the obnoxious and impecunious Mr. Yates.

The Crawfords' license menaces the established order of the home and family at Mansfield Park, and the novel concludes with the banishing of their sexual impurity and moral subversion. As siblings the Crawfords are close friends and confidantes, but Mary also takes a prurient interest in her promiscuous brother's sex life. Her partiality for Henry makes her blind to his sordid and dishonorable conduct with women. While Mary faults the Admiral for his rakishness, she condones exactly the same sort of behaviour in her brother, viewing him rather as the glorious 'hero of an old romance' (*MP*, p. 360). Mary is like a voyeur; she provokes and is titillated by Henry's multiple conquests of women in London, and she particularly relishes the sexual rivalry and jealousy he kindles at Mansfield between Maria and Julia. Moreover, Mary fans the flames of his passion for Fanny, even acting as her brother's accomplice in tricking Fanny into accepting a necklace which Henry gave her as a gift. As part of her devious strategy to arouse Fanny's ardour for Henry, Mary speculates about the 'sensation' their union might occasion in London. She even goes so far as to describe to Fanny 'the envyings and heartburnings of dozens and dozens' (*MP*, p. 360). The ultimate temptation for Fanny, in Mary's opinion, will be 'the glory of fixing one who has been shot at by so many; of having it in one's power to pay off the debts of one's sex!' (*MP*, p. 363).

Sensation, scandal, and sexual manipulation are Mary's major interests in life. While she herself does not indulge in sexual affairs, Mary experiences sex vicariously through her brother's exploits. Moreover, her love for Henry is narcissistic. As superficial, coldhearted, and decadent as her brother, Mary takes pleasure in Henry's appearance and notoriety, since she herself often profits by them. She luxuriates in being courted for her brother's sake and basks in his reflected sexual glory. In this way, Austen counterpoints the sibling relationships of Mary and Henry and Fanny and Edmund. Fanny's sexual feelings for Edmund (which rise to the surface when Edmund falls in love with Mary) are natural and acceptable because they are compounded with fraternal feelings which transmute mere sexual attraction. But in the case of the Crawfords, Mary's love for her brother is contaminated by her own concupiscence and perverted desire for sexual thrills and misconduct. Such a sibling love is unacceptable; it is dangerous both to the family and to society since it has the potential to wreak domestic havoc rather than to create domestic order.

The depravity of the Crawfords is compared to a disease which threatens to infect Mansfield. The heroine's reaction to the elopement of Henry and Mrs. Rushworth is one of nausea and revulsion: 'Fanny seemed to herself never to have been shocked before. There was no possibility of rest. The evening passed, without a pause of misery, the night was totally sleepless. She passed only from feelings of sickness to shudderings of horror; and from hot fits of fever to cold' (*MP*, p. 441). Avrom Fleishman points out that Fanny sounds as though she thinks there is something incestuous about Henry and Mrs. Rushworth's act, 'both families connected as they were by tie upon tie, all friends, all intimate together!' (*MP*, p. 441). But he does not investigate the implications of incest in this passage.[20] Paula Marantz Cohen stresses the resemblance between Maria and Fanny, asserting that Fanny's language suggests Maria has engaged in incest, an act which she herself engages in with Austen's approval.[21] However, Maria's act disrupts the family – unlike Fanny's, which consolidates it. The incestuous relationship between Henry and Mrs. Rushworth is based only on sexual appetite; moreover, it creates scandal. Therefore, it cannot gain Austen's approval. But the constructive relationship of cousins Fanny and Edmund, which blends spiritual, mental, and physical affinities, is not intended to shock or repel; on the contrary, the union enriches and improves the family at Mansfield and, in Austen's opinion, it should gain the reader's approbation.

At the end of the novel, chagrined by the corruption of the new order, 'Sick of ambitious and mercenary connections, prizing more and more the sterling good of principle and temper, and chiefly anxious to bind by the strongest securities all that remained to him of domestic felicity' (*MP*, p. 471), Sir Thomas blesses the marriage of his son and niece and retreats into the security of home in order to defend his principles and interests. Sir Thomas's protective attitude against the outside world typifies the tendency toward insularity in *Mansfield Park*. His retreat from the calculating and acquisitive outside world, like the alliance of Fanny and Edmund, is a stabilising movement. Indeed, the incestuous marriage of the cousins, brought up in the same household as brother and sister, completes the baronet's withdrawal into the protection and confinement of the home. One critic has remarked that 'the incestuous tendency in fiction is conceived less as an infantile fantasy than as a fear of change or death',[22] that incest betokens an inward, self-protective movement, but that, nonetheless, it is essentially self-repetitive and regressive. In Austen's view, however, the incestuous marriages are neither regressive nor negative (except in the case of a purely sexual relationship, such as that of Henry and Maria); instead, incest between like-minded members of the approved clan contributes to the moral good of the family and the home. In *Mansfield Park*, the incestuous alliance of the cousins may be regarded as symbolic of the author's endorsement of traditional moral values. As she abhors the infiltration and the undermining of unscrupulous, false types such as the Crawfords, Austen sees to it that Fanny and Edmund stay within the family and are sheltered from the danger and risk of external influences.

For Austen, the conjugal tie was on the whole less appealing than the fraternal tie. She, herself, had six brothers and a sister and never married. Since she disliked to write of matters of which she had little knowledge, Austen omits romantic scenes, particularly at the end of novels, and instead concentrates on scenes involving family members. *Mansfield Park* is no exception to this rule. At the conclusion of the novel, Austen's cavalier treatment of the change in Edmund and Fanny's relationship is noteworthy:

> Scarcely had he done regretting Mary Crawford and observing to Fanny how impossible it was that he should ever meet with such another woman, before it began to strike him whether a very different kind of woman might not do just as well or a great deal better; whether Fanny herself were not growing as dear, as important to him in all her smiles, and all her ways, as Mary Crawford had ever been; and whether it might not be a possible, an hopeful undertaking that her warm and sisterly regard for him would be foundation enough for wedded love. (*MP*, p. 470)

Austen's narrator abruptly sums up and understates the transformation from fraternal to conjugal love: 'I only entreat everybody to believe that exactly at the time when it was quite natural that it should be so, and not a week earlier, Edmund did cease to care about Miss Crawford, and became as anxious to marry Fanny, as Fanny herself could desire' (*MP*, p. 470). In several ways, this passage serves as an ironic commentary on the way such romantic 'discovery' scenes are usually written. The succinctness and unceremonious summary of Austen's scenes are in direct contrast to the overblown, protracted style of 'discovery' scenes in gothic fiction as well as in the novels of sensibility of contemporary writers. Instead of the romantic attachment between the two cousins, Austen stresses their fraternal regard and their having grown to maturity together: 'With such a regard for her, indeed, as his had long been, a regard founded on the most endearing claims of innocence and helplessness, and completed by every recommendation of growing worth, what could be more natural than the change?' (*MP*, p. 470). The critic who claims that the finale is 'a perfunctorily opted anticlimax the narrator washes her hands of, rather than a properly wished-for and well-deserved union towards which the parties have been moving all along' misses the point of the novel; on the contrary, the reader has been well-prepared for the union of the cousins throughout the work.[23] The love of Fanny and Edmund needs no further elaboration.

In the end, Mansfield remains immaculate and inviolable, undefiled by the morally incorrigible Crawfords, who come to regret bitterly their losses at the end of the novel. Despite the spirit and charm of the Crawfords, Austen condemns their irresponsibility, their lack of principles, and, most of all, their violation of the tranquillity of the family circle. In literature, verve and wit are sometimes the devil's tools, whereas dullness and virtue often go hand in hand. The choice between good and evil is after all supposed to be difficult. But Austen's perspective on the moral turpitude of Henry and Mary does not vacillate.[24] At the end of the novel, Austen disdainfully doles out poetic justice: Mary cannot put Edmund out of her mind and bitterly regrets the 'domestic happiness' (*MP*, p. 469) she might have had at Mansfield. As for Henry, Austen points out that he is vexed, regretful, and sometimes full of self-reproach and wretchedness 'in having *so requited hospitality, so injured family peace*, so forfeited his best, most estimable and endeared acquaintance, and so lost the woman whom he had rationally, as well as passionately, loved' (*MP*, p. 469, italics added). In the end, Austen makes it seem that Henry has committed a crime for which he must be punished.

Austen's awareness of the tension between conservatism and change resonates throughout the novel. Her own inclinations are manifest when, in the end, all of the approved characters seem to agree that Mansfield has been saved by the alliance of the cousins from the encroachment of the new order and negative values. Some critics have claimed that the overall mood of *Mansfield Park* is pessimistic, and that the stasis achieved is regressive. But such a reading becomes difficult to sustain at the conclusion of the novel, where the mood is obviously one of optimism and satisfaction; far from being regressive, the incestuous marriage not only proves to be restorative but also carries with it distinct moral and social benefits. Indeed, the marriage of Edmund and Fanny is the crux of Austen's moral vision in *Mansfield Park*. Mansfield is safe, and there is no doubt about its moral stature; and the union of Edmund and Fanny is a perfect marriage because of their spiritual affinities and their similarities of taste and temper: 'the happiness of the married cousins must appear as secure as earthly happiness can be. – Equally formed for domestic life, and attached to country pleasures, their home was the home of affection and comfort' (*MP*,

p. 473). For Austen, such a union is the only domestic establishment worth having, and in this case it is only available *inside* the family.

Other novels by Austen end with descriptions of the happiness of the hero and heroine, but *Mansfield Park* is the only novel in which Austen alludes to parenthood in the conclusion and promises a new generation: 'to complete the picture of good, the acquisition of Mansfield living by the death of Dr. Grant occurred just after they had been married long enough to begin to want an increase of income, and feel their distance from the paternal abode an inconvenience' (*MP*, p. 473). By referring to the impending birth of a child, Austen projects Fanny and Edmund into parental roles and endorses the domestic happiness of the married cousins who have loved, cherished, esteemed, and respected one another since they were children. The marriage is blessed – cousins can keep a family going. The union is fruitful, and the blissful pair look to the future with hope.

EMMA

At the beginning of Emma, Mr. Knightley is introduced as 'a very old and intimate friend of the family'. More important, he is connected with the heroine as the elder brother of Isabella's husband and is 'one of the few people who could see faults in Emma Woodhouse, and the only one who ever told her of them' (*E*, p. 11). For the major part of the novel, Mr. Knightley, Emma's brother-in-law and neighbor, acts as an elder brother or father figure to his young sister-in-law; he lectures her, criticizes her behaviour, protects, nurtures, and cherishes her. This relationship between the two creates a certain tension of desire and propriety. Yet, as they come to understand that their sensibilities are in harmony, their desires are cojoined with their sense of what is appropriate. In this regard, the novel – like all of Austen's novels – is satisfying as a fantasy or fairy tale because in the end the heroine marries her brotherly 'knight'. Indeed, Emma may be seen not only as a dramatization of the fantasy of incest but also as a dramatic presentation of the power of the unconscious.

As in the relationship between Edmund and Fanny, Austen stresses Mr. Knightley's fraternal regard for Emma and the advantages of in-family marriage. Mr. Knightley says of his brother near the end of the novel: '[John] is no complimenter, and though I do know him to have, likewise, a most brotherly affection for you, he is so far from making flourishes, that any other young woman might think him rather cool in her praise' (*E*, p. 464). Like John, Mr. Knightley has 'a most brotherly affection' for Emma; for he makes no 'flourishes', offers criticisms of her conduct, and proves his readiness to find Emma blameworthy when necessary. That is to say, measured against the exaggerated standards of popular fiction, his behaviour would seem neither romantic nor chivalrous, even in spite of the associations attached to his name.

And yet, Mr. Knightley takes a great interest in Emma; his concern is brotherly, but there are also clues along the way to his passionate feelings for her. He tells Mrs. Weston: 'I confess that I have seldom seen a *face or figure* more pleasing to me than her's. But I am a partial old friend . . . . I love to look at her' (*E*, p. 39, italics added). A little later, Mr. Knightley muses on the future of his 'sister':

> 'I have a very sincere interest in Emma. *Isabella does not seem more my sister; has never excited a greater interest, perhaps hardly so great.* There is an anxiety, a curiosity in what one feels for Emma. I wonder what will become of her . . . . She always declares that she will never marry, which, of course, means just nothing at all. But I have no idea that she has ever yet seen a man she cared for. It would not be a bad thing for her to be very much in love, with a proper object. I should like to see Emma in love, and in some doubt of a return; it would do her good. But there is nobody hereabouts to attract her; and she goes so seldom from home' (*E*, pp. 40–41, italics added).

His comments are revealing; he gives himself away when he notices Emma's face and figure, and when he remarks that 'I love to look at her', and that 'I should like to see Emma in love and in some doubt of a return'. He, himself, unconsciously hopes to be the object of his sister-in-law's affections: 'there is an anxiety, a curiosity in what one feels for Emma'. In short, Emma is both a woman whom Mr. Knightley describes as his 'sister', and a woman whom he also admires and desires. Although they are members of the same clan, so to speak, and Mr. Knightley has been used to thinking of Emma as his younger sister, his desire for her is in no way repressed as, at first, Edmund's feelings for Fanny are in *Mansfield Park*. That is to say, unlike Edmund's, in Mr. Knightley's case there seems to be no initial boundary or lingering taboo imposed between sibling love and the love that leads to marriage. In fact, Mr. Knightley appears to understand more immediately that these two types of love closely resemble each other in that they are relationships forged through trust, deep affection, and the common beliefs of members of the same family.

The major structural device of *Emma* is the endeavour of the heroine and Mr. Knightley, consciously or unconsciously, to retain and strengthen sibling ties. Sibling-like sparrings, disagreements, and peacemaking sessions constitute the dramatic structure of the novel. Moreover, Mr. Knightley, in the way of an elder brother, acts as Emma's teacher. As Juliet McMaster remarks, there are courses ranging from initiation rites to lectures in moral guidance and from examinations to graduation at the end of the novel.[25] In one scene, Mr. Knightley criticizes Emma's likeness of Harriet; and, although Emma realizes he is correct, she will not own to it. The 'brother' and 'sister', likewise, quarrel heatedly over Emma's matchmaking and her meddling in the affair of Robert Martin and Harriet. Later on, they patch up their differences at Hartfield. However, this potentially romantic scene between them becomes, significantly, a domestic scene created by a family connection; the two of them handle and admire their baby niece with 'all the unceremoniousness of perfect amity' (*E*, p. 98).

Still, the distinction between fraternal and passionate love is more blurred in *Emma* than in *Mansfield Park*. Austen writes about Emma and Mr. Knightley as if they are potential lovers, even though she stresses that they are closely related. Mr. Knightley becomes jealous of 'trifling, silly' (*E*, p. 206) Frank Churchill; Emma is astonished because Mr. Knightley, for once, does not show his usual 'liberality of mind' (*E*, p. 151). Unlike Emma, who does not understand her feelings of jealousy concerning Mr. Knightley until much later, Mr. Knightley discovers earlier in the novel the reasons for his instinctive dislike of Frank. He suspects Frank of some double dealing in his pursuit of Emma and fears the consequences for his sister-in-law: 'How the delicacy, the discretion of his favourite could have so lain asleep! . . . . He could not see her in a situation of such danger, without trying to preserve her. It was his duty' (*E*, pp. 348–9). When Emma tells Mr. Knightley that she can answer for Frank Churchill's indifference to Jane Fairfax, Mr. Knightley becomes instantly jealous and takes a hasty leave of Hartfield in order to compose his feverish feelings of irritation. In short, Mr. Knightley acts dutifully as Emma's champion and protector, as Edmund acts for Fanny in *Mansfield Park*. But, unlike Edmund, who urges on Henry Crawford in his wooing of Fanny, Mr. Knightley does not encourage Frank Churchill's suit. On the contrary, Mr. Knightley's incestuous love for Emma makes him hostile to the possibility of her choosing a romantic attachment outside the family. He becomes passionately jealous of his beloved sister-in-law's fondness of Frank, much as Fanny envies Edmund's love for Mary Crawford.

Emma, on the other hand, fails to detect the real causes of her feelings, violent dislikes, and jealousies until near the end of the novel; but then she always fails to see the truth. However, there are moments when her unconscious love makes a temporary breakthrough into half-awareness and manifests itself. There is, for instance, the scene in which she contemplates her image of the ideal man: 'General benevolence, but not general friendship, made a man what he ought to be. – She could fancy such a man' (*E*, p. 320). Mr. Knightley, we are aware, fits this description as though he were the prototype. Emma notices his 'tall, firm, upright figure' (*E*, p. 326) at the Crown ball and his frequent observations of her. And she is overjoyed when Mr. Knightley takes a turn dancing with the slighted Harriet: 'Never had she been more surprised, seldom more delighted, than at that instant. She was all pleasure and gratitude' (*E*, p. 328). At this point, Emma reveals no sexual jealousy of the humble Harriet, no fear of her captivating Mr. Knightley. Yet she cannot, at this point, allow these latent feelings to manifest themselves consciously. It seems plausible, from a Freudian perspective, that Emma's slow progress to awareness of her feelings for Mr. Knightley involves some repression. Her relation to him is symbolically oedipal: because of their ages, he is something of a father-figure to her as well as an elder brother.

Emma alludes to the incestuous implications of her relationship with Mr. Knightley when she asks him to dance with her at the ball: 'You have shown that you can dance, and you know we are not *really* so much brother and sister as to make it at all improper' (italics added). To which Mr. Knightley emphatically replies 'Brother and sister! no, indeed' (*E*, p. 331). He has loved Emma fraternally and passionately since she was thirteen. But because of the age difference of sixteen or seventeen years between them, Mr. Knightley has always assumed that Emma would marry someone her own age – someone like Frank Churchill. So he treats

Emma as an elder brother might treat her for fear of rejection, since he is so much older than she.

Unlike *Mansfield Park* and *Sense and Sensibility*, in which the hero's love for the heroine is not revealed as conjugal love until the end of the novel, in *Emma* the roles are reversed – Emma's fraternal affection for Mr. Knightley is not transformed until the conclusion of the novel. *Emma* is a mirror-image of the other works in that it retells the story of an incestuous love from another perspective; in this novel, the woman rather than the man discovers her true feelings at the end. *Emma* also reverses the pattern of Austen's other works in that the brother-hero acts as the redeemer of the sister-heroine rather than *vice versa*. Austen was steeped in the typical formulae of much Romantic poetry and also of numerous eighteenth-century novels, where the sister rescues her brother and operates as his spiritual guardian and conscience (as, for example, in Burney's *Evelina*). In *Mansfield Park*, Austen adopts a similar formula: Fanny serves as Edmund's deliverer from a dangerous liaison with Mary. And, in *Sense and Sensibility*, Elinor's marriage to Edward redeems him from the folly of his previous attachment to the unworthy Lucy. But in *Emma*, Austen transposes the usual pattern and shows Mr. Knightley acting as Emma's conscience and as her saviour.

The emotional climax of *Emma*, and the culmination of the latent love between Emma and Mr. Knightley, is the incident with Miss Bates.[26] Like an older brother, Mr. Knightley remonstrates with Emma for her cruel treatment of Miss Bates at Box Hill. Emma is dismayed, not so much because she has upset Miss Bates but because Mr. Knightley has shown serious disapproval of her: 'Never had [Emma] felt so agitated, mortified, grieved, at any circumstance in her life . . . . She felt it at her heart' (*E*, p. 376). Full of contrition, she soon visits Miss Bates to make up for her conduct. When he hears of Emma's penitence, Mr. Knightley is delighted:

> He looked at her with a glow of regard. She was warmly gratified – and in another moment still more so by a little movement of more than common friendliness on his part. – He took her hand; – whether she had not herself made the first motion, she could not say – she might, perhaps, have rather offered it – but he took her hand, pressed it, and was certainly on the point of carrying it to his lips – when, from some fancy or other, he suddenly let it go. – . . . . his manners had in general so little gallantry . . . but

she thought nothing became him more. – It was with him of so simple, yet so dignified a nature . . . . It spoke such perfect amity. (*E*, pp. 385–6)

The ardour of Emma's and Mr. Knightley's feelings – their surprise, hesitation, and pleasure – breaks through to the surface and is apparent in the many interruptions and dashes throughout the passage. As is often the case in Austen's novels, this romantic scene is also a domestic scene; it takes place in the parlour at Hartfield before the eyes of the unsuspecting Mr. Woodhouse. And even in this episode, Austen's emphasis is still very much on the spiritual quality of their relationship: the 'perfect amity' of the brother and sister-in-law, their mutual regard and gratitude, Mr. Knightley's simple, dignified nature.

The love of Emma and Mr. Knightley has originated and been disclosed in their relation as brother and sister; the unfolding of the love affair takes place within the family. When Emma understands the true nature of her love for Mr. Knightley, she still thinks of his regard for her as brotherly: '*from family attachment and habit, and thorough excellence of mind, he had loved and watched over her from a girl, with an effort to improve her, and an anxiety for her doing right, which no other creature had at all shared*' (*E*, p. 415, italics added). Even when Mr. Knightley proposes to Emma, Austen dismisses the romantic scene between them in the garden at Hartfield with a curt 'What did she say? – Just what she ought, of course. A lady always does' (*E*, p. 431). Instead, she stresses the fraternal attachment of the pair, just as she emphasizes the fraternal attachment of Fanny and Edmund at the end of *Mansfield Park*. Indeed, Mr. Knightley's reminiscences of Emma as a girl suggest that while he has always looked upon her as a sister, his fraternal love is also the love that leads to marriage: 'I have blamed you, and lectured you, and you have borne it as no other woman in England would have borne it . . . . God knows, I have been an indifferent lover' (*E*, p. 430). However, it matters not to Austen if Mr. Knightley has been an 'indifferent lover'; what matters is that he has been a good brotherly lover, without the gallant flourishes and blind affection of a passionate lover, such as the deceitful Frank Churchill. Instead, as in the union of Fanny and Edmund, the love of Emma and Mr. Knightley grows out of domestic happiness, years of warm friendship, and tender affection.

SENSE AND SENSIBILITY

Like Fanny's marriage to Edmund in *Mansfield Park* and Emma's marriage to Mr. Knightley in *Emma*, Elinor's marriage to Edward in *Sense and Sensibility* takes place very much within the family. Although marriage between a man and his sister's husband's sister was not prohibited in Austen's time, the union of Elinor and Edward, like that of Mr. Knightley and Emma, is incestuous in the special sense that we have defined. Throughout the novel Elinor and Edward treat one another as blood brother and blood sister; while they do not possess the childhood associations of Edmund and Fanny or Emma and Mr. Knightley, their relationship is still very much like that of siblings. Moreover, the relationship of Elinor and Edward is similar to that of Fanny and Edmund in *Mansfield Park* in another sense. Although the heroine loves the man from the outset of the novel, the fraternal love of the hero is not fully transformed into conjugal love until the end of the work.

As in *Mansfield Park* and *Emma*, there is a clear-cut distinction in *Sense and Sensibility* between the brotherly Edward and the passionate lover, Willoughby. Edward is introduced early on in the novel as the brother of Mrs. John Dashwood. Although he is 'pleasing' and 'gentlemanlike', with an 'open affectionate heart' and 'good understanding' (*SS*, p. 15), he is certainly not a dashing, handsome, or charming hero, and he cuts a poor figure beside the sexy Willoughby, much as Edmund Bertram cuts a poor figure beside charming, witty Henry Crawford in *Mansfield Park*, and as Mr. Knightley, 'a sensible man of seven or eight and thirty' (*E*, p. 9), seems old and rather dull when first compared with the young and handsome Frank Churchill. But Austen expresses disapproval in her novels of the gallant lover. In *Sense and Sensibility*, for instance, Elinor criticizes Willoughby's conduct: 'he was a lover; his attentions were wholly Marianne's, and a far less agreeable man might have been more generally pleasing' (*SS*, p. 55). Willoughby is apparently smitten with Marianne and spends his time making himself attractive and agreeable to her alone. He sacrifices general politeness and propriety in order to give Marianne his undivided attention. Elinor censures Willoughby for his disregard of decorum, his selfishness, his violence of feeling, and his irresponsible enthusiasm as a lover.

By way of contrast, Marianne criticizes her brother-in-law elect,

Edward, for his deficiency as a lover, his lack of spirit and sensibility. Edward is not a gallant man, but he is a humane one. Through most of the novel, while Elinor is unsure of Edward's affection for her, she admires and esteems him for his goodness of heart and mind, his benevolence and understanding. She treats him 'as she thought he ought to be treated from the family connection' (*SS*, p. 89). Edward seems to admire Elinor, but for the major part of the work he does not distinguish between her and Marianne; he seems to have fraternal feelings for both of them. In fact, early in the novel, Elinor misunderstands Edward's intentions. Since he is bound to Lucy, he cannot marry Elinor. His social conscience appears to act as a brake on any amatory feelings that may originate for Elinor, and so he loves her as one of his family. Thus, out of honour to his betrothed and also because he restrains himself from encouraging an aimless love relationship which could disrupt domestic peace, Edward regards Elinor as a sister. In fact, Edward's fraternal love is not metamorphosed into passionate love until Lucy elopes with Robert, and Edward can lift the taboo he has imposed on his feelings. But, earlier in the work, when Edward bids Elinor and Marianne farewell, 'it was the good wishes of an affectionate brother to both' (*SS*, p. 39). The eventual marriage of Elinor and Edward is endogamous in that, like Fanny and Edmund in *Mansfield Park*, they behave more like siblings than lovers until late in the novel; future spouses, in each case, are known more as members of the family than as lovers.

The main weapon Lucy Steele uses to beat down Elinor when she discovers the friendship between her and Edward is her spiteful reminder that Edward thinks of Marianne – and Elinor – 'quite as his own sisters' (*SS*, p. 130). Dismayed by Lucy's revelation about her betrothal to Edward, Elinor is bitter; but she always remembers that Edward is her relation and pays him the attention properly deserved by a brother-in-law. When Colonel Brandon tells Elinor that the living on his estate is vacant, for instance, Elinor exerts herself to tell her brother-in-law of his great fortune. Edward and Lucy have previously been unable to marry since Mrs. Ferrars cut her son off from the family fortune, and Edward has no means of support. With Colonel Brandon's living, Edward will be able to marry Lucy. His reaction to Elinor's tidings, however, is certainly not one of jubilation. This potentially romantic scene between the characters is turned into a domestic scene between two near relations; despite their initial embarrassment and distress and Edward's 'look so serious, so earnest, so uncheerful' (*SS*, p. 290) when Elinor gives him the news, there is no romantic interchange between them. Instead, Austen stresses their fraternal regard for each other's welfare and Edward's gratitude rather than his suppressed amour.

Later in the novel, another potentially romantic scene between Elinor and Edward is turned into a domestic scene. Freed from his engagement to Lucy, Edward rushes to Barton. Mrs. Dashwood and her three daughters are all sewing in the sitting-room when he arrives. After he informs them, much to their amazement, that Lucy has married his brother Robert, Edward picks up a pair of their scissors and spoils them and their sheath by cutting the latter to pieces. Both Edward's newly-charged passion for Elinor and his perplexity at the transformation in his situation are objectified by his actions. In this scene, there is no romantic dialogue between the hero and heroine, and Austen focuses on the domestic situation and the varying reactions of Mrs. Dashwood and her three daughters to their relation's tidings. At the end of the scene, Austen gives an abrupt summary of what ensues between Elinor and Edward: 'This only need be said; – that when they all sat down to table at four o'clock, about three hours after his arrival, [Edward] had secured his lady, engaged her mother's consent, and was not only in the rapturous profession of the lover, but in the reality of reason and truth, one of the happiest of men' (*SS*, p. 361). The 'rapturous' couple proceed to sit down for tea; their passion is tempered by their excellence of mind, 'perfect amity', fraternal estimation, and admiration for each other. Lovers are defined here as people who fit into certain domestic situations created by family connections. Austen stresses that the rightness of their union has very little to do with sexual passion.

The story of the incestuous love of Colonel Brandon and Eliza Williams, located at the heart of *Sense and Sensibility*, is the melodramatic material of gothic and sentimental novels. This narrative seems at first to be contrived and incongruous with the rest of the text; Austen dwells on the wretchedness of two fallen women, who are coincidentally mother and daughter. But, in fact, the story fits into and is another facet of the incest formula in Austen's oeuvre. Drawing on the eighteenth-century novel paradigm of the orphan girl who is raised with male relatives, Austen experiments in the story of Brandon and Eliza with a plot configuration she later developed more fully in *Mansfield Park*.

Eliza Williams is one of Brandon's 'nearest relatives' and his father's ward. Austen highlights the shared childhood associations of the cousins, how they were 'playfellows and friends' from their earliest years. Their fervent love for each other springs naturally from their domestic attachment. Unlike the impecunious Fanny Price in *Mansfield Park*, Eliza has a large fortune. For this reason, her uncle forces her to marry Brandon's elder brother, much to her chagrin. The marriage of Eliza and Brandon's brother has sinister overtones, for, as Brandon remarks, 'his pleasures were not what they ought to have been' (*SS*, p. 206); moreover, Eliza's husband treats her unkindly. To escape their misery, Brandon and Eliza arrange to elope; their plans, however, are betrayed by Eliza's maid.

Rather than tantalizing the reader with the incestuous implications of the relationship between Brandon and Eliza, Austen arouses sympathy for them and presses home the spiritual nature and sibling association of the bond between them. While Brandon and Eliza's proposed elopement defied parental authority, we lament that their scheme did not succeed. Austen seems to imply that the marriage of these two cousins, who cannot remember a time when they did *not* love each other, would doubtless have been a fulfilling union. As a result of the discovery of their proposed elopement, Brandon is banished from his home, and Eliza is allowed no freedom or company until she submits to her uncle's will. Worse is in store for Brandon's 'unfortunate sister' (*SS*, p. 207); her husband divorces her, and Eliza turns to prostitution, ends up in a spunging house, and dies of consumption. Years later, her daughter has an illegitimate child by Willoughby. Such is Brandon's attachment to Eliza that he falls in love with Marianne because of her resemblance to his sister. He wants to protect and console Marianne like an elder brother or father, as he once protected and consoled Eliza. In this respect, his love for Marianne seems more like a transfer or resuscitation of his former passion for Eliza. At the end of the novel, the unions of Colonel Brandon and Marianne and Edward and Elinor create a tight ring at Delaford. The two couples live almost within sight of each other, the Colonel and Marianne residing at the mansion-house, and Elinor and Edward close by at the parsonage. The ring closes the ranks against predatory outsiders, such as Willoughby and Lucy Steele, who threaten to lower moral standards and desecrate the temple of the home.

Although their situations differ, one point remains constant: Austen will not allow her heroes and heroines to marry on the ground of sexual magnetism or romantic love. She constructs marriages on the foundation of sibling ties.[27] The incestuous themes of *Mansfield Park, Emma,* and *Sense and Sensibility* offer a revolutionary development in the treatment of what had become a standard novel formula. Moreover, the in-family marriages provide a frame of reference in which to view contemporary events; they manifest Austen's desire to preserve the vitality of the home or the estate. Her attitude is one of self-defence during a time of transition and uproar. At the end of all of the novels, there is finally the promise of an untainted family circle. These, then, are the types of alliances that Austen most favours and approves. The marriages of Edmund and Fanny, Mr. Knightley and Emma, and Edward and Elinor, far from seeming illicit or immoral unions, become more nearly moral imperatives. For Austen, in fiction as in life, collateral relations should proceed from prudence and seek to permanence.

4

Sisterhood, Education and Marriage

All of Austen's novels are acknowledged to be about forms of courtship and marriage. The extent to which ties of sisterhood impinge on those of marriage in her fiction is less generally appreciated. For although the hero, in most cases, educates the heroine (and she, in her turn, may help to teach him), sisters often play an equally crucial role in the development of their siblings. The heroine forms a close alliance with a sister, a relationship that often proves highly conducive to their development as individuals. In some ways, those sisters with deep sororal bonds owe their moral, social, and emotional education to their sisters even more than to their suitors or husbands. All of Austen's novels follow the pattern of the *Bildungsroman*. Marriage is a goal the heroines attain, but the crucial stage in the lives of these women and their sisters is that of the initiation or apprenticeship to adulthood, and, during this period in their lives, Austen's heroines look to their sisters for counsel and approbation. Thus we find that Elizabeth educates Jane, Elinor guides Marianne, Eleanor helps to shape Catherine's mind, and Fanny refines Susan's understanding. In this way, devoted sisters in Austen's fiction prime each other for marriage. The suitor contributes to the teaching of the heroine, but his instruction is, in most cases, inaugurated and/or complemented by the education a sister provides.

At the end of *Pride and Prejudice, Sense and Sensibility, Northanger Abbey*, 'The Watsons', and *Mansfield Park*, the sororal unit remains strongly intact, even when the sisters go off to live with their husbands; indeed, so potent is this relationship in *Pride and Prejudice* and *Sense and Sensibility*, it may even be appropriate to say that the marriage is grafted onto the sororal union. On occasions, a sister-in-law takes on the role of a blood sister. In other words, the sister-in-law earns the title of sister in Austen's work because she

61

offers guidance and deep affection and takes on the moral obligations of a blood sister. But only sisters with fervent bonds succeed in
instructing one another because they have each other's best interests
in mind and at heart. Their desire to maintain such puissant ties of
sisterhood even after marriage suggests that, although marriage is
the goal of the sisters in the novels, they have every expectation of
continuing to learn from each other afterwards. That is to say, the
sister bonds provide edification not just about marriage, but about
the art of living well, of discriminating between true and false moral
values, and between appearance and reality. In Austen's fiction,
the narrative steers towards marriage, but not merely to satisfy
convention. The heroine gains the best of both worlds in four of the
novels in that she finds a husband and retains a sister. Furthermore,
this triad expands concentrically to comprehend other sisters (and
brothers). Therefore, the married couple become the centre of a
polity of peers. Their lives and actions touch upon those of other
members of the group.

As Sandra Gilbert and Susan Gubar have pointed out, Austen
often uses pairs of complementary sisters to consider the different
choices confronted by women and also to demonstrate how antithetical qualities of the self can be consolidated.[1] She was, of course,
by no means original in this respect; eighteenth-century sentimental
and didactic novelists regularly employed the double sister motif in
order to moralize on the courses of action available to and the ultimate fates of their female protagonists.[2] In all of her novels, Gilbert
and Gubar maintain, Austen counterpoints a quiet, modest, reticent
sister (or sister-in-law) – Jane Bennet, Elinor Dashwood, Eleanor
Tilney, Fanny Price, Isabella Knightley, Anne Elliot – against a
livelier, more demonstrative sister – Elizabeth Bennet, Marianne
Dashwood, Catherine Morland, Susan Price, Emma Knightley, Mary
Musgrove. The quiescent and the forward sisters respond, each
one according to her temperament, to situations and dilemmas in
their lives. In most cases, the individual responses of each of the
doubled sisters prove deficient. This reading implies that Austen the
writer experienced a kind of psychic struggle – a split betokening
conflicting desires for her female characters: for whereas she seems
to approve of 'unladylike' women who assert themselves in their
society, her works often end with the description of a rather 'lady-
like' retreat into the security of the home. Ultimately, according to
these critics, Austen solves the conflict by forcing the heroine to
submit to a man, that is, according to the conventions of marriage.

Gilbert and Gubar's argument uncovers what they refer to as Austen's 'double vision' – her acceptance of her readers' expectations, and at the same time, her secret yearning to sabotage female suppression.[3] Although their argument seems cogent enough, these commentators tend to emphasize the latter and fail to take fully into account Austen's deep-rooted belief in tradition. Austen's work does reflect justified frustration with women's economic dependence, the neglect of their education, and the unfair inheritance laws of the day; she censures male tyranny and intimidation and lauds sensible, spirited, morally independent women. But the kind of 'feminism' advocated by Austen is neither as theoretical nor as radical as some recent critics have claimed.[4] The sibships formed in Austen's texts synthesize male and female qualities to create a supportive, symbiotic coalition. Moreover, in Austen's novels, marriage is not an expression of female submission and limitation but one of female assertion and expansion, though not in a subversive sense. Indeed, by means of her marriage, the heroine, in most cases, constructs even more beneficial ties with her sisters. The campaign for marriage is simultaneously linked to the campaign for sisterhood – marriage to the suitor is as important to establishing a woman's station and well-being in life as the formation of intimate bonds with a sister or network of sisters, whether blood sisters or sisters-in-law. In many respects, the exemplary marriages in Austen's novels – Elizabeth and Darcy, Jane and Bingley, Elinor and Edward, Catherine and Henry, Fanny and Edmund, Emma and Mr. Knightley, Anne and Wentworth – mirror the ideal sister relationships – Elizabeth and Jane, Elinor and Marianne, Catherine and Eleanor, Fanny and Susan – in that they are characterized by rapport, empathy, and common values and assumptions. Austen's novels therefore have two major plots operating in tandem – the plot to win the husband and the plot to win the sister.[5]

In Austen's novels, sororal relationships are often synergistic. Intense relationships frequently form between siblings as a result of the inadequacy or defectiveness of parents or because of some collapse in the family structure. Sisters both educate and function as models for each other, becoming parents in place of negligent or missing ones. The examples of this cooperation among sisters are legion in Austen's novels. Left to their own devices by their detached father and foolish mother, Elizabeth and Jane Bennet teach each other. Likewise, Elinor guides Marianne, endeavouring to compensate for their dead father and the indiscriminate tutelage of their romantic, indulgent mother. Away from her sensible but naive parents, Catherine learns not only from Henry but also from her future sister-in-law Eleanor. Cloistered from their vulgar, indifferent parents, Fanny instructs Susan about books and manners while Susan draws Fanny's attention to the advantages of practicality and strength. Inasmuch as Austen promotes characters of independent thinking, she makes it clear that good sense alone will not serve without a partner to help sift through emotional, intellectual, and moral problems. And for Austen's heroines, such a partner is likely to be the sister early on and the suitor later (though still supplemented by the sister if possible); for, without the abiding sororal relationship, achieving a positive conjugal relationship is more formidable – particularly, as we shall see, since sororal and familial bonds in general help the heroines of Austen's novels to attain satisfying marital relationships.

In order to appreciate more fully this emphasis on sisterhood in her novels, we may wish to consider Austen's intimate relationship with her elder sister, Cassandra. In his biography of Austen, John Halperin describes Cassandra Austen's efforts to comfort Jane during her last illness:

> From 7 p.m. on 17 July until she died the next morning at 4.30 a.m. in the arms of her sister, Jane Austen, after praying for death, lay apparently insensible. What thoughts, if any, may have raced through the fading light of her mind we of course shall never know . . . . Surely some portion of her last earthly thoughts must have been of Cassandra, with whom she had always shared everything; Cassandra, who seemed always to be there, as she was now; Cassandra in whose arms she lay cradled; Cassandra, Cassandra.[6]

Austen's death marked the end of a period of thirty-five years in which the two unmarried sisters shared the same bedroom, confided their innermost thoughts to each other, and wrote and worked together.[7] The writing of fiction formed a means for Austen of bracing ties with her family, but especially those with her sister. Four of the Juvenilia – 'The Beautifull Cassandra', 'Ode to Pity', 'The History of England', and 'Catharine, or the Bower' – are dedicated to Cassandra, and Austen consulted her sister, more than any other member of her family, about her work. Moreover, Jane's relationship with the intelligent, undemonstrative Cassandra evidently formed the basis of the ideal sister relationships in her works. Mrs. Austen once remarked that her daughters were 'wedded to each other', and that if Cassandra were going to have her head cut off, Jane would insist on sharing her fate.[8] The complementarity and intellectual equality, devotion and esteem, admiration and fidelity of the 'wedded' Austen sisters matches that of the perfect marriages in Austen's novels.

The intimate ties of sisters in the late eighteenth and nineteenth centuries created what Carroll Smith-Rosenberg has termed 'a female world of love and ritual'.[9] Indeed, although her essay concerns women in nineteenth-century America, Smith-Rosenberg's descriptions are thought to be generally applicable to female relationships in Britain.[10] Living in close confinement at home, sisters played a pivotal emotional role in each other's lives. At a time when there were social restrictions on the intimacy between unmarried men and women, the supportive network of the female world was of the utmost importance. At the core of the female world was the nucleus of the family. Bonds between sisters formed the underlying structures around which bands of women friends and the network of female relatives were grouped. The woman's world, as clearly shown in Austen's novels, was delimited by the home, church, and the institution of visiting back and forth. The women visited friends and relatives, made purchases, had teas, read novels, took walks, and spent time at resorts, such as Bath, searching for husbands. When the time came, they looked after children together. During periods of absence, sisters often wrote long letters to one another, in which they provided details of day-to-day activities and shared their sorrows and joys. Indeed, Jane and Cassandra Austen wrote hundreds of letters to one another; their existing correspondence covers a twenty-year period beginning in 1796.

Relationships between women (whether related or not), unlike those between unrelated men and women, were characterized by freedom of emotional expression and physical contact. Women responded with trust and tenderness to each other (except when they competed for the same man) in this world of 'female support, intimacy, and ritual'.[11] And yet, as might be expected, not all displays of affection between women signified genuine feelings of sisterhood; some of the rituals were merely social conventions. In her study of female love, Lillian Faderman remarks that 'Jane Austen was one of the few women writers [of her time period] who seemed to scoff at the excesses of romantic friendship'.[12] Faderman refers, in particular, to the early story 'Love and Freindship', but the point may also be extended to include Austen's mockery of romantic or sentimental friendship to be discovered in the relationship of Isabella Thorpe and Catherine Morland. Such friendships delight in effusiveness, excessive embracing, and ecstatic language; the friends are transported with joy in each other's company and refer to their relationship as being that of sisters. This is especially true in the case of Isabella and Catherine when they contemplate their blissful state as sisters-in-law. But such affected sororal relationships in Austen's novels result in failure. In Austen's opinion, these women react to each other according to a stock sentimental standard. Their exaggerated feelings are mainly designed to attract the notice of men and afford an opportunity for mutual flattery; in this respect, they lack the true sympathy of close emotional response.

Although Austen criticizes the disingenuous, insincere nature of sentimental friendship, she also demonstrates that sisters, whether real or honorary, may have a passionate commitment to each other. That is to say, although the attachment of sisters in Austen's fiction is certainly not erotic or lesbian, they think constantly of each other, generally share the same ideas and values, promise to be faithful to each other, and hope to live together or near to each other even after they marry.[13] Moreover, if romance with a man has proved unsatisfactory, sororal love may act as balm to soothe and protect. In many ways, this world of female emotional support seems, temporarily, even to supplant heterosexual love. Although these sororal relationships unquestionably possess a romantic tone, Austen makes clear that her women are not antagonistic to men. Her heroines pursue marriage, but, at the same time, seek to build a loving relationship with a sister that may exist concomitantly with the marital alliance.

Although solidarity between siblings was extolled in Austen's time, the loyalty between the novelist and her sister, Cassandra, was singular. Cassandra was the most important person in Jane's life – her friend, confidante, and correspondent. Since they were the only girls in a family of many boys, their allegiance was intense. Their niece Anna described the sisters as being 'everything to each other. They seemed to lead a life to themselves within the general family life, which was shared only by each other. I will not say their true, but their *full*, feelings and opinions were known only to themselves.'[14] After Jane died, Cassandra wrote: 'I *have* lost a treasure, such a Sister, such a friend as never can have been surpassed, – she was the sun of my life, the gilder of every pleasure, the soother of every sorrow, I had not a thought concealed from her, & it is as if I had lost a part of myself' (*Letters*, pp. 513–14).

In her novels, Austen describes a number of profound sister relationships, many or all of which were doubtless based in part on her relationship with her 'dearest sister'. Jane and Elizabeth Bennet, Elinor and Marianne Dashwood, Emma and Elizabeth Watson, and Fanny and Susan Price are as devoted and complementary as Jane and Cassandra Austen were in real life. These and other heroines often create ties with other women who are metamorphosed into sisters, as in the case of Catherine Morland and her future sister-in-law, Eleanor, Elizabeth and her sister-in-law, Georgiana, and Emma and her former governess, Mrs. Weston. In some regards, the novels may be seen as works of wish-fulfillment. The sisters marry worthy suitors, but their marriages do not separate them. On the contrary, the sisters end up living in close proximity and become as much 'married' to each other as to their husbands.

The strong loyalty that existed between Jane and Cassandra Austen, although it made circumstances bearable, could not always overcome the tribulations of family life. The Austen household was not an idyllic place at all times. The novelist hated her homes in Bath and Southampton, and she and her mother were continually sniping at each other. More important, Mrs. Austen evidently preferred Cassandra to Jane. The Austen family regarded Jane as being of less consequence than Cassandra because she was the younger sister – Mrs. Austen stressed this even after Jane died. One biographer notes that Austen promoted the idea of Cassandra's superiority 'to benefit from the shield of Cassy's *savoir-faire*, guidance, and normalcy'.[15] This may well be accurate, but surely Austen suffered from some jealousy over the dominant position accorded her elder sister. The family's favouritism, and the author's subsequent feelings of ambivalence towards her sister on occasions, may account for the theme of sibling rivalry which recurs throughout Austen's fiction.[16]

In Austen's time, sisters sometimes jockeyed for position in the marriage stakes. Indeed, meeting the economic imperative to find a husband was made all the more difficult because of the decrease in the number of available men owing to the wars on the Continent. The insularity of the home could make sororal bonds of rivals both stifling and hostile. Savage sibling rivalry seethes, for instance, between Lucy and Nancy Steele in *Sense and Sensibility*; between Penelope and Margaret, who compete for the affection of Tom Musgrave, in 'The Watsons'; and between Maria and Julia, who both love Henry Crawford, in *Mansfield Park*. Marriage often helps to cement the relationship between certain sister-pairs in Austen's novels, but marriage campaigns sometimes cause conflict and erect insuperable barriers between them.

Although Jane and Cassandra apparently did not compete for the same suitors, and though they lived together blissfully and harmoniously most of the time, more than a ripple of competitiveness and jealousy was sometimes detectable in their relationship. Unlike Cassandra, who was briefly engaged to Thomas Fowle, who died of yellow fever in the West Indies in 1797, Jane had never been officially engaged (except for one night in December 1802 to Harris Bigg Wither). There are passages in the novelist's writing where one seems to detect a yearning for the right man to turn up in her life (if only to prove herself), as he had turned up in Cassandra's.[17] And yet, at the same time, the fear of losing the beloved sister to a man made Jane and Cassandra guard each other jealously. The threat of unbearable loneliness without each other may even have made them act selfishly (Cassandra apparently persuaded Jane to break off her engagement to Bigg Wither).[18] In any event, the ambivalent feelings among sisters in Austen's fiction seem to follow from the novelist's own emotions and experience as well as her observations.

Throughout her work, Austen produces a chequered effect by counterpointing sororal solidarity against antipathy between sisters. The repercussions of these strong and weak sororal relationships stimulate action in the novels and provide insight into individual character. Several narratives in Austen's Juvenilia concern rivalrous sisters – sisters who lack the deep friendship, reciprocal sense of responsibility, and mentorial spirit of the devoted sister pairs in the novels, or who are estranged by sexual competition. Her early piece entitled 'The Three Sisters', for example, anticipates the sororal rivalry between and alienation of Elizabeth and Lydia in *Pride and Prejudice*, the Steeles in *Sense and Sensibility*, Penelope and Margaret in 'The Watsons', and Maria and Julia in *Mansfield Park*.

'The Three Sisters' may be regarded, in some aspects, as the template of *Pride and Prejudice*. In this short piece, two families, the Stanhopes and the Duttons, reside in the same village, and each family has three daughters. Similarly, in *Pride and Prejudice*, the Bennet sisters and the Lucas sisters are friends and neighbours.

In 'The Three Sisters', two sisters, Sophia and Georgiana, form an alliance on account of their moral superiority to and shame of their competitive elder sister Mary. Likewise in *Pride and Prejudice*, the superior sisters, Jane and Elizabeth, criticize their precocious, competitive younger sister Lydia. In 'The Three Sisters', Mary fears that one of her sisters, or one of the Dutton girls, will marry before she does; largely out of jealousy, she decides to marry the hideous Mr. Watts, who, like Mr. Collins in *Pride and Prejudice*, is as willing to marry either of her sisters as to marry her. And so, like Charlotte Lucas in *Pride and Prejudice*, who resigns herself to marrying Mr. Collins out of fear of spinsterhood and the belief that one of her sisters will marry her suitor if she declines his offer, Mary becomes engaged to the wealthy but disagreeable Mr. Watts. The acquisition of Mr. Watts as a husband means that Mary will have a new carriage. Moreover, she relishes the thought of chaperoning her sisters to balls, much as Lydia delights in this fantasy in *Pride and Prejudice*. In 'The Three Sisters', as in *Pride and Prejudice*, the states of sisterhood and marriage intertwine. Mary's engagement to Mr. Watts is activated by sibling rivalry, and Sophia and Georgiana encourage their sister to enter into what will undoubtedly be an unhappy marriage.

Although Sophia and Georgiana gleefully conspire against Mary, they blame themselves for their sister's actions, just as Jane and Elizabeth feel responsible for what happens to Lydia in *Pride and Prejudice*. Georgiana confesses to her correspondent in 'The Three Sisters' that she and Sophia have been practising 'a little deceit' on their sister; they scheme and trick Mary into believing that if Mr. Watts were to make them an offer of marriage, they would accept him. Sophia and Georgiana feel guilty, and Georgiana seeks her correspondent's approval of her conduct. She claims, 'Mary will have real pleasure in being a married woman, & able to chaprone [sic] us all which she certainly shall do, for I think myself bound to contribute as much as possible to her happiness in a state I have made her choose' (*MW*, p. 63). In *Pride and Prejudice*, Jane and Elizabeth, who are as close as Sophia and Georgiana in 'The Three Sisters', fail to warn Lydia about Wickham's true nature: his deception, extravagance, and unreliability. Elizabeth reproaches herself because she and Jane withheld Darcy's information about Wickham; full of guilt, she exclaims: 'Oh, Jane, had we been less secret, had we told what we knew of him, this could not have happened!' (*PP*, p. 291).

In *Pride and Prejudice*, the author sharpens our consciousness of the inherent dangers of familial neglect. Austen's relationship with Cassandra seems to be relevant here. After her sister's death, Cassandra wrote: 'I loved her only too well, not better than she deserved, but I am conscious that my affection for her made me sometimes unjust & negligent of others, & I can acknowledge, more than as a general principle, the justice of the hand which has struck this blow' (*Letters*, p. 514). Like Jane and Cassandra Austen, Elizabeth and Jane Bennet isolate themselves in their own private world within the family and bask in their moral and intellectual primacy. Austen suggests that such exclusive, self-protective relationships may create prejudice and wound other family members. Even in a large family, like that of the Bennets, really powerful bonds are limited to two sisters. The sororal bond, which aids and improves Elizabeth and Jane, does not prevent Lydia from being vulgar, or stop silly, conceited Kitty from following her sister's lead in all things; nor does the bond help turn Mary into a sensible, sensitive individual. In *Sense and Sensibility*, Margaret Dashwood is younger than her sisters; moreover, although she has a great deal of Marianne's romance, she possesses little of her sense. Consequently, Margaret is left out of the superior circle of Elinor and Marianne, since she is not the intellectual equal of her sisters. Much the same is true in *Pride and Prejudice* where the three younger Bennet sisters are left out of the select circle of Elizabeth and Jane. Similarly, in *Mansfield Park*, Fanny and Susan choose to bond together in the attic, high above the lowly society of Mrs. Price and Betsey.

Even though Austen testifies to the attendant dangers of exclusivity, she also, in great part, vindicates the sisters' behaviour. The sisterly marriage of Elizabeth and Jane, like those of Elinor and Marianne, Fanny and Susan, and even Catherine and Eleanor, reinforces the motif of in-family marriage in the novels. For Austen, these premium relationships between sterling sisters create an inward, self-protective movement. Moreover, sibling solidarity is often restricted to two sisters because a close sororal bond is in many ways analogous to a good marriage in Austen's works. Love has been built up over a long period of time between the two women, as it has in the ideal marriage. In Austen's novels, individuals confirm their own worth in their relationships with their siblings as well as with other relations and friends in their group. Therefore, the author implies, it is only natural that they should turn for love to those who share the same mental endowments and ethical code. Those individuals in the family who are irredeemable and intractable must be left to their own devices, except when they need pecuniary assistance. Furthermore, to exonerate the sisters from the charge of exclusivity, we are told in the final chapters of their attention to teachable siblings after they marry. In *Pride and Prejudice*, for instance, Kitty becomes 'less irritable, less ignorant, and less insipid' (*PP*, p. 343) as she follows the example set by her elder sisters. And in *Sense and Sensibility*, the 'constant communication' between Barton Cottage and Delaford after Elinor and Marianne marry will undoubtedly work to the advantage of the impressionable Margaret. Thus the collective power of the sororal pairs escalates with the annexation of other enlisted siblings. And, as we have already seen, these sororal pairs form new, synchronized family circles with their husbands, brothers-in-law, and sisters-in-law.

Sororal relationships form the nucleus of another early piece 'Lesley Castle', a burlesque of the sentimental novel. Charlotte and Eloisa Lutterell are counterpointed against the majestic but pretentious Matilda and Margaret Lesley in much the same way that pairs of sisters are pitted against each other in the later works – Elizabeth and Jane Bennet against the haughty Miss Bingleys; Elinor and Marianne Dashwood against the mercenary, unscrupulous Miss Steeles; Emma and Elizabeth Watson against malicious, competitive Penelope and Margaret; Fanny and Susan against the proud, vain Miss Bertrams; and rivalrous Anne and Mary against the pleasant but vapid Musgrove sisters. Such counterpointing creates an effect of *chiaroscuro* in the fiction; the confrontations, disagreements, and sparring sessions between the sisters contribute to the dramatic structure of the works in that the 'dark' sisters serve to make us aware of the virtues of the 'light' sisters. Likewise, the luminous qualities of the latter set off the failings of the former.

Unlike the sentimental portraits of such tender, effusive sisters as Ellinor and Matilda in Sophia Lee's *The Recess*, Evelina and Polly in Frances Burney's *Evelina* (and, much later, Juliet and Lady Aurora in *The Wanderer*), or the melodramatic opposition of a virtuous and an erring sister such as Harriot and Sophia in Charlotte Lennox's *Sophia* (1762), or Marianne and Louisa in Jane West's *A Gossip's Story* (1796), Austen's sisters are far from being either paragons or monsters involved in far-fetched situations. Indeed, in 'Lesley Castle', Austen takes a swipe at fictional clichés by showing Charlotte and Eloisa Luttrell as absurdly divided and unsympathetic. When Eloisa's fiancé is thrown from his horse and in imminent danger of dying, Charlotte tells her sister not to cry about such a trifle. And, in the next moment, upset about the waste of victuals prepared for the wedding feast, Charlotte begins eating the food immediately and advises Eloisa to do the same. Charlotte's comic indifference and cold-heartedness anticipate the callousness of the Steele sisters, Maria Bertram, and Elizabeth Elliot. The other sororal pair in 'Lesley Castle', Matilda and Margaret Lesley, clash with and abuse their step-mother, Susan (a woman young enough to be their sister), who has only recently married their father. Susan is a hudibrastic imitation of the wicked stepmother of contemporary sentimental and gothic fiction. Instead of plotting to disinherit or to kill her stepdaughters, Susan makes petty and spiteful comments about their appearance. The sisters criticize their step-mother's 'diminutive figure' and excessive use of make-up, referring to her as an 'insignificant Dwarf'; Susan retaliates by insultingly calling her step-daughters the 'Scotch Giants' (*MW*, p. 123–4).

In 'Lady Susan', as in 'Lesley Castle', strong dislike exists between a mother and daughter. Moreover, as the attractive Lady Susan looks at least ten years younger than her real age, she and her daughter become more like sibling rivals than mother and child. As Gilbert and Gubar note, like the sister pairs in Austen's novels, Lady Susan and Frederica embody antithetical qualities; while Susan is assertive, vivacious, and sensual, Frederica is meek and passive.[19] The sexual competition between mother and daughter becomes explicit when Lady Susan suspects that her daughter's affection for Reginald has awakened a return in him. She exclaims jealously against Reginald's disloyalty and scorns her rival daughter. At the conclusion of the narrative, Lady Susan and Frederica apparently exchange places; Catherine Vernon hopes that in time her brother Reginald will marry Frederica, and Lady Susan marries Sir James, whom she had once intended for her own daughter. Thus, in 'Lady Susan', a family drama takes place at two levels: that is, not only between the mother and daughter but also between two rival 'sisters'. The conflict between Lady Susan's sense of maternal duty and her own personal interests serves to heighten the drama. And the daughter vies with her mother for the affections of the suitor or surrogate father. While the mood of the early narratives is buoyant, comic, and exaggerated, they nevertheless manage to explore serious issues on which Austen's novels seek to elaborate. For example, the dramatization of the sibling-like rivalry in a work such as 'Lady

Susan' enables Austen to test opposing fantasies: pleasure-seeking self-gratification on the one hand, and quiet, virtuous moderation on the other, a technique that she later refined in her longer fiction.[20]

Not only are sororal relationships important thematically, but they are also essential to the dramatic structure of the novels in that they express the moral and emotional crises that the female characters undergo. In this sense, thematic and structural concerns coalesce because both the process and the nature of the sisters' education involves overcoming crises, or learning how to deal with them. The sisters endeavour to redress their sibling's misfortunes or shortcomings by provoking each other either to take action or to reform. In *Pride and Prejudice*, Elizabeth saves her sister's relationship with Bingley; in the process, she learns from Jane the importance of impartiality and modesty. In *Sense and Sensibility*, Elinor and Marianne are both made unhappy by their situations with the men they love. Even so, Elinor still manages to teach her younger sister to control her emotions and be more prudent. In *Northanger Abbey*, Catherine Morland learns discrimination from her sister-in-law Eleanor; in addition, Eleanor persuades her arrogant father to accept the marriage of Catherine and Henry. And in *Mansfield Park*, Fanny and Susan manage together to transcend the depressing and degrading atmosphere of their parents' home.

In *Pride and Prejudice*, Jane and Elizabeth are intimates despite their differences in nature and temperament. Lively and witty, Elizabeth is quick to form judgements and to criticize, whereas Jane is quiet, self-effacing, and unwilling to denounce anybody. Austen counterpoints the two sisters in order to reflect upon the different approaches to life they represent. Elizabeth and Jane have few secrets from one another. Indeed, their freedom of expression in each other's company has a therapeutic effect, for, in times of trouble, they turn with trust and confidence to each other. When Elizabeth is mortified by Charlotte's engagement to Mr. Collins, she is soothed by her sister, 'of whose rectitude and delicacy she was sure her opinion could never be shaken' (*PP*, p. 128). Austen calls attention to the loyalty and mutual exchange between complementary sisters; they benefit from each other's contrasting attributes and responses to situations. This reciprocity contributes to the sisters' success in their apprenticeship to life and preparation for marriage. As they mature, they discover the usefulness and value of each other's point of view and course of action.

The ideal sister, like the ideal husband in Austen's works, is a caretaker and a teacher figure. In *Pride and Prejudice*, normal roles are reversed: the younger sister is more of an educator than the elder. Even so, the process of education works both ways, although in the case of Jane's influence on Elizabeth, it is more by process of osmosis than by active aid. While Elizabeth instructs Jane in right reason and good sense, Jane provides an example for Elizabeth of the virtues of tolerance and tact. Elizabeth regards her sister as more noble and kind-hearted than herself, but sometimes she becomes incredulous at and even exasperated by Jane's naivety and undiscriminating goodness, her inability to see a fault in anyone. '[W]ith more quickness of observation and less pliancy of temper than her sister' (*PP*, p. 15), Elizabeth remarks that Jane is 'too good. Your sweetness and disinterestedness are really angelic; I do not know what to say to you . . . . *You* wish to think all the world respectable' (*PP*, pp. 134–5). Elizabeth helps to make her gullible sister wiser and to improve her observation of others; that is to say, she takes the role of a parent. Moreover, as she watches her sister, Elizabeth becomes aware of her own deficiencies – in particular, her social and emotional prejudice. She discovers the value of Jane's 'excellent understanding and super-excellent disposition' (*PP*, p. 348).

Elizabeth applies herself *in loco parentis* on her sister's behalf to help rescue Jane's relationship with Bingley by means of her own relationship with Darcy. In other words, the sororal relationship between Elizabeth and Jane affects the dramatic structure of the novel. The vicissitudes in the relationship of Bingley and Jane mirror those in the relationship of Elizabeth and Darcy. Elizabeth rejects Darcy because of the unhappiness he has caused Jane and out of her thirst for revenge: 'Had not my feelings decided against you, had they been indifferent, or had they even been favourable, do you think that any consideration would tempt me to accept the man, who has been the means of ruining, perhaps for ever, the happiness of a most beloved sister?' (*PP*, p. 190). When Darcy approves of Bingley's match with Jane, Elizabeth agrees to marry him. Jane's contentment is as important to Elizabeth as her own. And likewise, Jane also requires her sister's happiness. When Darcy proposes a second time and Elizabeth accepts him, Jane tells her sister, 'Now I am quite happy . . . for you will be as happy as myself' (*PP*, p. 374). The sister is as important as the lover; indeed, she is even more valued than the lover on occasions.

It is clear that Jane and Elizabeth will continue to be as much married to each other as to their husbands. They have been close as children and young women; their early attachment, common mythology, and shared experience of learning means that they have ties that not even a conjugal relationship can provide. Their bonds are twofold: in addition to their blood ties, they have the spiritual ties of initiates who have gone through rites of passage together. Such a relationship, Austen suggests, will not jeopardise their marriages, but will serve, on the contrary, to empower them. This very notion is anticipated during the engagement of Jane and Bingley. In the absence of Jane, Bingley always attaches himself to Elizabeth; and when Bingley is gone, Jane seeks the same means of support. The brother-in-law becomes a surrogate brother or husband: this tie augments the family circle.

Darcy bolsters his merit in Elizabeth's opinion by his realization of Jane's worth and also by his behaviour to and actions on behalf of two other sisters: Elizabeth's younger sister Lydia and his own sister Georgiana. Elizabeth is overwhelmed by Darcy's goodness to Lydia even in the face of opposition from his formidable aunt Lady Catherine de Bourgh: 'he was the person, *to whom the whole family was indebted for the first of benefits*, and whom she regarded herself with an interest, if not quite so tender, at least as reasonable and just, as what Jane felt for Bingley' (*PP*, p. 334, italics added). Darcy becomes an even better prospect as a husband when he demonstrates his excellence as a brother to Georgiana, for whom 'there was nothing he would not do' (*PP*, p. 250), including rescuing her from scheming, seductive Wickham. In Austen's vision of society, the heroine must choose a husband who will contribute to and protect the honour and stability of the family. Like Colonel Brandon, Edmund Bertram, Henry Tilney, and Mr. Knightley, Darcy is an ideal brother and, therefore, promises to make an ideal husband.

By marrying Darcy, Elizabeth is able to maintain her 'marriage' to her sister Jane, aid her younger sister Kitty, and mould and enlighten a new sister. Elizabeth forges ties with Georgiana, who moves in with her brother and sister-in-law at Pemberley, having formed 'the highest opinion in the world of Elizabeth'. Elizabeth begins immediately to instruct her young sister-in-law, whose 'mind received knowledge which had never before fallen in her way' (*PP*, p. 388). Elizabeth educates Georgiana in the art of discrimination; she teaches her sister-in-law to be more sensible, more observant, and less in awe of her brother. If, as we are told, Elizabeth must teach her husband to laugh, then, clearly, she must do the same for her sheltered sister-in-law. Moreover, by Elizabeth's instructions, the naive Georgiana, who almost eloped with the perfidious Wickham, learns what constitutes a satisfactory marital relationship. In addition to all this, Kitty's character is upgraded as she makes amends for her earlier weaknesses. Given these circumstances, we begin to see that Elizabeth's marriage to Darcy does not compromise or limit her sisterly relationships. For Nina Auerbach, the world of the Bennet sisters is in a suspended state of 'agonized restraint' until Darcy assumes 'the mother's role' at the end of the work. Another critic claims that sisterhood in *Pride and Prejudice* 'as a source of emotional support . . . is . . . underdeveloped' since Elizabeth is estranged from her younger sisters.[21] On the contrary, it would seem that in marrying Darcy, Elizabeth takes on a powerful administrative role and actually extends her sororal ties concentrically; indeed, she is now able to cherish and influence Jane, Georgiana, and her younger sisters from a far more advantageous, powerful position as mistress of a magnificent estate. This arrangement, by which all members profit intellectually, emotionally, and socially (but only economically only in the case of Lydia), is Austen's vision of an ideal self-sustaining family, the microcosm of a model for an ideal society.

At the conclusion of *Pride and Prejudice*, we are told that Jane and Elizabeth, 'in addition to every other source of happiness, were within thirty miles of each other' (*PP*, p. 385). One commentator claims that 'such an understatement provides . . . [a] sign of the narrator's discomfort at making sisterhood figure centrally in the story's end'.[22] Such an interpretation betokens a failure to see that the stability and peace between the sisters is part of the resolution. Far from revealing discomfort at making sisterhood a major part of the conclusion, Austen emphasizes the significance of the sequestered family circle. The unified family circle of sisters, Jane, Elizabeth, and Georgiana, and the two 'brothers', Darcy and Bingley (devoted friends and companions who are now brothers-in-law), effects a securing of family ties. Thus, the conclusion is propitious beyond the satisfactory marriage of the heroine, the goal to which all the novels point.

The dovetailing of sisters' fates and the joint quests for a sororal relationship and marriage are also the major foci of *Sense and Sensibility*. The relationship of sensible, polite Elinor and romantic, impetuous Marianne dominates the novel. In *Sense and Sensibility* (originally titled 'Elinor and Marianne'), the fluctuations in the love affairs of the sisters are in tandem. The plot is geometrical. Tony Tanner comments on the importance of this for the resolution of the novel:

> At the end [of *Sense and Sensibility*] two parallelograms are formed which demonstrate on the one hand true harmony (Elinor and Edward, Marianne and Brandon), and on the other a merely apparent, superficial harmony (Lucy and Robert, John and Fanny Dashwood); as is often the case, Jane Austen helps to make us appreciate the value of the real thing by juxtaposing a travesty or parodic version of it. It is this geometry which provides the formal resolution to the novel . . . . But the body of the novel concerns itself with these things which complicate and cloud the emergence of that or any other geometry.[23]

Tanner's metaphor of the parallelogram may also be used to indicate the nature of sibling relationships in both *Pride and Prejudice* and *Sense and Sensibility*. The latter presents, on one plane, vital sibling relationships between Elinor and Marianne and Edward and Brandon and, on the other plane, a travesty of family harmony, in that Lucy and Robert, and John and Fanny prove to be worthless siblings. In *Pride and Prejudice*, Elizabeth and Darcy and Jane and Bingley constitute the parallelogram of harmony, whereas the marriages of Lydia and Wickham, Charlotte and Mr. Collins provide parodic versions of meaningful relationships. In *Sense and Sensibility*, Elinor and Marianne move gradually towards good marriages with deserving men, Edward Ferrars and Colonel Brandon. But the progress towards the resolution of the novel is complicated by the egocentric schemes of Lucy Steele and Willoughby, the conflicts between the sisters and their suitors, and the opposition in temperament and attitude between the sisters themselves.

   In *Sense and Sensibility*, as in *Pride and Prejudice*, Austen stresses the love and reciprocity of the complementary sisters and explores the choices they both represent. While Marianne is eager in everything, Elinor knows how to govern her feelings: 'Their means were as different as their objects, and equally suited to the advancement of each' (*SS*, p. 104). The sisters frequently debate matters, but Marianne usually ends up acknowledging and admiring her sister's more sensible opinion: 'That her sister's affections *were* calm, she dared not deny, though she blushed to acknowledge it; and of the strength of her own, she gave a very striking proof, by still loving and respecting that sister, in spite of this mortifying conviction' (*SS*, p. 104). Whatever their differences in temperament, the situation of the sisters is similar in their love lives; each misunderstands the intentions of the man she loves. But the real testing-ground for the two young women is not how they respond to their suitors, but how they understand, react to, and become involved with each other's needs and problems, in spite of their own miserable predicaments.

Above all, Elinor nurtures her younger, more vulnerable sister. Marianne learns the importance of discipline and self-control from her less demonstrative, more reticent sister. She comes to acknowledge the shortcomings of feelings alone and of any view of life based almost solely on emotion. After her near-fatal illness, she is willing to learn from Elinor's 'rational employment and virtuous self-control' (*SS*, p. 343). Whereas Marianne discovers how to regulate her feelings, Elinor finds out how to communicate hers. Sense by itself is not enough for complete understanding or happiness in life. Throughout most of the novel, Elinor disguises and confines her emotions for the benefit of others. At times, she feels obliged to behave hypocritically and seems to be restrained to a fault by the modes of her society. The whole task of telling lies when politeness requires it falls on Elinor. When Lucy Steele exclaims that Lady Middleton is full of sweetness, Marianne is silent, while Elinor hastens to agree. Yet, Elinor liberates her strong, pent-up emotions in her expression of overpowering love and relief when Edward reveals that Lucy married his brother: '[she] almost *ran* out of the room and *burst* into tears of joy' (*SS*, p. 360, italics added).

After facing and weathering the vicissitudes of their relationships with Willoughby and Edward, the sisters become more alike. Indeed, several commentators have insisted that when Elinor begins to sympathize with Willoughby following his histrionic explanation at Cleveland of his past actions, the two sisters seem to change places. Marianne, they suggest, becomes more sensible, while Elinor becomes more irrational.[24] Elinor's sense does seem to evaporate at the touch of Willoughby's charm; like Marianne, she is deceived by him. But, to a certain extent, Willoughby's scene with Elinor must be interpreted as ironic; that is to say, it is included for literary purposes to strike a balance between the opposites of sense and sensibility in the novel. Whereas Jane West in *A Gossip's Story* (1796) and Maria Edgeworth in *Letters of Julia and Caroline* (1798) recommend prudence by employing the formula of the sensible heroine who lectures and transforms her wayward sister, Austen refrains from offering sanctimonious homilies and presents authentic rather than allegorical characters.[25] For throughout *Sense and Sensibility*, Marianne is never wholly without sense, and Elinor is far from being completely bereft of sensibility. In short, although Austen exploits conventional schematic and geometric structures, she is never so committed to them as to risk undermining her deeper artistic and moral structures. Moreover, Elinor and Marianne do not exchange personalities in the way of two characters in a comedy or farce. Instead, the sisters become more balanced characters, having profited from each other's example and tutoring.

All the way through the novel, the sisters support and console one another. Austen chooses, in this way, to emphasize the depth of sororal love rather than marital love. Edmund Wilson points out that although Marianne's love for Willoughby is the 'most passionate thing' in Austen's fiction, the emotion of Elinor as she witnesses her sister's tragic liaison is most poignant, most deeply felt by the reader.[26] When Marianne, 'almost choked with grief' (*SS*, p. 182), learns of Willoughby's treachery, Elinor weeps violently with her, and they spend time in 'joint affliction'. And when Marianne asks Elinor why she kept the news of Edward's engagement to Lucy Steele a secret, Elinor replies: 'But I did not love only him . . . . I would not have you suffer on my account' (*SS*, p. 263). A touching remark, Austen reveals in it her own reverence for such generous, abiding, and unselfish adoration. Likewise, Marianne reveals her tenderness for her sister at Mrs. Ferrars' home, when the hostess and Fanny Dashwood are rude to Elinor about the screens she has made. Marianne's 'affectionate heart' cannot bear 'to see a sister slighted in the smallest point', and, urged by a strong impulse of sisterly love, she moves to her sister's chair, embraces her, and says 'Dear, dear Elinor, don't mind them. Don't let them make you unhappy' (*SS*, p. 236), before bursting into tears herself. However, the sisters sometimes argue and are occasionally jealous of and competitive with each other. Indeed, the underlying foundation of *Sense and Sensibility* is the tension between two sisters as temperamentally unalike as Elinor and Marianne.

These differences reveal themselves when, for example, the sisters distinguish between their male friends. While Marianne censures Edward for his lack of spirit and sensibility, Elinor denounces Willoughby for his reckless, egocentric ways. Invidious comparisons and a sense of rivalry over and about suitors proliferate in *Sense and Sensibility*. When Edward claims Elinor for his wife near the end of the novel, Marianne's feelings for her sister, as she regretfully thinks of Willoughby, are ambivalent: 'Comparisons would occur – regrets would arise; and her joy, though sincere as her love for her sister, was of a kind to give her neither spirits or language' (*SS*, p. 363). Similarly, on their journey to London, '[Elinor] must learn to avoid every selfish comparison, and banish every regret which might lessen her satisfaction in the happiness of Marianne' (*SS*, p. 159).

Sexual rivalry surfaces more in the relationship of Elinor and Marianne in *Sense and Sensibility* than that of Elizabeth and Jane in *Pride and Prejudice*. Austen's own relationship with her sister Cassandra may help to account for the presentation of the major sororal relationships in the two works. *Pride and Prejudice* was composed between 1796 and 1797. *Sense and Sensibility*, originally an epistolary novel, was probably first written in 1795. But it was completely rewritten between 1797 and 1798, after the novelist's unsuccessful romance with Tom Lefroy. Thomas Fowle had proposed to Cassandra and been accepted, but Tom Lefroy was not seriously in love with Jane and did not propose to her, apparently much to her chagrin. The novelist's feelings of disappointment and envy may well be reflected in *Sense and Sensibility* in the sibling rivalry between Elinor and Marianne.[27] The jealousy and antagonism between the principal sisters are more noticeable than in *Pride and Prejudice*, and Lucy and Nancy Steele, another pair of competing sisters, also accentuate the theme of sibling rivalry in the novel.

By the end of *Sense and Sensibility*, however, all tensions between the Dashwood sisters are eradicated. Marianne marries Colonel Brandon, a man of sense, virtue, and moderation, whose character and temperament closely resemble her sister's. Some critics have claimed that Marianne's marriage is the weakest part of the novel. For example, Tony Tanner argues that 'She is married off to Brandon to complete a pattern, to satisfy that instinct for harmonious arranging which is a part of the structure both of that society and the book itself. Her energy is sacrificed to the overriding geometry.'[28] However, since the portrayal and resolution of a sibling relationship dictates the dramatic structure of the novel, it is appropriate that Marianne learns from Elinor and then marries a man who resembles her sister to show that she has completed the tutoring process. It has been argued that the ending is only aesthetically appropriate, that the marriage of Marianne and

Colonel Brandon is a ploy to bring about an acceptable conclusion to a pattern that exists in Austen's novel. But, in addition, the ending is psychologically and morally appropriate. Marianne comes to see the correctness of choosing someone who, like her sister, will be a good partner and will complete her further education in the art of living and choosing well. The ending of *Sense and Sensibility* suggests not so much the completion of an ordered artistic pattern as a certain fidelity to an art grounded in a practical and realistic philosophy; Marianne chooses a sensible, virtuous, moderate but affectionate man who reminds us of her sister in attitude and nature. As Elinor has been a caretaker and role model for Marianne, so Colonel Brandon will be. Moreover, Colonel Brandon proves his worthiness as a potential husband by his warm-hearted, fraternal attentions to the Dashwood sisters (as well as his tenderness for Eliza, the woman brought up as his own sister).

To complete the picture of in-family domestic happiness at the end of *Sense and Sensibility*, a close, brotherly friendship, like the friendship of Darcy and Bingley in *Pride and Prejudice*, develops between Edward Ferrars and Colonel Brandon, who are alike in their principles, disposition, and even their manner of thinking. Elinor and Marianne, like Elizabeth and Jane, settle near one another in the same neighbourhood, indeed nearer to one another even than the Bennet sisters, who reside in adjacent shires: 'and among the merits and the happiness of Elinor and Marianne, let it not be ranked as the least considerable, that though sisters, and *living almost within sight of each other*, they could live without disagreement between themselves, or producing coolness between their husbands' (*SS*, p. 380, italics added). The two of them will live in close proximity at Delaford, their physical nearness symbolizing their new nearness in temperament and attitudes. In this way, the sororal relationship is sustained, even regenerated by the marriages. Elinor and Marianne look forward to a future of happiness and harmony with their husbands and with each other.

If the formation of *Sense and Sensibility* and *Pride and Prejudice* is, to use Tanner's metaphor, like that of two parallelograms of sibling relationships, then the structure of *Northanger Abbey* is more like that of a triangle, with Catherine, Eleanor, and Isabella constituting the three angles. As in the other early novels, the structure of *Northanger Abbey* still amalgamates the marriage quest with the quest to strengthen sibling ties. But in this novel the overriding theme is the creation of sororal bonds between sisters-in-law. There is a marked symmetry in the parallelogram-like sibling structures of *Pride and Prejudice* and *Sense and Sensibility*; compatible, synchronized sibling relationships are easily distinguished from dischordant versions. But in *Northanger Abbey*, the tension results from the heroine's inability throughout most of the novel to detect the differences between the genuine sister Eleanor and the parodic sister Isabella. As a result, the angles of the relationship between Catherine and her sisters are more acute, and the tension is increased.

The situation in *Northanger Abbey* is much altered from those in *Pride and Prejudice* and *Sense and Sensibility*, where the plot revolves around two devoted blood sisters.[29] Catherine's blood sister Sally is loyal to her, but the strong affection which survives and grows between Elizabeth and Jane, as well as between Elinor and Marianne, vanishes in this relationship. When Catherine leaves for Bath at the beginning of the novel, Austen comments ironically:

> Sally, or rather Sarah . . . *must from situation be at this time the intimate friend and confidante of her sister.* It is remarkable, however, that she neither insisted on Catherine's writing by every post, nor exacted her promise of transmitting the character of every new acquaintance, nor a detail of every interesting conversation that Bath might produce. (*NA*, p. 19, italics added)

Sally only appears on two other occasions in the novel: on the opening page when we are told that she is a quicker, cleverer child than Catherine; and near the conclusion, after Catherine returns in disgrace from Northanger, when Sally exclaims at her sister's sad situation with 'youthful ardour' (*NA*, p. 234). This demotion of the blood sister to the role of an insignificant character is an inversion of many novels of Austen's period in which the sister 'must from situation' be the 'intimate friend and confidante' of the heroine (or, in certain novels, the best friend is discovered to be the sister of the heroine).[30] Austen reverses the reader's expectations in *Northanger Abbey* and exchanges the blood sister for two potential sisters-in-law: one vain and venal, the other, generous and worthy. The genuine sororal relationship in *Northanger Abbey* is between Catherine and her future sister-in-law, Eleanor. In Austen's novels, a relationship between sisters-in-law often proves as powerful as that between blood sisters, and so Eleanor becomes a surrogate sister to the heroine at Northanger. In this way, the novelist offers in *Northanger Abbey* a variant on the theme of sororal relationships.

In the novel, the heroine's progress towards a desirable marriage with Henry Tilney is complicated by her relationship with her potential sisters, Isabella and Eleanor. Austen often anticipates the unfitness of a marriage by demonstrating the unfitness of a sibling relationship.[31] Deceitful, unscrupulous Isabella gushingly tells Catherine that she prefers her to her sisters, Anne and Maria, and claims that she will be more attached to Catherine's family than to her own after she marries James. Isabella's disrespect and lack of regard for her own family mark her as an objectionable sister. By contrast, according to Austen's logic, the relationship of Catherine and Henry evidently will prove to be an appropriate one. It is enough to know that Catherine is struck by Henry's high regard for Eleanor, as Elizabeth is struck by Darcy's solicitude towards Georgiana in *Pride and Prejudice*. In both novels, the suitor's treatment of his sister is an attraction for the heroine. The love, compliance, and sincerity of the fraternal relationship anticipate the same qualities in a marital relationship. The sister campaign is therefore as crucial as the campaign for the suitor. However, Catherine must learn to set apart her prospective sisters-in-law; that is, she must discern the differences between affectation and earnestness, flattery and esteem.

Henry Tilney, as numerous critics have argued, is Catherine's educator in that he dispels her visions of romance.[32] But Catherine also learns a great deal from her putative sisters. Susan Morgan points out that Isabella is Catherine's 'teacher in sentimental conventions'. Having gleaned her ideas from the romantic novels she reads, Isabella attempts to make a heroine of Catherine, as Emma tries to make one of Harriet in *Emma*.[33] Conversely, Eleanor plays a far more salutary role in the formation of Catherine's discrimination and moral vision. Indeed, Catherine spends more time with the well-educated Eleanor since she lives under the same roof with her at Northanger, than with either Isabella, or with Henry, who is away at Woodston.

Eleanor is regularly described in the text as 'elegant'; the word is derived from the Latin *eligere* meaning 'to choose' or 'to select',[34] and this root meaning is, in fact, indicative of Eleanor's role as Catherine's educator. As the heroine discovers and becomes ashamed of Isabella's 'inconsistencies, contradictions, and falsehood', so her relationship with Eleanor develops and is boosted.

She exchanges the 'decided pretension', 'boasted absence of mind', and 'resolute stilishness' of Isabella for the 'elegance', 'intelligence', and 'kindness' of Eleanor. A sign of Catherine's ripening judgement is her ability to penetrate Isabella's superficial, histrionic friendship, along with her realization that no friend, or sister for that matter, can be better worth keeping than the noble Eleanor. When she leaves Northanger and Eleanor, 'a long and affectionate embrace supplied the place of language in bidding each other adieu' (*NA*, p. 229). In place of the flowery effusions and hackneyed terms which she used in her greetings of and adieux to Isabella, Catherine has learnt that sincere sisterly regard need not be clamorous or exaggerated.

Like *Pride and Prejudice* and *Sense and Sensibility*, *Northanger Abbey* ends with a double marriage. Catherine marries the man who is closest to Eleanor in character, attitude, and values – Eleanor's brother Henry. But it is Eleanor's own prudent marriage that provides the means for Catherine's to take place. Eleanor's husband's accession to a fortune puts the General in an excellent humour, and Eleanor is able to soothe and influence her father into accepting the marriage of her brother and Catherine. The relationships of Eleanor and Catherine jibe; that is to say, their marital prospects are coupled. The sisters overcome familial conflict by interceding on each other's behalf.

In 'The Watsons' and the later novels, Austen's vision of sister relationships darkens. Sisterhood is still important to the dramatic structure of the novels, but Austen explores the weakening and loss of such ties. Indeed, where sister relations are concerned, the later novels bear out more often Austen's claim in *Mansfield Park*, that 'Fraternal love, sometimes almost every thing, is at others worse than nothing' (*MP*, p. 235). Attachment between sisters breaks down, and animosity holds sway over love between sisters. Sororal harmony either disappears or becomes muted. When we examine Austen's opus, we find that the process of education, to which sisters contribute a major part in the early novels, is still important in 'The Watsons' and *Mansfield Park*; however, in *Emma* and *Persuasion* the process falters. Moreover, in *Mansfield Park* and *Persuasion*, Fanny and Anne, in each case, the sister brought up *outside* the family, acquire the approved values, whereas the other sisters do not. Unlike Elizabeth Bennet and Elinor Dashwood, who have the constant love and attendance of a blood sister, the heroines of the later works are separated for long periods or estranged from their real sisters. As a result, substitute sisters are introduced into the novels, or a sister is acquired after a long period of waiting. The other alternative offered by Austen is that of an endogamous marriage of the heroine to a brother figure she has grown up with and with whom she shares the same values, for example, Fanny and Edmund and Emma and Mr. Knightley. And, indeed, fraternal ties come to preponderate over sororal ones in the three final works. We may ask why fraternal instead of sororal ties eventually become the cynosure of Austen's novels. Peters argues that 'the process of winning the sister becomes more complex and difficult . . . as the historical realities change.'[35] That is to say, Austen's later fiction evokes the economic and social disruption at the beginning of the nineteenth century. To counteract these effects, Austen's in-family marriages in her fourth and fifth novels become the ultimate means of shoring up the moral heritage. Whereas sisters provide emotional, social, and intellectual advantages, the brother-like husbands append economic benefits to their repertoire: Fanny is installed at the Mansfield parsonage, and Emma becomes mistress of Donwell Abbey, the estate to which all of Highbury (including Hartfield) belongs. While Peters's argument is certainly à propos, it is also important to underscore that Austen was much affected by the cult of brother/sister love in contemporary novels and in Romantic poetry. She put aside the double sister plot, an eighteenth-century fictional feature, which had been well-plumbed in her earlier work, and turned instead to the relations of cross-siblings.

As in the earlier novels, the sibship still fans out at the conclusion of *Mansfield Park* and *Emma*, but the union of brother and sister at its centre is the most concentrated, most intimate, most complete relationship. The same deep spiritual virtues of the sororal relationship are now compounded with physical unanimity, with the possibility of bearing children in the marriages of Fanny and Edmund and Emma and Mr. Knightley. Austen always emphasizes the nearness of siblings at the close of her novels – their living in the same shire, on the same estate within view of each other's houses, in the same house, or the frequency of their visits to one another. But a new dimension is introduced with the lodestar of the brother-sister relationship. Unlike sisters who may be apart for substantial periods of time (either because of marital commitments or, as in the case of Cassandra and Jane Austen, because they were visiting other relatives),[36] the wedded cross-siblings are together, for all intents and purposes, *all the time.*

The married brother-sister pairs therefore constitute the apotheosis of sibling relationships.

Between the two sets of three novels comes 'The Watsons', a watershed work as far as sororal relationships are involved. This unfinished fragment, written between 1804 and 1805, when Austen was about twenty-eight or twenty-nine and living in Bath, seems to reflect the sadness and impatience of her middle years. Austen hated moving from Steventon to Bath; she felt unsettled, miserable, and unfulfilled in the family's cramped lodgings in the uncongenial city. Moreover, her father died suddenly in 1805. She was reaching the end of her twenties, and though she had written a great deal, she had been unable to publish a line (and she had no satisfactory marriage prospects). In the fiction, Emma Watson, Fanny Price, and Anne Elliot feel themselves to be a 'burden to others'. Jane Austen undoubtedly felt this way herself at this time; she was the only member of her family without any independent means of support.[37]

In 'The Watsons', Elizabeth and Emma, like Elizabeth and Jane in *Pride and Prejudice* and Elinor and Marianne in *Sense and Sensibility*, constitute the intelligent, affectionate sister pair in their family. Although Elizabeth and Emma become close in the course of the novel, the division between them created by fourteen years' absence makes them less intimate than the Bennets or the Dashwoods. Elizabeth sometimes appalls and astonishes her younger sister by her unsophistication and her lack of shame about their impoverished home. But Elizabeth grows in Emma's esteem, and the mutual regard of the sisters increases with the knowledge of each other that their affectionate intercourse provides. Economic pressures and intolerable household arrangements, similar to those described in the Austen household, force the Watson sisters, except for Emma who has more pride and dignity than her siblings, to search frantically for husbands. As in the case of the Bingleys in *Pride and Prejudice* or the Steeles in *Sense and Sensibility*, sisterly feelings between Penelope and Margaret Watson are negligible where men are concerned. They seem to be absent as well when one or the other finds a situation in which she can promote her own advantage.

Unlike the novels of the early 'trilogy', 'The Watsons' does not end with a double marriage. According to Cassandra Austen, the novelist had planned for Emma to marry the clergyman Mr. Howard; matrimony would not appear to be in store for Elizabeth.[38] When she wrote this fragment, Jane Austen, like Elizabeth Watson

in the narrative, was in her late twenties; Austen obviously understood and empathized with the plight of the single, impecunious
woman, such as Elizabeth, who is aware of getting older and having
no happy prospects to look forward to. At one point in the novel,
Elizabeth says to Emma: 'we must marry . . . . my father cannot
provide for us, and it is very bad to grow old and be poor and
laughed at' (*MW*, p. 317). Likewise, Penelope and Margaret are
obsessed with finding a man. For example, when Tom Musgrave
visits the Watsons, husband-hungry Margaret competes to gain his
attention and is only satisfied when she has secured him from her
sisters. Austen bitterly reflects on the betrayal and malice such an
unbearable situation leads to: 'Could a sister do such a thing? –
Rivalry, treachery between sisters?' (*MW*, p. 316) cries Emma in
horror and amazement.

Against the dark background of the sparring and backbiting of
Penelope, Margaret, and Mrs. Robert, the loving relationship of
Emma and Elizabeth, as they make reparation for years spent apart,
is the only bright part of 'The Watsons'. But in this fragment, the
sister is no longer the saviour, unlike the earlier novels. Elizabeth
rescues Jane's relationship with Bingley, Elinor spiritually nourishes
Marianne, and Eleanor contributes to the teaching of Catherine
and influences her father into accepting Catherine and Henry's
marriage. But in 'The Watsons' only one of the sisters marries,
and Elizabeth is apparently resigned to spinsterhood and economic
dependence on relatives, a fate which undoubtedly terrified the
novelist in her younger years. The structure of this work is therefore
dramatically altered from that of the early novels; the power of the
sister is diminished, and sexual rivalry between siblings more accen-
tuated. In its harsher, less idealistic view of sororal relationships,
'The Watsons' sows seeds of doubt and dissension which, as we
shall see, come to full fruition in *Persuasion*.

Mansfield Park reveals a curious inversion of the double quest for
sororal ties and marriage. As in *Pride and Prejudice*, where Elizabeth
agrees to marry Darcy when he approves of Jane as a match for
Bingley and bails out Lydia, and as in *Sense and Sensibility*, where
Marianne marries a man who resembles her sister in temperament,
the marriages of Maria and Julia Bertram are closely linked, but for
different reasons. Maria's marriage to Mr. Rushworth is activated
in part by sibling rivalry. Maria is chagrined when Henry leaves
Mansfield after her father returns from Antigua. She fears her sister
will overtake her in the marriage race and win Henry. Therefore,

she hastens her marriage to the rich but doltish Rushworth out of disappointed affection for Henry and hatred for her rival sister. The relationships of Maria and Julia are again connected later on in the novel. When Maria elopes with Henry, Julia immediately absconds with Mr. Yates to compete and out of selfish alarm and fear that, as a result of her sister's behaviour, greater restraint and severity will be imposed on her. Thus, Maria's adultery induces Julia's folly. In both cases, the relationships of the sisters dovetail. But these sisters act out of egocentric and jealous motives, unlike the sisters in the early works who act out of love and loyalty.

As in *Northanger Abbey*, where Catherine is part of a triangular sororal relationship involving a virtuous sister and an errant one, in *Mansfield Park* Fanny is part of a triangle involving a false would-be sister, Mary Crawford,[39] and a true sister, Susan. In *Mansfield Park*, Austen again anticipates the unfitness of a marriage by showing the unfitness of a sister relationship. Edmund, spellbound by Mary's loveliness and scintillating conversation, encourages Fanny to think of her as a sister: 'And I observed that [Mary] always spoke of you as "Fanny" which she was never used to do; and it had a sound of most sisterly cordiality' (*MP*, p. 352). In order to get into Edmund's good graces, and because she perceives that Edmund takes Fanny's opinions seriously, Mary speaks affectionately to Fanny on the possibility of their becoming sisters, either, as first appears likely, through Mary's marrying Edmund or, much later on, through Fanny's marrying Henry: 'Who says we shall not be sisters? I know we shall. I feel that we are born to be connected' (*MP*, p. 359). The situation is superficially comparable to the scene in *Northanger Abbey* where Isabella Thorpe remarks that there are 'more ways than one' (*NA*, p. 145) that she and Catherine may become sisters. Yet, like Isabella and John Thorpe, Mary and Henry disregard sacred family structures. And, as we have already seen, for this reason, they must be banished from Mansfield.

Mary's benighted attitude toward familial structures is set against the enlightened attitude of Fanny to create an effect of *chiaroscuro* in *Mansfield Park*. Although Fanny does not esteem her slatternly mother and vulgar father, she governs her feelings and never openly criticizes them. In contrast, Mary roundly condemns her uncle and guardian, the Admiral. We are made aware of the Admiral's serious breach of moral conduct regarding the abuse of his wife and installment of his mistress in his home. Austen seems to imply, nonetheless, that it is imprudent and unwise to air such vituperative criticism publically – the Admiral is, after all, a relative. While Mary is expunged, Fanny gains a sister as a reward for her endurance and filial duty. *Mansfield Park* differs from the earlier works in that, although strong ties are formed between Fanny and Susan later in the novel, Fanny has been brought up without sisters until this time. Maria and Julia have always ignored her, and Fanny's favourite sister Mary died when she was a child. Fanny has a very close relationship with Edmund, but when he falls in love with Mary Crawford, he pays his cousin less attention. She has no female ally, no intimate ties with a sister to sympathize with her sadness and chagrin at Edmund's love for the undeserving Mary Crawford, or to console her for her degradation at the hands of Mrs. Norris. Later on in *Mansfield Park*, by forging ties of sisterhood with Susan, Fanny makes up for her earlier lack of deep sororal bonds.

Like the sororal pairs in the earlier novels, Fanny and Susan educate each other. Susan looks to her elder sister as an 'oracle' and is 'a most attentive, profitable, thankful pupil' (*MP*, p. 418). Heartened by Susan's enthusiasm, Fanny sets out to fix her sibling's principles and to inspire taste and discrimination in her, much as Sir Thomas and his family, particularly Edmund, have taught her. In this way, Fanny prepares Susan for her entry to Mansfield. In addition, Fanny becomes firmer and more assertive as a result of her relationship with Susan. For example, she subscribes to a circulating library and finds herself, 'amazed at doing anything *in propria persona*' (*MP*, p. 398). Thus, Fanny comes to respect and learn from her more resolute sister; for Susan has a determined nature and is more useful than the weaker, less assertive Fanny, who alone and under similar degrading circumstances in Portsmouth, or elsewhere, could only have gone away and wept. Their meetings become a forum for the exchange of ideas and attitudes, and, in this way, the two sisters become closer.

At the conclusion of *Mansfield Park*, the potent relationship of the two sisters contributes substantially to Fanny's happiness and the preservation and invigoration of Mansfield. When Fanny returns to Mansfield, Susan accompanies her and eventually takes her sister's place in the household. Fanny marries her cousin Edmund, a man she (and the reader) have thought of throughout the novel as her brother. Moreover, it seems possible that the fates of the sisters will be interlaced in another way. As in *Emma*, where two sisters, Isabella and Emma, marry two brothers, John and George Knightley, it is plausible that Susan might wed her penitent cousin, Tom, to complete the loving and enclosed family at Mansfield. The sisters, though divided in temperament and ways, and having been separated for many years, may look forward to a future in which they will be closely connected.

In *Emma*, the themes of sororal solidarity and sororal rivalry seem distinctly less central. Unlike the heroines of the first four novels, Emma has no strong ties to a blood sister or sister-in-law. Emma is fond of her sister Isabella; however, insuperable intellectual barriers weaken their relationship. Emma is 'quick and assured', while Isabella is 'slow and diffident'; moreover, Isabella is far away and too busy coddling her husband and three children to maintain a powerful bond with her sister. Three other women have the potential to become honorary sisters to Emma, but the permanent love and nurturing which dominate the sororal relationships in previous works fade in *Emma*. Mrs. Weston has brought Emma up, and she sometimes acts like an elder sister to her former charge:

> . . . there was not a creature in the world to whom [Emma] spoke with such unreserve . . . not any one, to whom she related with such conviction of being listened to and understood, of being always interesting and always intelligible, the little affairs, arrangements, perplexities of her father and herself. (*E*, p. 117)

But at the beginning of the novel, Emma's former governess marries and, therefore, Emma loses this potential sister. As a result, Emma is lonely and disoriented, and she seeks a close friend to replace Mrs. Weston. Her choice of foolish Harriet Smith has unfavourable consequences. Emma tries to teach Harriet, but, in fact, she herself is in as much need of teaching as her protegée. As in the case of Isabella and Catherine Morland, the relationship of Emma and Harriet is largely artificial and foolish; the two women stroke each other's egos and abet each other in ill-judged schemes. Emma's other potential honorary sister, Jane Fairfax, would probably be the most appropriate choice since Jane is intelligent and discriminating. Indeed, the people of Highbury have always imagined that Jane Fairfax and Emma would be as intimate as sisters; they are the same age, and they both possess talent and refinement. However, although there is an unacknowledged rivalry between the two women, such as we have noted in certain sororal pairs in Austen's fiction, they lack the affection, intimacy, and openness of sisters.

In *Emma*, it would seem clear, Austen makes a radical departure from her previous works; she concentrates on a heroine who is without the support and guidance of a sister. The brotherly suitor alone is Emma's role model and protector; no sister, natural or potential, provides any effective education. In place of a sister, Mr. Knightley sustains Emma emotionally and prepares her for marriage – to himself. Nonetheless, it is implied that the arrogant, snobbish heroine would undoubtedly have benefited from the constant advice and restraint of a sensible sister, as Marianne does in *Sense and Sensibility*. Instead, Mrs. Weston, Emma's governess, indulged her charge, letting her do just as she liked and imposing few checks. And, as we have noted, Isabella was overshadowed by her younger, brighter sister. Since Emma has not had the advantage of the crucial education of a shrewd, strong-minded sister, she suffers emotional and intellectual effects. Austen, however, appears to imply in the conclusion of *Emma* that the heroine, now that she is married, will begin to learn from her sister: Isabella will provide an excellent model of parental unselfishness, dependability, and duty for her complacent, egocentric younger sister. *Emma*, then, demonstrates the weight of beneficent sisterhood by underscoring the disadvantages its absence creates.

In *Persuasion*, originally titled 'The Elliots', no strong ties exist between Elizabeth, Anne, and Mary Elliot, only rivalry, jealousy, and coldness. Arguments, disagreements, and battles between sisters constitute the dramatic structure of this novel. Marriage and sisterhood are nowhere intertwined, and the heroine is isolated morally and intellectually. The depiction of sororal relationships in this work, the last of Austen's completed novels, is far less idealistic than that of previous novels. Her first four novels derive a great deal of their dramatic tension from the conflict between opposing pairs of sisters. By the end of *Pride and Prejudice, Sense and Sensibility, Northanger Abbey*, and *Mansfield Park*, a laudable sororal pair plainly establish their moral authority and help to reanimate the family circle from within. A sister pair is even established at the end of *Emma*; although Emma and Isabella are not devoted siblings, it seems likely that Emma will learn from her sister. But in *Persuasion*, no such pair emerges. To be sure, Louisa and Henrietta Musgrove are, for the most part, congenial sisters. But, as Admiral Croft remarks, it is difficult to 'know one from the other' (*P*, p. 92), which seems to imply that they are insignificant. By no means the moral touchstones in the novel, the Musgrove sisters lack the rich individuality and dynamic inner resources of the sister pairs in Austen's earlier fiction. In addition, they lack the complementary qualities of the devoted sisters, qualities which enable the sisters to enhance each other's understanding and character. Whereas Austen appears to be preoccupied with forging harmonious sororal structures in her early fiction, in *Persuasion* she constructs a preeminently male network of individuals who team up to protect and defend their interests and those of their country. Indeed, such is the fidelity of the 'brother officers' of the navy that Wentworth claims he would bring 'any thing of Harville's from the world's end, if he wanted it' (*P*, p. 69). Significantly enough, the date of Anne and Wentworth's engagement coincides with that of Napoleon's escape from Elba,[40] emphasizing the centrality of 'the dread of a future war' (*P*, p. 252) in people's minds, including Jane Austen's, during this period. And, indeed, war on the domestic front between sisters prevails in *Persuasion*.

The conflict between the Elliot sisters is driven by fundamental differences in attitude, intellect, and values. Because Anne fell in love as a young woman with penniless Wentworth and therefore threatened to degrade the family name, her father and eldest sister have punished her for years with their lofty contempt and indifference, regarding her as 'nobody'. Indeed, so strong is Elizabeth's disdain for Anne that she turns completely from the society of so deserving a younger sister to bestow her affection on the social climber Mrs. Clay. As for Mary, she and Anne only tolerate each other. Endowed with her own share of the 'Elliot self-importance', Mary laments her loss of status in marrying a member of the untitled gentry. To attract attention, she feigns illness and puts on airs. The Musgroves, however, pay her scant attention, and thus kind-hearted Anne is always forced to soothe and console her miserable sister and to give way to her ill-judged claims. Indeed, Anne spends much time with Mary, arranging and organizing domestic affairs for her, and trying to convince her selfish sister that she is not ill-used by anyone.

Feelings between the Elliot sisters are further exacerbated by an unacknowledged but nonetheless fierce sexual rivalry. Competition evidently rankles between Mary and Anne, since Charles Musgrove proposed to Anne before finding a more willing partner in her younger sister. And Elizabeth pursues her cousin Mr. Elliot, who is attracted to Anne. Anne, however, is indifferent to her cousin and earnestly wishes that Mr. Elliot 'might not be too nice, or too observant, if Elizabeth were his object' (*P*, p. 140). Near the end of the novel, when Anne accepts Wentworth's proposal of marriage, her ill-humoured sister Elizabeth acts nonchalantly and 'did nothing worse than look cold and unconcerned' (P, p. 248). Secretly she is mortified since both of her younger sisters are now married, and she is not. For her part, Mary, though more bearable in nature than Elizabeth, responds by congratulating herself on Anne's less prestigious marriage:

> She had something to suffer perhaps when they came into contact again, in seeing Anne restored to the rights of seniority, and the mistress of a very pretty landaulette, but she had a future to look forward to of powerful consolation. Anne had no Uppercross-hall before her, no landed estate, no headship of a family; and if they could but keep Captain Wentworth from being made a baronet, she would not change situations with Anne. (P, pp. 250)

Like Elizabeth Bennet, Elinor Dashwood, and Eleanor Tilney, who actively help their sisters to seal their marriages to their suitors, Mary believes she has been 'instrumental' to her sister's connection with Wentworth because she kept Anne with her during the autumn. In fact, Mary parodies the loyal, cooperative sisters of earlier fiction in her passivity and covetousness; her contribution to her sister's marriage is coincidental, and her only concern is that Anne's husband is more affluent than those of Louisa and Henrietta.

More solid ties do exist in *Persuasion* between the Musgrove sisters. Anne envies the mutual understanding and concordance of Louisa and Henrietta. In particular, she admires their good humour and affection, of which she has known so little with her own sisters. But even their bonds become tenuous when they both compete for the love of Wentworth. Their marriages near the end of the novel are symmetrical but not interconnected. Anne Elliot describes Louisa and Henrietta as 'two sisters, who both deserve equally well, and who have always been such, the pleasant prospects of one should not be dimming the other – that they should be equal in their prosperity and comfort' (P, p. 223–4). But Louisa and Henrietta are not the heroines of *Persuasion*; they are certainly not Anne's equals in discernment and character, and their major purpose in the novel is to provide a contrast to the Elliot sisters by spotlighting the coldness of the latter's sororal ties.

In *Persuasion*, Austen writes as a satirist of a *whole* society more than she does in any other work (except the unfinished works *Sanditon* and 'The Watsons'). Rather than focusing on a particular family or group of characters, she takes a wider critical view. Families are in upheaval: the Elliots are divided, and the Musgrove household is noisy and chaotic. The only families who seem to escape censure are those of naval officers, but even they are not idealized. Admiral and Mrs. Croft have no permanent abode and no offspring. And although the Harvilles' home is a 'picture of repose and domestic happiness' (*P*, p. 98), its lowliness appalls Anne at first. Anne is fortunate to have grown up outside her own family and to have spent much of her youth, after her mother died, with Lady Russell. Her marriage to a naval officer ensures that she will be away from her own family a great deal. And judging by the letters in the novel from Elizabeth and Mary to Anne – Elizabeth's cold and curt, Mary's from Lyme full of complaints, jealous digs, and gleeful comments when she breaks the news that Anne's supposed admirer Captain Benwick has proposed to Louisa – the correspondence after Anne marries and leaves home will be meagre. Anne maintains contact, it is true, with Lady Russell; however, Lady Russell, a surrogate mother and elder sister for Anne, had advised her protegée badly eight years before and almost ruined her life. Although she is a worthy person, she lacks understanding and penetration: moreover, her snobbery and poor judgement have made her a false and inadequate sister to Anne. Anne also finds some consolation in the person of her sensible, considerate sister-in-law Mrs. Croft. But since Mrs. Croft is much older, they will probably not communicate as peers, and so she will be more of a mother or aunt figure to her young sister-in-law. Furthermore, unlike the devoted sisters of previous novels, Mrs. Croft is not part of the 'female world'; she has given this world up to participate in the male arena of Admiral Croft and therefore does not meet the requirements for a sororal companion.[41] There is, finally, Mrs. Smith, who visits Anne and Wentworth after they marry and would seem to qualify as a sisterly friend, but her relationship with Anne is likewise ambiguous. Her trustworthiness and reliability have been weakened as a result of her prevarication concerning Mr. Elliot. In the end, then, unlike other female protagonists, Anne has no estate to look forward to and, perhaps more importantly, no strong ties to a sister to support and cherish throughout her life.

   Like the hero and heroine at the conclusion of previous novels, Anne and Wentworth are at the center of a well-knit circle of relatives; however, they only receive 'a prompt welcome . . . in *his* brothers and sisters' (*P*, p. 251, italics added), for they have little or nothing to do with Anne's family. In a muted way, Wentworth and Anne find some semblance of extended familial relations in that they join forces with Admiral and Mrs. Croft and Wentworth's brother, the former curate of Monkford. But, we hear little of the curate, and while Wentworth and Sophia Croft reveal some fondness for each other, they are apart a great deal and by no means share the same values or opinions, especially on the subject of women accompanying their naval husbands on sea voyages. As for the Elliot side of the family, it is quite obvious that Wentworth has no affectionate ties to his haughty father-in-law or malicious sisters-in-law, Elizabeth and Mary. Anne feels her own inferiority because she has 'nothing of respectability, of harmony, of good will to offer in return for all the worth' (*P*, p. 251) of his siblings. More telling still is the fact that Anne and Wentworth go outside the family to attain happiness; their domestic establishment will be the brotherhood of the navy, a profession 'more distinguished in its domestic virtues than in its national importance' (*P*, p. 252). Indeed, the hardships and dangers of a naval life seem to pull sailor brothers closer to each other and to their families.

Thus, at the close of *Persuasion*, while a sibship is imposed (as at the end of all the other novels), it is an unconventional sibship in that it lacks the organic quality of the in-family confederacies of intimate sisters and brothers. Moreover, unlike all the other novels, the narrative movement in *Persuasion* is a centrifugal rather than a centripetal one; close siblings are brought in from outside the family. Another significant difference is that this sibship entirely omits or demotes warm sororal relations. And these unsatisfactory or absent sororal relations have profound implications dramatically and thematically. Women who do not have the support of strong sister relationships, or who are isolated from sororal ties, suffer debilitating effects. They do not possess the substantive moral force, nor do they share in the opportunity to educate and be educated by other women. They suffer, that is to say, from the absence of such mutual influence and help as sisterly relations may provide. And so, while Austen maintains her idealistic moral vision in this work in her depiction of a fraternity, the harsh reality of the possibility of sororal breakdown and impotence is also present. The sister, in the person of Anne Elliot, is the moral touchstone in the novel. But the scope of her powers is severely limited. And, in this way, the author darkly underscores how the danger of sororal collapse signifies wider repercussions in society at large. The analogy between familial and social constructs, that is to say, may be best appreciated when one considers the consequences of, in either case, denying truly worthy agents of morality and vision the support and alliance they merit.

5

Fairy Godmothers and Ugly Sisters: The Cinderella Motif in Austen's Fiction

At the core of all of Austen's novels lies the Cinderella story, or, rather, several mutations of the popular fairy tale. Each novel tells of a provincial girl who falls in love with and eventually marries a worthy man. Moreover, all of the novels recount a young lady's entry into society and her earliest speculations in the marriage market. Yet Austen does not resignedly reproduce the Cinderella story; instead, she transforms the novelistic paradigm of the fairy tale into an original artistic pattern. This paradigm, passed down from Richardson's *Pamela*, in which a poor servant girl marries her rich master and becomes a model wife,[1] was rooted in a middle-class ideology obsessed with rising up the social ladder. It filtered down through the eighteenth-century novel, saturating the works of such female authors as Charlotte Smith, Frances Burney, and Jane Austen, all of whom both conformed to and subverted the pattern. In particular, we can imagine the cynical, witty Austen taking on the typical Cinderella novel formula with a grimace. But although she frequently twists and disfigures components of the Cinderella dream in order to highlight the misconceptions and false expectations to which they give rise, Austen ultimately exploits the crucial elements of fantasy. All her novels, for instance, offer examples of wish fulfillment: they have happy endings, and the heroines attain or even surpass their dreams of love.

Although Austen seems to take pleasure in debunking popular romance plots, particularly in early chapters of her novels, at the end of her works she appears to reimpose a fantasy-like finale. This is especially true in her presentation of the confederacies of brothers and sisters, in which ideally suited men and women, who have applied themselves to the building of abiding ties, coexist harmoniously and ameliorate the prospects of their society. In this regard, the fairy tale formula acquires gravity in Austen's novels. To be sure, its infrastructure comes under stress, and the dream descends to earth from its sentimental heights. However, despite these alterations, the mythic pattern of her novels remains firmly anchored in the paradisiacal world of the galvanized family clique. That is to say, Austen retains the outlines but then recolours or repaints the canvas of the Cinderella story. Formerly decked out in pastel, Rococo-style hues and exaggerated proportions, the canvas changes to one of more sombre colors and the restrained, less frivolous style of late eighteenth-century neoclassical art.

The Cinderella story, as Huang Mei has noted, is 'a narrative about female desire and ambition'.[2] In her overhauling of the Cinderella tale, Austen operates in the tradition of Frances Burney, who exposed the collusion of fear and love of the 'ideal, authoritative male' in the female dream of romance in *Evelina*.[3] Austen also draws on the tradition of Charlotte Smith. In *Emmeline*, Smith reveals a resourceful heroine who proves her ability to protect herself and, moreover, comes to understand the dangers of far-fetched fantasies.[4] But Austen creates a new dimension in her revision of the Cinderella paradigm, in which she fastidiously distills and merges the processes of art and life. She employs the Cinderella plot convention as a medium to transmit works of fiction which are documents of sororal affirmation and amplification. And yet, Austen's intention is neither combative nor threatening to male dominance; instead, her revamped versions of the Cinderella story justify the inclusion of a new kind of relationship with the hero, of a more democratic marriage grounded in fraternal ties. Her reinterpretation of an accepted pattern stresses the shared responsibility of the sexes. Moreover, the sibships, which incorporate substitutes for the unworthy siblings of the fairy-tale paradigm, offer a triumphant social and moral vision. Paradoxically, Austen's down-to-earth approach to love generates a fantasy-like bliss; the characters create their own happiness in the finales of the novels.

Critics have offered manifold interpretations of the language and meaning of the Cinderella fairy tale in Austen's fiction. D. W. Harding asserts that Austen's works are about the 'Cinderella theme with the fairy godmother omitted' (which, as we shall see, in four of her works is a disputable claim). According to Avrom Fleishman, *Mansfield Park* chronicles 'the accession of a Cinderella to dominance'. Joseph Wiesenfarth argues that the Cinderella myth 'appeals to the rightness of personal merit achieving social recognition as well as to the fitness of genuine love finding happy marriage'. Derek Brewer, on the other hand, maintains that in Austen's family dramas 'Cinderella will be shown to be less of a Cinderella than she seems'. Despite all these readings, however, the significance of the 'ugly sister' and 'fairy godmother' motifs in Austen's fiction, closely linked with the themes of individual edification and social progress, have, in the main, escaped the notice of commentators.[5] Austen's modification of the Cinderella paradigm buttresses the centripetal movement in nearly all of her fiction. From the youthful works to the novels of her maturity, Austen promotes the ideal of the fellowship and unanimity of the family network.

Several of the narratives in the Juvenilia are small-scale experiments in the Cinderella story that simultaneously embrace and diverge from its conventions and devices. These caustically humorous pieces mock melodramatic, facile novels of the sentimental mode by defiantly laughing in the face of the urgent need of the insecure Cinderella figure to survive or thrive by dint of marrying a rich man. In other words, the Cinderella subtext in certain Juvenilia elicits laughter and apprehension: laughter at the absurdity of the fight for a man (usually an unprepossessing suitor), and apprehension of possible mental or psychological abuse inflicted by female tyrants or rivals, or by ill-matched husbands who may become despotic persecutors. In 'The Three Sisters', Austen inverts the Cinderella theme, as she does later in *Emma*. The ugly sisters, Georgiana and Sophia, deceive their boastful, competitive sister, Mary – the satirical Cinderella figure – into accepting the hideous 'Prince Charming' figure, Mr. Watts. In 'Lady Susan', the antagonist combines wicked stepmother figure and ugly sister. As Gilbert and Gubar have noted, Lady Susan also resembles the wicked queen in 'Snow White'.[6] Obsessed with her own self-image, the monster woman manipulates and traps her innocent daughter to prevent her from usurping her position. In this way, Austen depicts female vulnerability and the barriers it sets against the bonding of women.

Female generational conflict also materializes in 'Catharine, or the Bower'. Catharine's guardian aunt Mrs. Percival, the fairy godmother in this narrative, is good-hearted but strict and tenacious in her protection of Catharine. Away from her aunt, the orphaned heroine weeps and seeks solace in a tranquil bower, a version of Cinderella's kitchen hearth. The ambivalent, fear-provoking portrait of Mrs. Percival anticipates that of Lady Russell in *Persuasion*, another well-meaning godmother who becomes overzealous in the protection of her charge when she cajoles Anne into rejecting Wentworth's proposal. Moreover, the Prince Charming type in this narrative also prefigures other predatory males in Austen's novels. If Austen had completed the piece, unreserved, lively, and exceptionally attractive Edward Stanley would undoubtedly have been exposed as a deceitful cad, since he has all the attributes of later cads – Wickham, Willoughby, Henry Crawford, and Mr. Elliot – in Austen's novels.

Thus, danger threatens the vulnerable Cinderella figure both from the outside world and from within the family in several of these early narratives; she must learn to protect and assert herself against intimidating and, in some cases, unappetising suitors, as well as be wary of rivalrous, interfering female relatives. The dangers to her, then, are twofold: there is the hazard of marrying and becoming dependent on an indifferent man and also the peril of being exploited or controlled by family members for the sake of monetary or social aggrandizement. Ultimately, Austen resolves these threats by uniting Cinderella with a man who loves her first as a sister, or with one who has demonstrated disinterested kindness to and stewardship of either his own or the heroine's siblings. The brotherly lover, therefore, immunizes the heroine from the dangers posed by both the outside world and by inferior members of the family. Austen introduces other safeguards as well, banishing the ugly sisters (or wicked stepmother), and ennobling the benevolent, collaborative sister (or sister-in-law), who flanks the heroine in the configuration of siblings drawn together at the end of at least four of the novels.

The Cinderella theme continues to be of consequence in the early novels and becomes even more pronounced in the second 'trilogy'. D. W. Harding argues that in *Northanger Abbey, Sense and Sensibility*, and *Pride and Prejudice*, Austen handles the Cinderella theme more simply than in the later novels. For Harding, the three heroines of the early works are alienated from the other members of their family because they prove to be more sensitive and/or possess better judgement. Indeed, their happy marriages are their recompense 'for being different from the rest, and a consolation for the distresses entailed by being different'. At the end of each of the novels, the heroine, who is either morally superior to her sisters or has learnt to be so, is rewarded with marriage to her prince. The neglected sister triumphs; her virtue is recognised by all, and she marries well.[7]

But Austen's handling of the fairy tale in the early works is not so simple or straightforward as Harding claims. He dismisses the relationship the heroines of the first 'trilogy' fashion with a sister or sister-in-law. He also fails to see that Austen's major method of deepening the Cinderella story is to present the female protagonists more dynamically, thereby allowing us to witness their growth in self-knowledge and perception. The Cinderella-like heroines go through a period of suffering and degradation, often at the hands of unworthy sisters and parents, and then emerge, as it were, from the rite of passage, to realize their highest potential both socially and emotionally. Home is important but inadequate and unstable throughout most of Austen's novels because of the incompetence or absence of parents and, just as frequently, because of sibling rivalry. But, by the end of the works, home has been reactivated from within by the synergized network of worthy siblings.

The novels take stock of the protagonists' attitudes to parent-figures. As in a fairy tale, mothers or stepmothers in Austen's novels and in a number of the Juvenilia are either absent or guilty of foolishness, neglect, and/or coldheartedness. For examples, we need look no further than the tyrannical Lady Susan, vulgar Mrs. Bennet, callous Mrs. Ferrars, apathetic Mrs. Price, nonchalant Lady Bertram, and abusive Mrs. Norris. The mother may also be dead and, therefore, unable to protect or influence her child; such is the case of Emma Watson, of Emma Woodhouse, and of Anne Elliot. For their parts, fathers, too, are far from blameless; their sins are those of detachment (Mr. Bennet), indifference (Mr. Price, Sir Walter Elliot), and ineptitude (Mr. Morland, Mr. Woodhouse). In other cases, they are simply absent owing to ill health (Mr. Watson) or death (Mr. Dashwood).

There is, of course, no sense in suggesting that Austen ever adheres rigidly to the Cinderella paradigm. Our interest is more properly focused on her success in altering the paradigm to suit her purposes. In some versions of the tale, the father harbours incestuous desires for his daughter and ill-treats her when she refuses his advances. However, in Austen's works, incestuous desires are, in special cases, sanctified and transferred to sibling figures. Moreover, the mother (or a sister) is frequently a persecutor but not necessarily owing to any innate perversity or evil. Quite often, the heroine's mother figure is insensitive, careless, or ignorant rather than cruel and wicked. Nonetheless, the mother's neglect and inadequacy, or her opportunistic ambition for her daughter, exact a mental toll on the heroine and contribute to her emotional isolation. To counteract this persecution by mothers and by ugly sisters, another family member (usually a favoured brother or sister) comes to the rescue. For example, Elizabeth Bennet makes Jane's life more bearable at home (and *vice versa*), and Edmund Bertram nurtures his adopted sister, Fanny.

Above all, it is important to note that the Cinderella theme in Austen's fiction reinforces the idea of the sanctity of the family and the exclusionary tendency of approved relationships. In the fairy tale, the heroine breaks out from the family circle, but in Austen's novels the protection of the enclosed family circle is emphasized, particularly at the conclusion of her works.[8] And it is here that we discover a crucial difference between Austen's fiction and the fairy tale paradigm, a difference embodied in the narrative structure. Austen never concerns herself primarily with the desires of the individual but rather with the necessities for achieving moral order. Her novels find resolution for an approved group, not merely for a likeable heroine or an attractive couple. So while Austen excoriates foolish female ambitions and unrealistic dreams, she still presents a validated way to find a partner. Husbands, however, do not appear magically in Austen's fiction. To gain the novelist's stamp of approval, heroes must fit the bill not only of the loving prince but also of a husband and relative who will serve to forward the welfare of the family group.

Austen's heroes may initially appear to be insufferably dull; on the surface, Edward Ferrars, Colonel Brandon, and Edmund Bertram cut a poor figure beside the 'sexy' cads. But gallant, dashing types in Austen's novels invariably prove to be deceitful rogues, false 'Prince Charming' figures. On the other hand, although they may be lacking charisma and prove far from flawless, Austen's heroes always reveal a kind of inner beauty; they usually possess sense, humanity, strong domestic habits, and a belief in the sanctity of the home. These mixed heroes differ from those of Frances Burney. For example, the insecure Cinderella heroine in *Evelina* is overwhelmed by the faultlessness of Lord Orville, the prince who rescues her from ignominious dependence; moreover, she is awed by her saviour's superior judgement and acts in order to please him.[9] In Austen's works, by contrast, the fraternal nature of several of the relationships begets an egalitarian, symbiotic relationship; this symbiosis consequently eliminates the elements of fear and awe.

Another major revision Austen makes to the Cinderella paradigm is that the heroes must wait (and often a long time) for some opposition to be overcome before their marriages can take place, unlike the prince in the fairy tale who quickly falls in love with Cinderella and, without any opposition, marries her soon after their first meeting. For instance, Darcy is at first rejected by Elizabeth, and he hesitates several months before he proposes to her again; Colonel Brandon patiently bides his time for Marianne to get over her infatuation with Willoughby before declaring his love to her; and Wentworth, like Darcy, is at first rejected by the heroine, and, for this reason, he tarries eight years before asking Anne a second time. That is to say, Austen does not offer the reader instantaneous gratification; on the contrary, the hero and heroine may take years to establish bonds and to find out where their mutual interests lie.

The message underlying these alterations to the fairy tale paradigm is plain: in the ideal society, which for Austen is a type of meritocracy, happiness comes to those who deserve it. One must earn the right to happiness through the cultivation of cardinal virtues: patience, judgement, discretion, and, above all, good sense. On the other hand, to Austen's way of thinking, those who rely solely on fate or good fortune have little right to expect happiness, particularly if they do nothing to prepare themselves for the opportunity. Unlike the fairy tale, where it is enough for the heroine to be beautiful and pure, and for the hero to be handsome and wealthy, Austen's novels manifest her insistence on the necessity of strong moral character in love and marriage. The heroines earn their virtuous princes by overcoming a series of obstacles; furthermore, it is their charity, perspicacity, and excellence of mind that enable them to prosper. It is not enough to hope and dream of romance; men and women must prepare themselves to be deserving partners.

Hundreds of different versions of the Cinderella myth exist, but the most popular is that of Charles Perrault. The earliest English version of the Cinderella story is Robert Samber's translation (1729) of Perrault's tale first published in his *Histoire ou Contes du Temps Passé* (1697). Another widely-known variant is that of the Grimm brothers, who revised and published a set of folktales entitled *Kinder und Hausmärchen* (1812), which included the tale 'Ash Girl'.[10] Perrault's version of the fairy tale substantially alters the heroine of the tale passed down to and polished by the Grimms. The hardy, shrewd, intelligent, and active Cinderella of Grimm reverts to the coy, malleable, self-debasing, passive heroine of Perrault's version. Furthermore, Cinderella's treatment of her ugly sisters proves significantly different in the two versions. In Perrault's tale, Cinderella meekly forgives her sisters for their cruelty and jealousy, lodges them in the palace, and marries them off to two nobles of the court. By way of contrast, in the German story, Cinderella does not forgive her sisters; pigeons peck out their eyes, and thus they are punished for their wickedness with blindness.

Parts of the different versions of 'Cinderella' emerge in Austen's works. Austen must have read (or have had read to her) as a child the popular Samber/Perrault version of the story, since it was probably the only complete translation of the fairy tale available to her. The Grimms' collection was published in German in 1812; therefore, it is unlikely that she read their version of the story. However, it is plausible that Austen was aware of similar tales in which a hardier Cinderella was depicted. In any case, Austen reassesses the Cinderella story, opening the fairy tale to the outside world and bringing it to bear upon the relation of the individual to the family and to society as a whole. A recognition of the various elements of the Cinderella myth provides insight into the nature of the heroine as well as into Austen's evolving perspective of the family and society.

Austen offers various Cinderella dreams of love in *Pride and Prejudice*. Darcy's pursuit of Elizabeth (in spite of her inferior relatives) is the material of fairy tales. Elizabeth, however, refuses to be bowled over by this highly eligible bachelor. Incensed by his treatment of Jane and, to a lesser extent, of Wickham, she rejects his offer of marriage even though she is secretly flattered by his attentions. Indeed, in Elizabeth's deluded mind, Darcy has taken on decidedly beastly or villainous proportions. In one sense, Elizabeth revels in a private 'fantasy of power',[11] that is, she prides herself on her superior wit and ability to appraise others. But when she reads Darcy's letter and later visits the majestic Pemberley, she realizes that she has overestimated her powers of perception and comprehension. Pemberley's owner is not a monster of pride and snobbery but a kindly master and brother, although he is far from being perfect – among other things, he must cultivate a sense of humour. Although Elizabeth's 'fantasy of power' with respect to her infallibility of judgement is proved false, in another way her fantasy comes true. The marriage of Elizabeth and Darcy at the close of the novel fulfills the heroine's fantasy in that, despite Darcy's higher social status, their union is one of equals and is very much 'to the advantage of both' (*PP*, p. 312). Unlike Georgiana, who is in awe of her brother, and Caroline Bingley, who obsequiously simpers in his presence, Elizabeth spars with, defies, and laughs at Darcy. Even more important, she influences and enlightens Darcy, making him more tolerant, more gracious, and more conscious of his ability to inflict injury on others (especially in the case of Jane) and to give aid to people when they most need it. Moreover, far from being a taciturn, love-besotted Cinderella waiting passively for her prince, Elizabeth indirectly tests Darcy. The fairy tale gender roles are reversed; figuratively speaking, Elizabeth exercises her power of choice and makes certain that Darcy's foot fits the slipper. That is not to say that this Cinderella figure has the ascendancy; she herself is as much humbled and enlightened as the prince. But, in *Pride and Prejudice*, the prince must establish that he is as meritorious as the heroine.

Elizabeth also demonstrates her power in that she gives her sister Jane the opportunity to attain her fantasy and marry her prince. Hence, the wise sister in the novel replaces the supernatural, maternal figure in the fairy tale. Acquiescent, gentle, and forgiving, Jane fits the archetypal Perrault Cinderella model. At first, she endures a period of degradation; the cold, jealous Bingley sisters treat her haughtily, and Lydia taunts and temporarily deposes her. But Jane's patience and unselfishness are rewarded, although, to be sure, not without the help of Elizabeth, who heads off Lydia's threats to Jane and urges Darcy to reactivate Bingley's suit.

The story of Charlotte Lucas provides another version of the Cinderella myth. Her marriage of convenience to Mr. Collins not only laces the narrative with black comedy but also debases the Cinderella story. Moreover, it serves to illustrate the structural opposition at work in Austen's novels between fantasy and disillusion: desire for security and bliss in marriage (although Charlotte has long ago denounced all thoughts of the latter) and dread of being trapped for a lifetime in a loveless union to an intellectually inferior, undiscriminating mate. Charlotte, that is to say, is a Cinderella who is satisfied with the position of comfortably married woman, even if her husband is no Prince Charming. Elizabeth is shocked by her friend's consent to Mr. Collins' proposal. And yet, significantly, it is neither his lack of physical attractiveness nor his modest living to which she objects but, rather, his palpable and embarrassing lack of sense. And this is where the significance of the sister or sisterly figure lies in Austen's fiction. In many of her novels, the heroine plays fairy godmother to a beloved sister, or she herself is aided by a sisterly fairy godmother. She must help her sister to choose wisely in love and marriage. In this way, the sisters help each other to overcome hardship, to assimilate each other to marriage, and, eventually, to fare well.

In *Pride and Prejudice*, Elizabeth undergoes a series of crises and important stages in her passage from innocence to experience, all of which she learns how to manage. Indeed, both Jane and Elizabeth discover what Edmund Bertram in *Mansfield Park* refers to as 'the most valuable knowledge we could any of us acquire – the knowledge of ourselves and of our duty, to the lessons of affliction' (*MP*, p. 459). Such knowledge sets Jane and Elizabeth apart from the rest of their family; they learn to endure the hostility of the proud Bingley sisters and the gaucherie and jealousy of their own sisters and mother. As in the Cinderella story, a ball, or rather several balls, become testing-grounds and, in some ways, combat zones for the heroine. Like the ugly sisters in the fairy tale, Elizabeth's silly, conceited siblings embarrass and compete with her for the attention of the handsome suitor Wickham at the Netherfield ball. (After she 'wins' the competition and marries Wickham, Lydia is quick to point out that she must now take precedence over her elder sisters since she is a married woman). And the balls also test Elizabeth's patience, for her mother's stupidity and vulgarity in public chagrin her. Thus, like Cinderella, Elizabeth experiences a period of humiliation and degradation. Mrs. Bennet scolds her, Lady Catherine de Bourgh tries to control her actions, and her younger sisters, particularly the imprudent Lydia, threaten to damage or even annihilate her marriage prospects by their vulgarity and foolishness.

According to Bruno Bettelheim, the story of Cinderella presents each of the stages in personality development necessary to attain self-fulfillment. Similarly, in *Pride and Prejudice*, Elizabeth must pass through a series of experiences and obstacles to gain self-knowledge and to discover what it means to love truly. Bettelheim bases his model of the cycle of crises on Erik H. Erikson's and refers to the stages of the sequence as basic trust, autonomy, initiative, industry, and identity.[12] In Austen's novel, Elizabeth must first learn to trust Darcy, to distinguish between Wickham's wickedness and Darcy's goodness as a brother and master. She then learns to accept her own unique role and make the best of it; that is, she discovers how she can wield her special qualities of wit and discernment to cooperate with and to affect the actions and lives of others. She must use her initiative and direct affairs at home after Lydia elopes with Wickham, since her father is discomposed and shocked, her mother incapable of any exertion and requiring constant attendance, and her other sisters defective in intelligence and judgement. She works hard to help Lydia and compose her family, and her industry is rewarded with some success. Finally, she accepts Darcy, after he reconciles himself to her family's shortcomings, and when she has overcome all her own prejudices. After much suffering, she finally wins her prince. And the handsome, noble Darcy is indeed a princely figure. One of the richest men in England, he reigns over a large, imposing estate in Derbyshire. But, more important, he is also a man of intellectual resource and fine discrimination. Elizabeth and Darcy establish their own family at the close of *Pride and Prejudice*. Away from the uncemented, unstable world of her parents, Elizabeth builds a new, improved family unit with her husband, sister, sister-in-law, and brother-in-law. And, as we have noted, Austen stresses the self-sufficiency of such a family circle, with its strong spiritual as well as consanguineal ties.

In the Cinderella story, as in most fairy tales, the ending is 'closed'. The characters have seemingly learnt everything they need and are going to learn. Cinderella and her prince will live happily ever after, and the ugly sisters are either forgiven or punished for their sins. The family picture at the end of Austen's novels, however, is not static; the finale is rather more open-ended. At the conclusion of *Pride and Prejudice*, it seems clear not only that Elizabeth and Jane have acquired greater self-knowledge, but also that they will continue to learn from each other and from their husbands. Elizabeth and Jane will benefit from their husbands' knowledge of and information about the world and from their sense and understanding (limited though the latter may be in Bingley's case). For their part, Darcy and Bingley will have to learn to practice courtesy and tact with Mrs. Bennet as their mother-in-law. By escaping the Bennet household, Jane and Elizabeth, with their husbands, are able to create a resuscitated family circle more conducive to their self-development and to that of their sisters. Moreover, unlike the story of Cinderella, which takes place out of time and out of space, Austen's novels are grounded in decorum and economic and social realities. The moral of Austen's work, therefore, is neither exaggerated nor saccharine in the way of the fairy tale. As Mary Poovey points out, 'Austen redeems romance by purging it of all traces of egotism.'[13] That is to say, the fulfillment of individual desires is far from sufficient for Austen. The Cinderella dream has been extended to incorporate not merely the happiness of the hero and heroine but that of a network of interrelated individuals. In this respect, Austen expands the limits of the ideal to encompass more diverse prospects.

Sense and Sensibility also features two Cinderella-like figures. At the beginning of the novel, Elinor and Marianne lose their position and their inherited estate to unworthy relatives, much as Cinderella loses hers in the fairy tale. Elinor, like Elizabeth Bennet, is neglected by her mother, who pays more attention to her sisters. But, after much hardship and misunderstanding, she marries a virtuous, affectionate man. In many ways, the wise sister, Elinor, acts as fairy godmother to her younger, susceptible sister in *Sense and Sensibility*, much as Elizabeth acts as Jane's in *Pride and Prejudice*.

Despite her cleverness, Marianne seems more like the dreamy and romantic heroine of Perrault's story. Indeed, her ambition in life is to be a kind of fantasy heroine, to love and to be loved immoderately. And the adventurous, sexy Willoughby seems to fit her requirements perfectly. Marianne's dream, however, does not ignore economic factors: two thousand pounds a year is a prerequisite for her earthly paradise. Hence her yearning for love and her concern for what she terms a 'proper establishment' in life are concomitant. That is why at the end of the novel, in chameleon-like fashion, she transfers her passion for Willoughby to the Colonel. Her love blooms in the company of a devoted man and in the wealthy environs of Delaford. Thus, in the story of Marianne, Austen drastically alters the Cinderella myth in that Marianne is not sacrificed to an 'irresistible passion'; instead, she marries an older man who seeks to protect his health with flannel waistcoats. Yet, at the same time, Austen reimposes the dream in both a romantic and an economic sense; Marianne comes to love Colonel Brandon wholeheartedly at the same time that she scales the heights of upward mobility to become mistress of an estate and patroness of a village.

In the same novel, Lucy Steele's story offers yet another version of the Cinderella myth; however, her establishment in life is most carefully distinguished from Mariannne's. To be sure, Lucy attains upward mobility, but she and Robert are not united in either affection or virtue, and so the dream is parodied, vitiated. Their unromantic union lacks the magic generated by esteem, mutual interests, and devotion. In Austen's fiction, such magic arts are often learned from a precious sibling relationship. In the case of Marianne and Elinor, Elinor has dispensed magic in that she acts as an advisor, teaching her sister qualities that prepare her for an ideal marital union with, as it turns out, Colonel Brandon. By contrast, the price of sibling betrayal and moral bankruptcy is made evident in the union of Robert and Lucy; without the agency of a fairy godmother (dimwitted, treacherous Nancy offers no support), Lucy has not been tutored in such magical arts.

Emma, the Cinderella-like heroine of 'The Watsons', seeks to escape from her humble, depressing surroundings and the deceit and vulgarity of her sisters Penelope and Margaret by establishing a strong sororal bond with her elder sister Elizabeth. Another ambivalent fairy godmother figure, Elizabeth is simple-minded and unsophisticated but also affectionate and kind-hearted. At the beginning of the narrative, Elizabeth proposes that Emma go to a ball in her place. She instructs and cautions her inexperienced sister about the other guests and takes pleasure in providing transportation (an old chair rather than a glamorous carriage) for her sister and all her finery. Even though she may at times be an erring, bumbling fairy godmother, Elizabeth provides constant emotional and moral sustenance to compensate Emma for the vices of her inferior sisters. Emma also finds solace in the company of her invalid father, 'a man of sense and education' (*MW*, p. 361). Her father's bedroom becomes Emma's oasis of refuge, a substitute for Cinderella's kitchen hearth. For most of her years, Emma has been brought up by an aunt, and like Cinderella, she enjoyed love and high esteem in the early part of her life. Her fall from this favoured position to the degradation and poverty of her parental home occurs suddenly, as does her restoration to a more exalted position as the wife of the scholarly, gentlemanly Mr. Howard at the projected conclusion of the novel. Indeed, the plot of 'The Watsons' would seem very like a fairy tale in that the heroine's fortunes are subject to rapid shifts of fate. Yet, as in *Pride and Prejudice*, the heroine does not merely wait for a change in fortune. She learns to manage her own destiny.

Deficiencies in the surrounding familial members become important for propelling the heroine on her path to self-realization and development in several of Austen's novels. Elizabeth Bennet, Elinor Dashwood, and Emma Watson must establish a new family circle that is itself a microcosm of a reinvigorated society. Furthermore, the heroine upholds and preserves traditional moral values and helps to reestablish family harmony. The heroines gain status and independence as they form their own family circles and secure their positions as mistress of a home or even of an estate. As in a fairy tale, in *Pride and Prejudice, Sense and Sensibility*, and 'The Watsons', wrongs are eventually righted, genuine love turns into happy marriage, and those who have learnt the virtues of tolerance and perseverance are elevated socially. Yet none of these conclusions arises out of or implies a simplistic formula. And the moral knowledge to be drawn from these works is not aimed at children. Virginia's Woolf's remark that George Eliot's *Middlemarch* was 'written for grown-up people'[14] is equally applicable to the novels of Austen. The human qualities and relationships on which Austen dwells and of which she approves are mature and, above all, practical.

The Cinderella story reappears in quite a different form in *Northanger Abbey*. Austen consistently provides in this novel a *reductio ad absurdum* variant of the Cinderella theme. Unintelligent and only passably attractive, Catherine differs from her predecessors in Austen's novels in that she is unfit to be a princess. Unlike the heroines in romantic tales, she possesses neither stunning beauty, grace, nor wit. She is a virtuous, 'deserving' character, but her attributes are not distinguished; still, like the Perrault Cinderella, she has a candid, guileless, and unpretentious nature, and she shows herself capable of strong but simple affections. Henry loves Catherine because of her lack of sophistication, her blunted sense of irony, her honesty, and her gullibility: he has never met anyone like her before. For Henry, Catherine is an endless field in which to sow new ideas for his personal influence and amusement. At the end of *Northanger Abbey*, the narrator confesses that Henry is attracted to Catherine, not because he is smitten by her loveliness but out of gratitude; the narrator goes on to acknowledge that Henry's love 'is a new circumstance in romance . . . and dreadfully derogatory of an heroine's dignity' (*NA*, p. 243). Nonetheless, the Cinderella pattern, substantially reformed and recoloured, is reaffirmed at the end of the novel.

Austen presents in the same novel another ambivalent fairy godmother figure in the person of Mrs. Allen. Her passion is dress; she spends much time teaching Catherine about grooming and providing her charge with a beautiful outfit of the newest fashion for her *entrée* into life, much as the fairy godmother transforms Cinderella's rags into a dazzling gown. But Mrs. Allen is ineffective as a moral guide because she is so concerned with outward appearance. When Catherine asks the Allens for their advice about the propriety of driving in an open carriage with John Thorpe, Mr. Allen admonishes Catherine and points out that such schemes are 'not right', whereas Mrs. Allen's only comment is that a clean gown soon gets soiled in an open carriage. Later on in the novel, the wise surrogate sister Eleanor replaces Mrs. Allen as fairy godmother to Catherine; Eleanor teaches the heroine to be more prudent and less fanciful.

Like Cinderella, Catherine experiences hardship, but she also learns to distinguish between what is estimable and what is reprehensible. The ugly siblings Isabella and John Thorpe scheme to gain Catherine's purported wealth. And General Tilney, the wicked parental figure in the novel, also plans to acquire Catherine's money. As tyrannical and mercenary as the stepmother in the fairy tale, the General exposes his inordinate pride and cruelty when he forces Catherine out of Northanger; Catherine fathoms that 'in suspecting General Tilney of either murdering or shutting up his wife, [she] had scarcely sinned against his character or magnified his cruelty' (*NA*, p. 247). Austen suggests that life is indeed fraught with dangers, and that people do in fact treat each other inhumanly, but not necessarily in the spectacular style of the romantic novel or fairy tale. Instead, she applies the corrective of realism and brings life to bear on the fairy tale. What is wanted in a spouse is not physical beauty (or, at least, physical beauty alone). Although Henry prizes Catherine's innocence, she must learn by experience and through the guidance of her suitor and her adopted sister, Eleanor, to become wise to the facts of existence while retaining her childlike capacity for wonder and her readiness to embrace life's possibilities. Thus *Northanger Abbey* offers what is, in many ways, the most clear-cut example of the moral sense in which Austen deviates from the Cinderella myth. Far from prospering by the superficial attainment of fashionable clothing or by indulged fantasies, the heroine nearly succeeds in ruining her chances for a fulfilling life. For, in Austen's novels, no character succeeds by behaving foolishly or by nurturing dreams of implausible outcomes.

In *Emma*, Austen overturns the Cinderella theme in manifold ways. As D. W. Harding argues, the Cinderella theme is now demoted to the sub-heroine Jane Fairfax, and, in some ways, Emma becomes more like one of the ugly sisters. Similarly, in the story of Harriet Smith, Austen deflates the theme of the noble, morally refined child raised in lowly circumstances, for Harriet is gormless and turns out to be the illegitimate daughter of a tradesman.[15] A virtuous, sweet-tempered character, Harriet's foot is still too large to fit the glass slipper. Moreover, fairy godmothers do not exist in *Emma*. Mrs. Weston, Emma's putative 'sister' and surrogate mother, is weak and ineffective as a guide; she has always spoilt Emma and let her have her own way, instead of disciplining and restraining her. Interfering, tactless Mrs. Elton lampoons the fairy godmother with her plans for the improvement of the impoverished but fair Jane Fairfax. And the heroine herself turns out to be totally unfit as a fairy godmother as is indicated by her absurd schemes for the elevation of Harriet.

Instead of a fairy godmother, Austen presents a godfather/brother – Mr. Knightley – who cossets and counsels his young charge. As opposed to the intervention of a spell, Austen stresses the importance of Mr. Knightley's moral instruction. In true Cinderella style, Austen's other heroines move gradually away from expulsion or negligence and suffering to bliss and consolation at the end of the novel. But Emma moves from her superior position as the rich mistress of Hartfield at the beginning of the work to another superior position as the future mistress of Donwell at the end. Moreover, Emma is faulted as a character more than any other heroine. She hopes to become more worthy of her husband, unlike most of Austen's other women, who have to forgive their husbands for sinning against them. Elizabeth forgives Darcy for his pride and arrogance. Elinor forgives Edward for his foolish engagement to Lucy. Fanny forgives Edmund for falling in love with Mary Crawford. And Anne forgives Wentworth for his resentment. But, at the close of *Emma*, the heroine acknowledges her haughtiness and snobbery and resolves to be more rational, humble, and circumspect in future.

In *Pride and Prejudice* and *Sense and Sensibility*, Austen leans more toward independent, resourceful heroines in the persons of Elizabeth and Elinor, both of whom resemble the hardier Cinderella model of Grimm. But in *Mansfield Park* and *Persuasion*, Austen depicts a patient, undemanding heroine, more like the Cinderella of the Perrault version of the fairy tale. This transformation in the portrayal of the heroine has profound thematic implications. Separated from the family unit and without the protection of sister ties for prolonged periods, Fanny, and more particularly Anne, are exploited and degraded like servants rather than treated like family members. In the case of Anne, such a situation can only be rectified by completely removing the heroine from her unstable family and by forming a new familial unit through marriage to her prince. Fanny eventually forges new ties of sisterhood with Susan, and the two of them literally replace the ugly Bertram sisters at Mansfield. But circumstances are very different for the heroine in *Persuasion*; Anne forges no ties with her sisters, and she remains alienated even at the end of the novel. Separated from Kellynch and from her sisters, and with no estate to look forward to, Anne loses both her station and her '"grounds" of being and action'.[16] Without the usual reference points of devoted sibling ties and a structured inheritance, Anne appears disoriented, even though she gains her prince.

Mansfield Park opens like a fairy tale with the description of three sisters, Miss Ward, Maria, and Frances. And, indeed, the triangle of sisters is employed in many of Austen's works. *Sense and Sensibility* tells the story of the three Dashwood sisters (although the youngest one is considerably less important in the narrative than the other two). The three Elliot sisters dominate *Persuasion*. In addition, the Ward sisters in *Mansfield Park* remind us of Mary, Sophia, and Georgiana in 'The Three Sisters', as well as the three Miss Simpsons in another early piece entitled 'Jack and Alice', who represent Ambition, Envy, and Shame. In *Mansfield Park*, Maria Ward marries a baronet, and all exclaim on the greatness of the match; however, as Janice Simpson has noted, the Cinderella plot is debased in the story of Miss Ward's meteoric rise up the social ladder, for she is trapped in a loveless marriage to Sir Thomas.[17] The next Miss Ward does not fare much better. After waiting several years, she is obliged to attach herself to a clergyman named Norris who possesses little private fortune. For her part, Frances disobliges and embarrasses her family by making an imprudent marriage to a poor lieutenant and is consequently banished from the family circle.

The same structure is repeated in the next generation. Maria aspires to marry the affluent but foolish Mr. Rushworth. Julia envies her sister's flirtation with the spirited Henry Crawford. As for Fanny, she is segregated from her step-sisters and degraded to a shameful Cinderella-like role, much as Harriet Smith and Jane Fairfax are relegated in *Emma* (Harriet becomes Emma's lackey, and

Jane Fairfax fetches and carries things for her senile grandmother and garrulous aunt in their meagre household). Obliged to perform errands, Fanny must also endure the abuse of her Aunt Norris, who frequently reminds her niece, 'You must be the lowest and last' (*MP*, p. 221). Excluded and taunted by Maria and Julia, Fanny weeps and is left to her own devices in the cold schoolroom without a fire, the equivalent of Cinderella's kitchen hearth.

In Cinderella fashion, Fanny goes through stages of suffering and mortification. The heroine's progress from segregation to owner-ship, from degradation to an essential, even exalted place in the family, with the variations of tension, rivalry, love, and loyalty forms the dramatic structure of *Mansfield Park*.[18] At Mansfield, Fanny must endure her cousins' selfish domination as well as the rivalry of another ugly sister, Mary Crawford, who persecutes Fanny by flirting with Edmund and by reminding Fanny that her love for Edmund can only be cousinly. Furthermore, she suffers the cruel remarks of her Aunt Norris, the wicked stepmother figure at Mansfield, who favours her rich, selfish nieces over poor, virtuous Fanny.

Like Cinderella's stepsisters, the Miss Bertrams compete with and come into conflict with each other. Brought up by an anxious, but reserved and unaffectionate, father and an indolent mother, haughty and irresponsible Maria and Julia have no sincere respect for family ties. When Sir Thomas leaves for Antigua, we are told: 'The Miss Bertrams were much to be pitied on the occasion; not for their sorrow but for their want of it' (*MP*, p. 32). Heartless as siblings, Maria and Julia not only ill-treat their lonely cousin Fanny, but, during their brother Tom's illness, choose to remain in London. In this way, Maria and Julia serve to educate both Fanny and the reader as to what it means to be ugly sisters. It is not so much their physical appearance (on the contrary, the sisters are very attractive) as their moral characters that are ill-formed. The heroine in Austen's novels must develop those qualities of loyalty to and respect for the family in order to become worthy of a prince.

The second stage of Fanny's period of suffering takes place at her parents' comfortless home in Portsmouth. Mrs. Price, like the stepmother in the fairy tale, ignores her daughter and prefers her other children. Mrs. Price and Betsey shame Fanny by their self-indulgence and boorishness; indeed, they injure all her feelings of honour, duty, and tenderness by their behaviour. Fanny wonders what she has done to forfeit her mother's affection:

> Mrs. Price was not unkind – but, instead of gaining on her affection and confidence, and becoming more and more dear, her daughter never met with greater kindness from her, than on the first day of her arrival. The instinct of nature was soon satisfied, and Mrs. Price's attachment had no other source. (*MP*, p. 389)

Austen suggests in such portraits that a real mother – Lady Susan, Mrs. Bennet, Mrs. Price – can by her neglect become a wicked stepmother. It is not far-fetched to say that this was perhaps how the mature Austen saw her own mother. The novelist resented her mother's neglect of and indifference to her, and, to a certain extent, she seems to have vented her hostility and disappointment in her descriptions of foolish, cold-hearted mothers in the novels. At one point in *Mansfield Park*, Fanny wonders why her mother does not love her: '[She] had probably alienated love by the helplessness and fretfulness of a fearful temper, or been unreasonable in wanting a larger share than one among so many could deserve' (*MP*, p. 389). Like Mrs. Price, Mrs. Austen had many children and doted on her sons. She favoured Cassandra over Jane, much as Mrs. Price favours Betsey over her other daughters.[19] All of this may help explain why Austen found 'Cinderella' so appealing and used the theme so often. Impoverished and neglected, she may have thought of herself as Cinderella.

In *Mansfield Park*, Fanny conquers her disappointment in her mother's lack of affection and establishes ties with her sister Susan, to whom she acts as a fairy godmother. While her cousins bring disgrace on Mansfield, Fanny becomes stronger as a character because of her developing relationship with Susan. Fanny succeeds in this regard and becomes a member of the family at Mansfield owing to her moral qualities and reverence for such ties, but her ugly sisters are punished for their sins and lack of veneration for family ties. Thus, Fanny and Susan replace the ugly sisters; Fanny marries Edmund, and Susan is 'established at Mansfield with every appearance of equal permanency' (*MP*, p. 472). Some commentators have claimed that Fanny and Edmund's relationship is loveless, that Fanny gains her prince but not his passion.[20] But, in fact, their passion has been ripening since they were children. We hear little about their courtship because we have observed how well-suited they are throughout the novel; and Austen implies that nothing could be more natural than for them to seal their love with a physical union. The ending of the novel is, in this sense, a true fantasy, that of the marriage of a brother and sister.

As Fleishman suggests, the major thrust of the Cinderella motif in *Mansfield Park* lies not so much in the matter of inheriting property, but in Fanny's acquisition of 'a commanding position in the affections of the family'.[21] Moreover, it is also appropriate to say that the influence of the Cinderella motif lies in the lesson to be learnt from suffering and the need for strength and self-knowledge. As Wiesenfarth remarks, Austen 'allows [mythical] patterns to fulfill the expectations they create only when they come to exist within a moral framework that satisfies her sense of what the true values in human life are'.[22] At the conclusion of the novel, Sir Thomas acknowledges 'the advantage of early hardship and discipline, and the consciousness of being born to struggle and endure' (*MP*, p. 473). Interestingly enough, Charlotte Bronte borrowed, consciously or not, the phrase 'born to struggle and endure' for *Jane Eyre*, the heroine of which is yet another Cinderella figure.[23]

In *Persuasion*, the Cinderella story is deferred. At the outset of the novel, we are told of a sad event that took place many years ago. A spirited, brilliant young man courted a fair and gentle woman. The couple were remarkably suited; indeed, the narrator claims that '[it] would be difficult to say which had seen highest perfection in the other, or which had been the happiest; she, in receiving his declarations and proposals, or he in having them accepted' (*P*, p. 26). But their blissful period of courtship was brought to an abrupt halt, thwarted by her snobbish father and interfering godmother (who took the place of Anne's beloved mother after she died). Thus, when we encounter Anne eight years later, she is a Cinderella in a state of suspended animation. Her prince found her, and the shoe fitted; however, parental persuasion intervened to prevent fulfillment of the relationship. And so we find Anne Elliot at twenty-seven, still dependent on her family, still in love with the memory of Wentworth, and still isolated from her kith and kin on account of her superior taste and feelings.

Disregarded by Elizabeth, used by Mary, and estranged from her conceited father, Anne leads a forlorn existence. Like the younger sister in Perrault's version of Cinderella, Mary is not so repulsive and unsisterly as Elizabeth; but she possesses no empathy or understanding to make her respect Anne. Faced with these imperfect conditions, Anne does not languish or pine for her lost love; instead, she endeavours to be of service to others, particularly to her sister Mary. In the tradition of the gentle Perrault Cinderella, Anne accepts her sister's exploitation of her, for 'to be claimed as a good, though in an improper style, is at least better than being rejected as no good at all' (*P*, p. 33).

Fairy godmothers are rendered effete in this novel. Unlike all of the other heroines, Anne does not act as fairy godmother to a sister, nor is she aided by a fairy godmother (or godfather or brother in the case of Mr. Knightley and his impact on Emma) of her own. Like Mrs. Weston in *Emma* and Mrs. Allen in *Northanger Abbey*, Lady Russell proves an ineffective guide. Indeed, Anne laments throughout *Persuasion* her loss of eight years' happiness because she allowed herself to be persuaded by Lady Russell into rejecting Wentworth's marriage proposal. And although Anne tries to act as a fairy godmother in her efforts to influence or support her sisters, her attempts are either severely hampered or aborted. Mary scarcely changes her attitude; she is as patronising and egocentric at the end of the novel as at the beginning. And when Anne offers to go with and succour Louisa after her fall at Lyme, Mary immediately butts in and, full of jealousy, claims that Anne is 'nothing to Louisa' (*P*, p. 115), that she is Louisa's sister and, therefore, the proper person to take the place of Harriet.

In many ways, *Persuasion* is not so innovative a work as some critics have claimed.[24] To be sure, there are narrative and thematic changes and developments, but the fairy-tale ending is still imposed. Anne's magical 'loss and return of bloom'[25] captivates Wentworth. But the magic does not merely make her as superficially beautiful in his eyes as she was at nineteen. Instead he acknowledges her 'steadiness of principle' (*P*, p. 242), her 'excellence of . . . mind' (*P*, p. 242), and the balance in her character of 'fortitude and gentleness' (*P*, p. 241). Whereas the fairy tale Cinderella impresses the prince with her outward appearance and innocence, Anne inspires Wentworth's love with her generous heart and firmness of mind. On the basis of these deeper qualities, Anne disproves Marianne Dashwood's theory that 'a woman of seven and twenty . . . can never hope to feel or inspire affection again' (*SS*, p. 38). At twenty-seven, Anne has reached new heights: having 'been forced into prudence in her youth, she learned romance as she grew older' (*P*, p. 30). The hero and heroine are no longer 'boy and girl' (*P*, p. 221) but mature lovers. Indeed, the second time around, they are 'even more exquisitely happy' (*P*, p. 240).

For Austen, romance is possible even at a later age. But what makes this relationship so deep is that Wentworth and Anne have learned to appreciate each other's worth.

As we have seen, Austen's works are far more than fairy tales even though fantasy-like finales are prescribed. At the end of all of the novels, the heroine, like Cinderella, marries her prince, who has waited a long time for the marriage to take place. But they do not marry merely on the basis of brief encounters or a glass slipper; their love is based on familiarity and tested feelings built up over a period of time. Moreover, we have noted that sibling love (as well as sibling rivalry) is a crucial feature of Austen's alterations to the Cinderella paradigm. For devoted sisters, incestuous lovers, and sibships all contribute to the education of the Cinderella figure by which means she becomes a true heroine rather than a mere object of desire for a prince. In this way, Austen exposes the prominence of siblings in moulding disposition, desire and future prospects. Heroines (and heroes) earn their happiness by proving themselves worthy; they do not merely have the right size foot, and their happiness is not the result of luck or fate. Austen draws on the fairy tale precisely to show the difference between those who hope to achieve a good life through sorcery or chance, and those who learn through trial and error and who cultivate the qualities of sense, sympathy, and forbearance. Their rewards, like their qualities, are not momentary or evanescent like the fairy tale ending, but perdurable and real.

6

Patrimonial Issue: Dutiful and Prodigal Brothers

As Elizabeth Bennet wanders around the Pemberley estate, she muses on Darcy's responsibilities and obligations: 'As a brother, a landlord, a master, she considered how many people's happiness were in his guardianship! – How much of pleasure or pain it was in his power to bestow! – How much of good or evil must be done by him!' (*PP*, pp. 250–1). While the dynamics of sororal and cross-sibling relationships steal the limelight, brotherly relations remain in the wings of Austen's novels. Nonetheless, the decisions and directions of brothers either affect or serve as a catalyst for all of the action in the novels. Elder brothers, in particular, have the ability to improve or ruin the lives of their sisters and younger brothers, whether temporarily or permanently. In this way, Austen reveals her acute sensitivity to and comprehension of the inner workings of the contemporary economic and social arena. The guardianship of brothers and the unequal fortunes doled out by the system of primogeniture may not be the major focus of her works, but they do serve as the underpinnings for her narratives. Thus, fraternal roles and relations become the prism through which expectations and prescriptions for other family members are refracted.

Austen frequently counterpoints inimical brothers – Robert and Edward Ferrars, Tom and Edmund Bertram, Henry and Frederick Tilney – to examine such matters and themes as inheritance laws, fraternal hierarchy, and the potential for use or misuse of fraternal power. These configurations of antithetical brothers, a throwback perhaps to Cain and Abel, help to brace the narrative structure of the novels. Like the double sister plot, the double brother plot in eighteenth-century novels and drama provides a convenient springboard for authors to moralize about opposing viewpoints and attitudes. The works of Fielding and Sheridan come immediately to mind. These authors, however, do not merely offer static depictions

119

of vice and virtue in their portraits of brothers. Instead, they delight in scenes that expose, on the one hand, the virtues of the erring brother, and, on the other, the fraudulence of the ostensibly pious and respectable brother. In *Tom Jones* (1749), for instance, although Tom allows himself to be kept by Lady Bellaston, his benevolence and charity to others are exemplary; meanwhile, his half-brother, Blifil, maintains a saintly exterior but secretly plots the downfall of Tom. Likewise, in *The School for Scandal* (1778), the spendthrift libertine Charles Surface refuses to sell his uncle's portrait out of affection for him, while his sanctimonious brother Joseph courts a woman for her fortune and later attempts to seduce Lady Teazle. Both Fielding and Sheridan use the dramatic methods of sentimental comedy. Vice and virtue are modified; characters are either worse or better, rather than being simply black or white. But still their techniques of contrasting characters are facile. Austen, writing later on in the century, either rejects such patterned types or renders them less simplistic, less artificial in order to create better art. In this way, she may employ her characters as more nearly realistic and persuasive touchstones for the moral values in her work.

Among the middle and upper classes of Austen's time, brotherly solidarity was severely affected by the laws of primogeniture. As we have already seen, although sisters tended to have intense relationships, they sometimes fought over suitors and marriage. Among brothers, however, fraternal war over land, property, money, and parental favour frequently terrorised familial peace much more drastically than competition over lovers. While primogeniture secured the independence of the eldest son in a well-to-do family, cadets or younger sons had to be provided for by means other than inheritance of the family estates – either through a profession, a sinecure, or marriage to an affluent heiress.[1] In *Mansfield Park*, Mary Crawford expresses her astonishment at Edmund Bertram's desire to enter the church, for she maintains, 'there is generally an uncle or a grandfather to leave a fortune to the second son'. Edmund coolly reminds her that this practice is 'not quite universal' (*MP*, p. 92). Indeed, according to certain historical evidence, Mary Crawford's generalization only applied to one out of three second sons.[2] The distribution of wealth and land in favour of the eldest brother, the need and urgency to look for a position in life, and the toil of a profession provoked in some cases resentment and covetousness in the younger brother. Hence, in Austen's novels, we come to see how economic pressures, opposition of interest, and parental partiality arouse hostility between brothers. And, in the case of Edward and Robert Ferrars in *Sense and Sensibility*, such jealous feelings are further exacerbated by competition over a woman, although this sexual contest is very much subordinated to economic rivalry.

Polite society of Austen's time sanctioned close-knit circles of trusting, intimate female relatives and friends; however, as Smith-Rosenberg points out, 'men appear[ed] to be an other or out-group, segregated into different schools, supported by their own male network of friends and kin, socialized to different behavior'.[3] As children and adolescents, brothers sometimes had close relationships. But as they grew older, circumstances often caused them to drift apart. While sisters lived quietly at home and depended on each other for companionship, brothers went out into the world and attended university or acquired a profession or business interests, any or all of which frequently kept them away from home and served to cool any strong fraternal bonds they may have formed as youngsters. Furthermore, as they matured, their awareness of hierarchy within the family also increased. In Austen's *Mansfield Park*, for instance, when Edmund and Tom Bertram argue about the propriety of putting on a play during their father's absence, the elder Tom haughtily reminds his brother of his superior status: 'Manage your own concerns, Edmund, and I'll take care of the rest of the family' (*MP*, p. 127). In this way, Tom claims his birthright and exercises his power as the eldest brother, even though he turns out to be a poor steward for his sisters. With these words, he also emphasizes the distinctions between himself, the present Mr. Bertram and future Sir Thomas, and his brother, Mr. *Edmund* Bertram, a form of address that Mary Crawford finds pathetically 'younger-brother-like' (*MP*, p. 211).

A similar type of rank was evident in sororal relations in Austen's time. The eldest daughter was formally distinguished by being addressed by her surname only, as in Miss Bennet, Miss Bertram, Miss Austen. But while envious feelings were sometimes generated among sisters by the superiority granted to the eldest daughter and also by the precedence accorded married sisters, jealousies between brothers were more incisive since, in their case, the family honour and wealth were more obviously at stake. For example, Robert Ferrars, in perhaps the most vicious and disturbing instance of sibling rivalry in Austen's novels, claims that as punishment for sullying the family name by marrying Lucy Steele, his brother 'must be starved, you know; – that is certain, absolutely starved' (*SS*, p. 300). Moreover, solidarity between adult brothers was also affected by the contemporary system of manners and mores. Whereas society promoted close contact and freedom of emotional expression between women, it disapproved of such overt intimacy between men, who were expected to interact calmly and unemotionally.

In most families, following established tradition, the eldest son took the family name and estates. Younger sons were settled by profession, sinecure, a family fortune, or marriage. But a daughter did not have the opportunity to attain independent social standing. Women of the aristocracy and of the gentry in Austen's time had to find a home with a husband. Marriage was of much greater consequence to a woman than to a man, especially in a large family with little money, like the Austens, the Bennets, or the Watsons. In the event that she did not marry (unless she had independent means of her own), a woman often had to live with and rely on the support of a brother, or go out to what Jane Fairfax calls the 'governess-trade'. In the former case, a woman gained respectability but was also severely limited by the arrangement. Both wealthy and impecunious women lacked mobility; even impoverished men, such as midshipman William Price, could go where they pleased, whereas women were not at liberty to do so and always had to be chaperoned. Although Georgiana Darcy has great expectations, she lives with a hired companion while her brother visits and travels with freedom and impunity. And whereas Eleanor Tilney remains in seclusion at Northanger, Henry lives independently at Woodston and attends to business.

On account of his economic and social advantages, a brother's guardianship of and largesse toward his siblings, especially his sisters, constitute a primary index to character in Austen's novels. Darcy, for example, is an excellent brother. The housekeeper at Pemberley comments: 'Whatever can give his sister any pleasure is sure to be done in a moment' (*PP*, p. 250). And even the vengeful Wickham grudgingly allows that Darcy is 'a very kind and careful guardian of his sister' (*PP*, p. 82). Similarly, Henry Tilney protects his sister's interests, warmly thanking Catherine for becoming his sister's companion at Northanger and thus alleviating her loneliness. In contrast, John Dashwood and Robert Watson are parsimonious, inconsiderate brothers, who uncharitably urge their sisters to marry well so that they will not be left on their hands. John Dashwood, in particular, abuses his power as head of the household by refusing to offer his stepmother and half-sisters adequate assistance according to his father's last request. Thus, a brother's instability, infirmity of purpose, or abeyance of guardian-ship, creates major complications and precipitates action in many cases in Austen's works.

Letters to sisters seem to constitute for Austen an important key to the quality of a brother. In *Mansfield Park*, during a discussion about letter-writing, Mary Crawford exclaims:

> 'What strange creatures brothers are! You would not write to each other but upon the most urgent necessity in the world . . . . You have but one style among you. I know it perfectly. Henry, who is in every other respect exactly what a brother should be, who loves me, consults me, confides in me, and will talk to me by the hour together, has never yet turned the page in a letter.' (*MP*, p. 59)

Henry Crawford is remiss since his letters are so brief, whereas the worthy brothers William and Edmund, and considerate brothers such as James Morland in *Northanger Abbey*, write long, affectionate letters to their sisters. Letters reinforce the idea of fraternal respon-sibility. Estimable brothers who write loving letters are attuned to familial permanence and stability. They keep the family structure intact by showing the right kind of fraternal devotion and respect rather than abdicating this important role and behaving in a com-pletely egocentric and extravagant manner, as, for example, Henry Crawford does in *Mansfield Park*. Even though they are far apart, Fanny and William Price stay close by sending detailed letters, in which they discuss their plans to live together. Fanny tells Edmund, 'I cannot rate so very highly the love or good nature of a brother, who will not give himself the trouble of writing any thing worth reading, to his sisters, when they are separated' (*MP*, p. 64). Austen's own experience may be relevant here. She sometimes complained that her sailor brothers did not write to her often enough; there may be some wish-fulfillment in Fanny's references to William's lengthy, lively letters.[4]

Austen was very much aware that in her society a brother's stewardship and moral character were often crucial to maintaining a family's reputation. In her novels, when feelings between brother and sister, or sister and sister, are strained, the consequences are usually limited to the immediate family or social circle; however,

animosity between brothers often forebodes more serious consequences for the family's standing in the community at large. As
fraternal rivalries and their graver consequences might serve to
overshadow the dramatic tensions between brother and sister, or
sister and sister, Austen largely confines herself to two types of
fraternal rivals: the dutiful brother and the prodigal brother. And
whereas the fairy tale archetype of Cinderella provides a useful analogue for discussing Austen's sister/sister relations, her portrayal of
brother/brother relations follows more nearly the sibling paradigms
presented in the biblical parable of the prodigal son.

In this parable, the younger of two sons takes his inheritance,
travels for some years, spends the whole of his money, and then
returns home begging for his father's forgiveness. The moral of the
parable concerns the importance of charity, but the drama of the
parable lies in the elder son's reaction to his father's celebration
of his dissipated brother's return. The elder son is angry; he resents
that his brother, who 'hath devoured [his] living with harlots' (Luke
15:30), is feted with the fatted calf, while he, who has always been
dutiful, has never received any credit. The father's favouritism
creates tension and rivalry between the two brothers. And despite
the Christian moral of the parable, one sees that the dutiful son is,
in some ways, justified in his anger and hostility.

This same kind of conflict between brothers, and its accompanying moral and emotional tensions, can be found in several of
Austen's novels. In *Sense and Sensibility*, no love is lost between
Edward and Robert Ferrars. Edward's modesty and worth contrast
with the conceit, foolishness, and extravagance of his younger
brother, Robert. Something like the father's liberality with the
wastrel younger brother is evident in the actions of the mother
in this novel. Mrs. Ferrars' favouritism, unfairness, and emotional
blackmail create tension between the two brothers and appall members of their social circle. John Dashwood exclaims in horror: 'Can
anything be more galling to the spirit of a man . . . than to see his
younger brother in possession of an estate which might have been
his own?' (*SS*, p. 269). The prodigal son Robert, full of gay uncon-
cern, cares not about his brother's suffering. Elinor notices Robert's
'happy self-complacency . . . while enjoying so unfair a division of
his mother's love and liberality, to the prejudice of his banished
brother, earned only by his own dissipated course of life, and
that brother's integrity' (*SS*, p. 298). Robert laughs immoderately
and indulges in *Schadenfreude* at the news about Edward's living

at Delaford: 'The idea of Edward's being a clergyman, and living in a small parsonage-house, diverted him beyond measure; – and when to that was added the fanciful imagery of Edward reading prayers in a white surplice, and publishing the banns of marriage between John Smith and Mary Brown, he could conceive nothing more ridiculous' (*SS*, p. 298).

Money and property constitute the major source of dissension between Robert and Edward, but they also become rivals in romantic matters. When Robert first meets Lucy, he superciliously remarks that she is an awkward, unsophisticated, uncaptivating country girl. Later on, however, he takes a greater interest in her, especially when Lucy begins to take an interest in him, and, instead of talking of Edward, they talk only of Robert, 'a subject on which [Robert] had always more to say than on any other' (*SS*, p. 376). The fact that Edward is apparently taken with Lucy adds to her charms in Robert's eyes. Robert avenges himself on his virtuous brother by marrying Edward's fiancée. Unrepentant for his unbrotherly conduct, he meets with just deserts – he 'wins' the selfish, shallow, cold-hearted Lucy. Still, he is 'proud of his conquest, proud of tricking Edward, and very proud of marrying privately without his mother's consent' (*SS*, p. 376).

Variations on the paradigm of the prodigal son can be traced in other of Austen's novels. In *Northanger Abbey* and *Mansfield Park*, roles are reversed. The younger son is virtuous and concerned with the family honour and reputation, while the elder is dissipated and reckless. In *Northanger Abbey*, Henry Tilney fulfills the role of the dutiful son and Captain Tilney that of the prodigal son. The significant characteristic of the prodigal son is irresponsibility, and this is manifested in Captain Tilney's thoughtless flirtation with the engaged Isabella Thorpe as well as in his disregard for filial duty and respect. Another candidate for the role of the prodigal son in *Northanger Abbey* is John Thorpe; in his behaviour he resembles the prodigal son in the parable who strays from home and returns only after he has wasted all his funds with riotous living. John Thorpe also abdicates his fraternal role in that he shows no respect for his family. After a long absence from his relatives, John slightly and carelessly touches Isabella's hand and rudely tells Catherine that he did not come to Bath to drive his sisters around and look like a fool. He bestows affection on his mother by publically telling her that she looks like an 'old witch' and on his sisters by observing that they both look ugly. Like Henry Crawford, John Thorpe is faulted as a brother for his disregard for the sanctity of the home and dislike of a permanent abode.

In *Sense and Sensibility*, Mrs. Ferrars wrongs her elder son by overlooking his integrity and by possessing a strong attachment to the younger, less deserving sibling, perhaps because he resembles her. But in *Mansfield Park*, the sense of unfairness to the younger brother works two ways. Austen faults Sir Thomas as a parent; he fails to punish Tom for his extravagance and only begins to appreciate Edmund's worthiness at the end of the novel. For his part, Edmund lacks the power to do anything about his situation because the tradition of primogeniture thwarts him. When Sir Thomas reprimands Tom for robbing his brother Edmund of more than half the income which ought to be his, 'Tom listened with some shame and some sorrow; but escaping as quickly as possible, could soon with cheerful selfishness reflect, 1st, that he had not been half so much in debt as some of his friends; 2dly, that his father had made a most tiresome piece of work of it; and 3dly, that the future incumbent, whoever he might be, would, in all probability, die very soon' (*MP*, p. 24).

By way of contrast, Edmund is as generous and considerate as Tom is selfish and irresponsible. When Tom becomes ill, Edmund rushes to his brother's bedside. Fanny's estimation of Edmund rises even higher when she sees him as the 'attendant, supporter, and cheerer of a suffering brother' (*MP*, p. 430). The prodigal son motif reappears later on in *Mansfield Park* in that the elder son repents after his catastrophic illness, much as the biblical prodigal son admits and atones for his sins. While Robert Ferrars remains incorrigible even at the end of *Sense and Sensibility*, in *Mansfield Park* Tom rejoins the family and becomes a steadier, more dutiful, less selfish son and brother. Indeed, as we have already noted, Tom participates in the incestuous movement in the novel: it seems likely at the end that he will marry his cousin Susan to complete the picture of in-family domestic happiness after his brother marries his cousin Fanny.

The paradigm of the prodigal son is also apparent, in some senses, in *Pride and Prejudice*. Intense rivalry and antagonism exist between Darcy and Wickham, who would seem to fulfill the roles of the dutiful elder son and the prodigal younger son. Wickham is not Darcy's blood brother, but he is Mr. Darcy's godson. Brought up like brothers, Wickham and Darcy were 'companion[s] from childhood, *connected together ... in the closest manner*'. Wickham tells Elizabeth: 'We were born in the same parish, within the same park, the greatest part of our youth was passed together; inmates of the same house, sharing the same amusements, *objects of the same parental care'* (*PP*, p. 124, italics added). Like the elder son in the biblical story, Darcy becomes angry at his father's fondness and high opinion of the undeserving Wickham. Wickham claims that Mr. Darcy's uncommon attachment to him irritated Darcy: '[Darcy] had not a temper to bear the sort of competition in which we stood – the sort of preference which was often given me' (*PP*, pp. 123–4). As a young man of about the same age and almost as close to Wickham as a brother, Darcy has the opportunity to see Wickham in unguarded moments when he reveals a vicious side to his nature. Darcy resents his father's love for the wastrel Wickham and sees him as a threat to his position.

Austen deviates from the biblical paradigm in that the prodigal son, Wickham, does not repent for his sins, and the father figure, who is willing to forgive his foster son's excesses, perishes. In his will, Mr. Darcy recommends his son to promote Wickham's advancement, and, if Wickham should take clerical orders, to give a valuable family living to Wickham as soon as it becomes vacant. The tension between the foster-brothers is clear: the dutiful son feels obliged to recognise the prodigal son only because of his father's wishes, but in reality he distrusts and finds his brother illaudable. Moreover, after a certain point, the true and deserving elder son Darcy is unwilling to help the younger son. Darcy gives the idle, dissipated Wickham a generous sum of money, but refuses to hand him the living. For Austen, charity only goes so far, and she prizes those who show sense and discrimination in their benevolence. Not only is Wickham unrepentant for his extravagance and dissipation, he proves himself ungrateful and objectionable by his cruel behaviour. Out of resentment and a desire for revenge, Wickham schemes to elope with and acquire the fortune of Georgiana Darcy, who loves him because her 'heart retained a strong impression of [Wickham's] kindness to her as a child' (*PP*, p. 231). His plot fails, and he is banished from the family circle at Pemberton. But he continues to persecute his foster-brother by criticizing and violently abusing Darcy in public and by telling lies about Georgiana.

Ironically, Darcy and Wickham become brothers-in-law (with Darcy's help) at the end of the novel. Darcy must learn to suppress his feelings not only in his relationship with his vulgar mother-in-law and silly sisters-in-law, but also against 'a sentiment so natural as abhorrence against a relationship with Wickham. Brother-in-law of Wickham! Every kind of pride must revolt from the connection' (*PP*, p. 338). In this regard, Mr. Bennet makes a telling comment about Darcy, Bingley, and Wickham: 'I adore all my three sons-in-law highly . . . Wickham, perhaps, is my favourite' (*PP*, p. 387). To be sure, Mr. Bennet has no sensible reason for favouring the unrepentant Wickham, because his other sons-in-law are virtuous, dutiful, and conscientious. But his delight in irony and the absurd overshadows his true paternal responsibility. His attitude highlights the importance not only of the need for good intentions on the part of the son, but also of the need for a strong parental figure to create the right environment for familial strength.

In *Emma*, Austen presents two brothers who are dutiful not only to their family but also to each other. Both have an admirable fondness for domestic peace and tranquillity. John and George Knightley are undemonstrative but loyal siblings who possess the 'true English style [of brothers], burying under a calmness that seemed all but indifference, the real attachment which would have led either of them, if requisite, to do every thing for the good of the other' (*E*, pp. 99–100). Their relationship would seem to be almost a utopian vision of how brothers ought to behave – that is to say, with genuine affection for each other and good sense with regard to their family.

In both *Persuasion* and *Sanditon*, the family structures are, for the most part, fragmented and neurotic. In *Persuasion*, Wentworth and Anne establish ties with his siblings only and, more importantly, they go *outside* the family and become part of the brotherhood of the navy. Charles Musgrove seems to fulfill the role of the dutiful elder son in his family, but he is inconsiderate and shallow and lacks the integrity of other dutiful sons, such as Edward Ferrars, Henry Tilney, Edmund Bertram, and John and George Knightley. Moreover, Austen scathingly attacks the Musgroves' late prodigal son, who is described as 'thick-headed, unfeeling, unprofitable Dick Musgrove, who had never done anything to entitle himself to more than the abbreviation of his name, living or dead' (*P*, p. 51).

The strength of family structures seems to become still more attenuated in *Sanditon*, which Austen had intended to call *The Brothers*. Austen expresses doubt as to the continuance of a vigorous family estate, nurtured and protected by a strong, dutiful son and brother. In this fragment, there is a *reductio ad absurdum* version of the paradigm of the prodigal son. The brother who seems to fulfill the role of the dutiful elder son is disoriented, eccentric, and foolish.

Tom Parker, the enthusiastic property-dealer, is a family man and fond of his wife, children, and siblings. Although sanguine and gentlemanly, he has far more imagination than judgement. Two brothers appear to be possible candidates for the role of the prodigal son. Sidney Parker, who appears only at the end of the narrative, is lively, clever, satirical, and mocking. He travels a great deal and apparently, like Henry Crawford and John Thorpe, has an aversion to a permanent abode. The other candidate for the prodigal son, Arthur, is a sickly, indolent creature rather than an extravagant, rakish wanderer. The disorientation, cynicism, and hypochondria of the brothers may be seen as a familial and social symptom; no clear deserving and dutiful heir emerges to control and defend the best interests and peace of the home.

Austen probes and transgresses inherited literary plots, motifs, and formulae in her manipulation of brother/sister, sister/sister, and brother/brother relations. In pirating the Cinderella myth, for example, Austen calls into question the conventional fictional prescription for marital happiness while averring the possibility of a fantasy-like union in which sisters play a key part. Likewise, in exploiting a well-established biblical analogue of the prodigal son, Austen opens the roles and responsibilities of brothers to negotiation. In contrast to the tensions stirred up by fraternal rivalries over property, wealth, and birthright, Austen proposes the concordance of idealized sibships, which, as we have noted, are often formed through in-family marriages. Amalgamating male and female values and dynamics, these configurations of brothers and sisters illuminate and reappraise the meaning of the general criteria for 'marriage.' The sibships modify and surpass the traditional narrative closure and proffer a vision of social restitution.

Notes

CHAPTER 1 INTRODUCTION

1. Marilyn Butler, 'History, Politics, and Religion' in J. David Grey, A. Walton Litz, and Brian Southam (eds), *The Jane Austen Companion* (New York: Macmillan, 1986), p. 198. For a classic 'subversive' reading of Austen's work, see for example Marvin Mudrick, *Jane Austen: Irony as Defense and Discovery* (Princeton: Princeton University Press, 1952). See also Mary Evans, *Jane Austen and the State* (London: Tavistock Publications, 1987). Evans disputes Austen's alleged conservatism and argues that she 'advances a radical critique of the morality of bourgeois capitalism'.
2. For useful analyses of sibling relationships and childrearing practices during the late eighteenth and early nineteenth centuries, see Lawrence Stone, *The Family, Sex, and Marriage in England 1500–1800* (New York: Harper and Row, 1977), pp. 115–16, 266, 449–80, 669–72; Randolph Trumbach, *The Rise of the Egalitarian Family* (New York: Academic Press, 1978), pp. 224–29, 239–42; and Priscilla Robertson, 'Home as a Nest: Middle-Class Childhood in Nineteenth-Century Europe' in *The History of Childhood*, ed. Lloyd deMause (New York: Psychohistory Press, 1974), pp. 414–23.
3. See Walter Houghton, *The Victorian Frame of Mind* (New Haven: Yale University Press, 1957), pp. 341–8 for a fuller discussion of Victorian attitudes toward home and the family.
4. Evans, p. 76.
5. V. S. Pritchett, *George Meredith and English Comedy* (New York: Random House, 1970), p. 28.
6. See John Halperin, *The Life of Jane Austen* (Baltimore, MD: Johns Hopkins University Press, 1984), pp. 17, 52–9.
7. For further discussion of this period in English history, see J. H. Plumb, *Georgian Delights* (Boston: Little, Brown and Company, 1980); Warren Roberts, *Jane Austen and the French Revolution* (New York: St. Martin's Press, 1979); G. E. Mingay, *The Gentry: The Rise and Fall of a Ruling Class* (London: Longman, 1976); E. P. Thompson, *The Making of the English Working Class* (Harmondsworth, Middlesex: Penguin, 1968); and David Thomson, *England in the Nineteenth Century* (Harmondsworth, Middlesex: Penguin, 1978), pp. 11–19.
8. B. C. Southam (ed.), *Jane Austen: The Critical Heritage* (London: Routledge and Kegan Paul, 1968), p. 128.

CHAPTER 2 ANTECEDENTS AND SUCCESSORS

1. Sigmund Freud, *Totem and Taboo*, trans. by James Strachey (New York: W. W. Norton, 1950), pp. 5–6.

2. Freud, *Totem and Taboo*, pp. 6–7. See also J. G. Frazer, *Totemism and Exogamy* (London, 1910) on the universality of the incest prohibition and the importance that primitive societies, as well as civilized, attached to it, and Claude Lévi-Strauss, *The Elementary Structures of Kinship*, rev. edn, trans. James Bell *et al.* (Boston: Beacon Press, 1969) on the concomitance of the development of the incest prohibition with that of culture.

3. This book does not incorporate the analyses of anthropologists Richard Handler and Daniel Segal, whose book, *Jane Austen and the Fiction of Culture* (Tucson: University of Arizona Press, 1990), was published while my manuscript was in production. Handler and Segal's work would seem to support and reaffirm my own argument since they stress that Austen's texts 'implicitly examine the [incest] taboo, even in the word's absence' (p. 40). Adopting an ethnographic approach, they claim that 'Austen's heroines make decisions about marriage that fail to conform to the most generally held suppositions about courtship, romance, advantage, and marriage itself . . . . the heroines' marriages should be regarded not as antisocial behavior but . . . as alter-cultural. It is not that these marriages violate social rules . . . rather, they call into question the criteria which, in general, distinguish the category *marriageable* from the category *nonmarriageable*' (pp. 86–7).

4. See Jean-Louis Flandrin on consanguinity, matrimonial alliance, and spiritual kinship in *Families in Former Times* (London: Cambridge University Press, 1979), pp. 19–23. The assimilation of affinity to consanguinity derived from the concept that husband and wife, although they were not related, were 'as one,' or 'of one flesh'. That is, when a man and a woman married, they assumed each other's relationships, using the same terms for the same individuals with the addition of 'in-law' or 'step'. See Sybil Wolfram, *In-Laws and Outlaws: Kinship and Marriage in England* (New York: St. Martin's Press, 1987), pp. 16–7, 64–5.

5. See Trumbach's discussion of prohibited degrees of marriage in *The Rise of the Egalitarian Family*, pp. 18–33 and Wolfram's commentary on incest, pp. 21–51. It is also worth noting here that Jane Austen's brother Charles remarried Harriet Palmer, the sister of his deceased wife Frances Fitzwilliam Palmer, in 1820. Critics speculate that biographers J. H. and E. B. Hubback may have stinted in their treatment of Charles in *Jane Austen's Sailor Brothers* (London: Bodley Head, 1906) because Charles had committed what was regarded by Victorians as an incestuous crime. See, for example, J. David Grey, 'Our Little Brother' in *Persuasions*, 3 (1981) 9–11.

6. See also Wolfram on the extended in-law relationships between the relatives of a husband and wife in *In-laws and Outlaws*, pp. 65–6. Even in the late nineteenth century, the term in-law was loosely used to apply to individuals connected by marriage. In Trollope's *Dr. Wortle's School* (1880), Robert Lefroy asks Mr. Peacocke, 'Are you my brother-in-law, or are you not?' (Chapter 7). Robert Lefroy is the brother of Ferdinand Lefroy, Mrs. Peacocke's first husband.

After Ferdinand supposedly died, Mrs. Peacocke remarried. Thus, Robert alludes to his former relationship with Mrs. Peacocke and even attempts to extend his family circle for mercenary reasons by addressing his former sister-in-law's present husband as his brother-in-law.

7. Freud, *Totem and Taboo*, p. 7.
8. See Paula Marantz Cohen, 'Stabilizing the Family System at Mansfield Park', *English Literary History*, 54 (Fall 1987) 671.
9. For a list of eighteenth-century novels dealing with the subject of incest, see J. M. S. Tompkins, *The Popular Novel in England, 1770–1800* (Lincoln: University of Nebraska Press, 1961), p. 66. See also Montague Summers, *The Gothic Quest: A History of the Gothic Novel* (London: Fortune Press, 1938), pp. 391–2 for a list of gothic novels which deal with incest and Sandra Sandell '"A Very Poetic Circumstance": Incest and the English Literary Imagination, 1770–1830', unpublished dissertation, University of Minnesota, 1981, pp. 11–29 for useful insights into the incest motif, especially in Sir Walter Scott's *The Antiquary*.
10. Interest in incest reached towering heights in the eighteenth century, but it was no means a new subject in literature. The issue of incest and its prohibition is an important subject in three of the seventeenth-century plays of Dryden, *Don Sebastian* (1689), *Oedipus* (1679), and *Love Triumphant* (1694). For more information on the preromantic treatment of incest in literature, especially in Milton, Ford, Dryden, and Otway's *The Orphan* (1680), see Jean H. Hagstrum, *Sex and Sensibility: Ideal and Erotic Love from Milton to Mozart* (Chicago: University of Chicago Press, 1980), pp. 41–5, 54–8, 93–5.
11. See Nancy Fix Anderson, 'Cousin Marriage in Victorian England', *Journal of Family History*, 11 (1986) 286–7.
12. This was particularly so in the case of the Romantic poets and their sisters, for example, William and Dorothy Wordsworth. See James B. Twitchell, *Forbidden Partners: The Incest Taboo in Modern Culture* (New York: Columbia University Press, 1987), p. 98.
13. Percy Bysshe Shelley, *Letters of Percy Bysshe Shelley*, ed. Frederick Jones (Oxford: Clarendon Press, 1964), Vol. 2, p. 154.
14. Hagstrum, p. 180.
15. See Wolfram on Reformation changes in prohibited degrees of marriage, pp. 23–30.
16. Frances Sheridan, *Memoirs of Mrs. Sidney Bidulph* (New York: Pandora Press, 1987), p. 114. All further references to this work appear parenthetically in the text.
17. See Wolfram, 'Degree Reckoning in Mourning', pp. 52–63.
18. Margaret Doody, *Frances Burney: The Life in the Works* (New Brunswick: Rutgers University Press, 1988), p. 161.
19. Frances Burney, *Evelina* (London: J.M. Dent, 1967), p. 337. All further references to this work appear parenthetically in the text.
20. Frances Burney, *The Wanderer* (London: Pandora, 1988), p. 107. All further references to this work appear parenthetically in the text.
21. Doody, *Frances Burney*, p. 65.

22. *The Diary and Letters of Madame D'Arblay*, Vol. III (London: H. Colburn, 1854), p. 201.
23. Doody, *Frances Burney*, pp. 105, 161, 277–8.
24. *Jane Austen: A Family Record*, ed. William Austen-Leigh and Richard A. Austen Leigh, rev. by Deirdre Le Faye (Boston: G.K. Hall, 1989), pp. 25, 91.
25. On *Evelina*, see *Letters*, pp. 180, 388, 438; on *Camilla*, see pp. 9, 13, 14. Austen also makes allusions to Burney's *Cecilia* and *The Wanderer*, pp. 254, 334.
26. On this subject, see for example, Marilyn Butler, *Jane Austen and the War of Ideas* (Oxford: Clarendon Press, 1975); Mary Poovey, *The Proper Lady and the Woman Writer: Ideology as Style in the Works of Mary Wollstonecraft, Mary Shelley, and Jane Austen* (Chicago: University of Chicago Press, 1984); and Claudia Johnson, *Jane Austen: Women, Politics, and the Novel* (Chicago: University of Chicago Press, 1988).
27. See Margaret Doody, 'Jane Austen's Reading' in J. David Grey (ed.) *The Jane Austen Companion*, pp. 360–1.
28. See *Letters*, p. 173.
29. In his deconstructionist reading of *Mansfield Park*, David Musselwhite argues that the hard-headed Austen was obsessed with making money from her fiction, and that this novel was written to appeal to a much broader audience, that of the 'urban and industrious' middle class, by using the sensationalist formula of *Lovers' Vows*. See David Musselwhite, *Partings Welded Together: Politics and Desire in the Nineteenth-Century English Novel* (London: Methuen, 1987), pp. 16–42. I am more struck by how Austen incorporates the bestselling formula of sensationalism in the shape of incest in her work, and how she undermines and desensationalizes it.
30. In Radcliffe's *The Romance of the Forest* (1791), for example, Adeline is pursued by her uncle and surrogate father, the Marquis of Montalt.
31. See Gary Kelly, *English Fiction of the Romantic Period, 1789–1830* (London: Longman, 1989), p. 115.
32. See William Patrick Day's commentary on siblings in American gothic novels in *In the Circles of Fear and Desire: A Study of Gothic Fantasy* (Chicago: University of Chicago Press, 1985), pp. 125–9.
33. Tompkins, pp. 62–3. See also Alan Richardson on the distinctions between sibling love in the eighteenth-century novel and in English Romantic poetry in 'The Dangers of Sympathy: Sibling Incest in English Romantic Poetry', *Studies in English Literature*, 25 (1985) 737–754.
34. N. I. White, *Shelley*, II (1940; New York: Octagon, 1972), pp. 422–3.
35. Much of what I say here and in the following paragraphs is indebted to Twitchell's discussion of Romantic art in *Forbidden Partners*, pp. 77–126.
36. Twitchell, p. 80.
37. Twitchell, p. 119.
38. Twitchell, p. 126.
39. *Letters*, p. 379.
40. Twitchell, p. 119.

41. Susan Morgan, *Sisters in Time: Imagining Gender in Nineteeth-Century British Fiction* (Oxford: Oxford University Press, 1989), p. 39. Morgan is referring here to the romantic attitudes in general of Austen's heroes and heroines. I take Morgan's point even further and argue more specifically that the relationships of many of Austen's heroes and heroines are relatively equal because they are rooted in intense sibling-like relationships.

42. See Jack Goody, *The Development of the Family and Marriage in Europe* (London: Cambridge University Press, 1983), p. 33. For the canon law forbidding first cousin marriage in the Orthodox Church, see *The Pedalion of St. Nicodemus* (Athens, Greece: Astir, 1957), p. 741.

43. Trumbach, p. 19.

44. See Anderson, p. 286.

45. Thomas Hardy, *The Well-Beloved*, New Wessex Edition (London: Macmillan, 1975), p. 160. All further references to this work appear parenthetically in the text.

46. See, for example, Robert Gittings, *The Young Thomas Hardy* (Boston: Little, Brown and Company, 1975), pp. 111–25, 216–17, and John Fowles, 'Hardy and the Hag' in Lance St. John Butler (ed.) *Thomas Hardy after Fifty Years* (London: Macmillan, 1977), pp. 34, 38–9.

47. See J. Hillis Miller on Hardy's debt to Shelley in his essay on *The Well-Beloved* in *Fiction and Repetition: Seven English Novels* (Cambridge, MA: Harvard University Press, 1982), pp. 147–8.

48. On the debate over inbreeding in the second half of the nineteenth century, see Anderson, pp. 291–297.

49. On Darwin's influence on Hardy, see George Levine, *Darwin and the Novelists: Patterns of Science in Victorian Fiction* (Cambridge, MA: Harvard University Press, 1988), pp. 22, 227–34, 239 and Roger Ebbatson, *The Evolutionary Self: Hardy, Forster, Lawrence* (Brighton: Harvester Press, 1982), pp. 1–40.

50. Thomas Hardy, *Jude the Obscure* (Harmondsworth, Middlesex: Penguin, 1978), p. 137.

51. Richard Steele in *The Spectator*, ed. Donald F. Bond (Oxford: Clarendon Press, 1965), 496 (1712), Vol. IV, p. 260, as quoted in Trumbach, p. 21.

52. Francis Hutcheson, *A System of Moral Philosophy*, Vol. 2 (New York: Augustus Kelley, 1968), p. 172.

53. *Encyclopedia Britannica*, 'Cousin Marriage', 1981 edn.

CHAPTER 3   INCESTUOUS SIBLING RELATIONSHIPS: *MANSFIELD PARK, EMMA* AND *SENSE AND SENSIBILITY*

1. Elizabeth Jenkins, 'Address' to the General Meeting of the Jane Austen Society (Report for the Year 1980), p. 26.

2. Such a marriage was regarded very differently in nineteenth-century Russia. A man's sister or brother could not marry his wife's brother or sister since they were regarded as relatives. For example, in

Tolstoy's *War and Peace* (1866), if Natasha had married Prince Andrew, his sister Maria would not have been able to wed Natasha's brother Nicholas. See Wolfram, *Inlaws and Outlaws*, pp. 66, 75.

3.   R. F. Brissenden, '*Mansfield Park*: Freedom and the Family' in John Halperin (ed.), *Jane Austen: Bicentenary Essays* (Cambridge: Cambridge University Press, 1975), p. 169.

4.   Julia Prewitt Brown, 'The Victorian Anxieties of *Mansfield Park*' in *Jane Austen's Novels: Social Change and Literary Form* (Cambridge, MA: Harvard University Press, 1979), p. 99.

5.   Claudia L. Johnson, *Jane Austen: Women, Politics, and the Novel* (Chicago: University of Chicago Press, 1988), p. 119.

6.   Johanna H. Smith, '"My Only Sister Now": Incest in *Mansfield Park*', *Studies in the Novel*, 19 (1987) 1.

7.   See Brissenden, p. 169; Brown, p. 99; Johnson, p. 115; and Smith, p. 2.

8.   As several critics have noted, in *Mansfield Park*, Austen tries to come to terms with a new social reality. See Brown, pp. 80–100, and Avrom Fleishman, *A Reading of Mansfield Park: An Essay in Critical Synthesis* (Minneapolis: University of Minnesota Press, 1967), pp. 19–42.

9.   Smith, p. 13.

10.   Brissenden, p. 166.

11.   Anderson, p. 286.

12.   There is clearly an autobiographical reference here. Jane Austen's sailor brother Charles brought back a topaz cross on a gold chain from one of his sailing expeditions in 1801. The brother's gift in real life becomes the cousin's gift in the novel. See Halperin, *Life*, p. 236.

13.   See Marilyn Butler, *Romantics, Rebels and Reactionaries* (Oxford: Oxford University Press, 1981), pp. 98–103, for a more detailed discussion of Austen's attitude towards social changes, especially the centrifugal movement within communities.

14.   Austen followed the fates of the Prince Regent and his estranged wife Princess Caroline with fascination. The novelist supported the Princess and strongly disapproved of the scandalous affairs and lax morals of the future George IV and his court; however, she grudgingly dedicated *Emma* to the Prince Regent, who was a great patron of the arts and an ardent admirer of Austen's novels, at the request of his librarian, the Reverend James Stanier Clarke. See Halperin, *Life*, pp. 215, 282–3.

15.   Huang Mei, *Transforming the Cinderella Dream: From Frances Burney to Charlotte Bronte* (New Brunswick: Rutgers University Press, 1990), p. 80.

16.   Alistair M. Duckworth, *The Improvement of the Estate: A Study of Jane Austen's Novels* (Baltimore: Johns Hopkins University Press, 1971), pp. 54–5.

17.   See Fleishman, pp. 24–9, on the foreign source and radical content of *Lovers' Vows*.

18.   See Butler, *Jane Austen and the War of Ideas*, p. 232.

19. See also Musselwhite who contends that *Mansfield Park* derives its characters from the dramatis personae in *Lovers' Vows*, pp. 25–6.
20. Fleishman, p. 65.
21. Cohen, p. 686.
22. Brown, p. 99.
23. Johnson, p. 114.
24. John Halperin compares Mary Crawford to Becky Sharp and Milton's Satan and points out that, as in Thackeray's *Vanity Fair* and Milton's *Paradise Lost*, Austen's moral perspective on false values never wavers. See 'The Novelist as Heroine in *Mansfield Park*: A Study in Autobiography', *Modern Language Quarterly* 44 (1983) 137.
25. Juliet McMaster, *Jane Austen on Love* (Victoria, B.C.: English Literary Studies, 1978), p. 61. McMaster also notes that pedagogic relationships between heroes and heroines act as aphrodisiacs in Austen's novels and have both emotional and sexual implications.
26. See McMaster, p. 58.
27. For a contrasting argument to my own, see Sandra Gilbert and Susan Gubar, *The Madwoman in the Attic* (New Haven: Yale University Press, 1979). The authors argue that 'the happy ending of an Austen novel occurs when the girl becomes a daughter to her husband' (p. 154).

CHAPTER 4   SISTERHOOD, EDUCATION AND MARRIAGE

1. Gilbert and Gubar, pp. 156, 162.
2. Kelly, p. 123.
3. Gilbert and Gubar, pp. 154, 160–3, 168.
4. On Austen as a subversive feminist, see Allison G. Sulloway, *Jane Austen and the Province of Womanhood* (Philadelphia: University of Pennsylvania Press, 1989) and Mary Evans in *Jane Austen and the State*, who views Austen's novels as a radical challenge to a 'self-interested patriarchy' (p. 53).
5. Susan Sniader Lanser points out that 'Austen creates double plots in the early novels, generating marriages for the women that preserve their sisterhood,' but adds that she betrays 'ambivalence at giving sisterhood the last and unconventional word' (a claim I will later dispute). See '"No Connections Subsequent": Jane Austen's World of Sisterhood' in Toni A. H. McNaron (ed.), *The Sister Bond: A Feminist View of A Timeless Connection* (New York: Pergamon, Athene Series, 1985), pp. 54, 57. Also on the subject of sisterhood, Christine Peters remarks that '[W]hile an Austen heroine needs a husband, a man is not enough' and argues for 'a broader definition of the marital bond'. See 'Jane Austen's Creation of the Sister', *Philogical Quarterly* 66 (Fall 1987) 474. And Nina Auerbach comments on the 'purgatorial existence' female relatives lead in Austen's fiction, a very different point of view to my own. See *Communities of Women: An Idea in Fiction* (Cambridge, MA: Harvard University Press, 1978), p. 47.

6. Halperin, *Life*, pp. 351–2.
7. Halperin, *Life*, p. 23.
8. James Edward Austen-Leigh, *Memoir of Jane Austen* (Oxford: Clarendon Press, 1926), p. 17.
9. Carroll Smith-Rosenberg, 'The Female World of Love and Ritual: Relationships between Women in Nineteenth-Century America', *Signs* 1 (1975) 1–29. Much of what I say in this paragraph is indebted to Smith-Rosenberg's discussion of the ties between sisters.
10. On the similarities between female relationships in England and the United States, see Linda Hunt's *A Woman's Portion: Ideology, Culture, and the British Female Novel Tradition* (New York: Garland, 1988), pp. 49–50.
11. Smith-Rosenberg, pp. 27–28.
12. Lillian Faderman, *Surpassing the Love of Men: Romantic Friendship and Love between Women from the Renaissance to the Present* (New York: William Morrow and Company, 1981), p. 427.
13. Smith-Rosenberg argues that, from a twentieth-century perspective, such relationships seem paradoxically 'sensual and platonic' (p. 4). To understand the context of sororal relationships in the late eighteenth and early nineteenth centuries, we should realize that such distinctions were alien, that sexual and emotional responses were viewed as 'part of a continuum . . . of affect gradations' (pp. 28–9).
14. Quotation from Jane Aiken Hodge, *Only A Novel: The Double Life of Jane Austen* (New York: Howard, McCann and Geoghegan, 1972), p. 114.
15. Park Honan, *Jane Austen: Her Life* (New York: St. Martin's Press, 1987), pp. 36–7.
16. Halperin, *Life*, p. 64.
17. Halperin, *Life*, pp. 71, 133–4, 162.
18. Halperin, *Life*, pp. 133–5.
19. Gilbert and Gubar, p. 156.
20. The date of the composition of *Lady Susan* is disputed, but it most probably belongs to the years 1793–4, the period of the late Juvenilia. See Brian Southam, *Jane Austen's Literary Manuscripts: A Study of the Novelist's Development through the Surviving Papers* (Oxford: Oxford University Press, 1964), Chapter 3.
21. Auerbach, pp. 39, 55; Judith Lowder Newton, *Women, Power, and Subversion* (Athens, GA: University of Georgia Press, 1980), p. 169.
22. Lanser, "No Connections Subsequent", in McNaron (ed.) *The Sister Bond*, p. 57.
23. Tony Tanner, *Jane Austen* (Cambridge, Mass.: Harvard University Press, 1986), pp. 78–9.
24. See for example Everett Zimmerman's commentary on Willoughby's interview with Elinor in 'Admiring Pope no more than is proper: *Sense and Sensibility'* in Halperin (ed.), *Jane Austen: Bicentenary Essays*, pp. 112–22.
25. Margaret Kirkham, *Jane Austen: Feminism and Fiction* (Brighton: Harvester, 1983) pp. 86–7. See also Kenneth Moler, *Jane Austen's Art of Allusion* (Lincoln: University of Nebraska Press, 1968), pp. 44–6, 61.

26.   Edmund Wilson, 'A Long Talk About Jane Austen' in Ian Watt
       (ed.), *Jane Austen: A Collection of Critical Essays* (Englewood Cliffs,
       NJ: Prentice Hall, 1963), p. 39.
27.   Halperin, *Life*, pp. 60–2, 65, 83.
28.   Tanner, p. 100.
29.   The composition of *Northanger Abbey* is disputed, but it seems likely
       that this novel was Austen's third, written between 1798 and 1799,
       revised over a period of several years, and published posthumously
       in 1818. Austen's novels may be divided into two sets of three
       novels – the first and the second 'trilogies'. *Pride and Prejudice, Sense
       and Sensibility,* and *Northanger Abbey* were composed between 1796
       and 1799 when Austen was in her early twenties. The novels of
       the second trilogy – *Mansfield Park, Emma,* and *Persuasion* – were
       composed between 1811 and 1816 when the author was in her mid
       to late thirties. See Halperin, *Life*, p. 57.
30.   Janet Todd, *Women's Friendship in Literature* (New York: Columbia
       University Press, 1980), pp. 306–7.
31.   Lanser makes a similar point in '"No Connections Subsequent"', in
       McNaron (ed.), *The Sister Bond*, p. 61.
32.   McMaster notes that Henry shares some characteristics with Henry
       Higgins, and that Catherine represents Galatea, pp. 47–8. See also
       Laura G. Mooneyham on Henry's role in Catherine's education in
       Romance, Language and Education in Jane Austen's Novels (New York:
       St. Martin's Press, 1988), pp. 17–22.
33.   Susan Morgan, 'Guessing for Ourselves in *Northanger Abbey*' in
       Harold Bloom (ed.) *Modern Critical Views: Jane Austen* (New York:
       Chelsea House Publishers, 1986), pp. 112–13.
34.   Joseph Wiesenfarth makes the same point about the word "elegant"
       and its origins but applies it to an exploration of language in *Emma*.
       See *'Emma*: Point Counter Point' in Halperin (ed.), *Bicentenary Essays*,
       p. 210.
35.   Peters, p. 475.
36.   Cassandra regularly visited her brother Edward at Godmersham,
       especially during his wife Elizabeth's numerous confinements. After
       Elizabeth died of childbirth in 1808, Cassandra spent months with
       Edward looking after his children. Austen wrote many letters to her
       sister during her absences, in which she expressed her feelings of
       loneliness without Cassandra. See Halperin, *Life*, pp. 156, 165–8.
37.   Halperin, *Life*, pp. 137, 140–1.
38.   Austen-Leigh, *Memoir*, p. 364.
39.   See Gilbert and Gubar on the similarities between and antithetical
       responses of Fanny and Mary, pp. 164–67.
40.   Joseph Wiesenfarth, 'Austen and Apollo', in *Jane Austen Today*,
       ed. Joel Weinsheimer (Athens: University of Georgia Press, 1975),
       p. 60.
41.   Peters, p. 492.

CHAPTER 5   FAIRY GODMOTHERS AND UGLY SISTERS: THE CINDERELLA THEME IN AUSTEN'S FICTION

1. See Huang Mei's chapter, 'Cinderella as the Paragon' in *Transforming the Cinderella Dream*, pp. 1–30, on Richardson's formulation of the Cinderella novel convention and his subsequent influence, in this respect, on eighteenth- and nineteenth-century women writers.
2. Huang Mei, p. 67.
3. Huang Mei, p. 38.
4. Huang Mei, pp. 32–3, 56, 69.
5. See D. W. Harding, 'Regulated Hatred: An Aspect of the Work of Jane Austen', in Watt (ed.), *Jane Austen: A Collection of Critical Essays*, p. 173; Fleishman, p. 64; Wiesenfarth in Halperin (ed.), *Bicentenary Essays*, p. 216; and Derek Brewer, 'Mainly on Jane Austen,' chap. in *Symbolic Stories: Traditional Narratives of the Family Drama in English Literature* (Totowa, NJ: Rowman and Littlefield, 1980), p. 149.
6. Gilbert and Gubar, pp. 36–39, 156.
7. Harding, 'Regulated Hatred,' in Watt (ed.), *Jane Austen: A Collection of Critical Essays*, p. 173.
8. Brewer also notes: '[e]xogamy is the rule in the European story and life alike. But the pattern is different in Jane Austen's novels' (p. 164).
9. Huang Mei, p. 36.
10. Much of what I say in this and the following paragraphs about the various versions of the Cinderella myth is indebted to Alan Dundes (ed.), *Cinderella: A Folklore Casebook* (New York and London: Garland Publishing, Inc., 1982), pp. 14–29, 294–301. See also Bruno Bettelheim's discussion of sibling rivalry in 'Cinderella' in *The Uses of Enchantment: The Meaning and Importance of Fairy Tales* (New York: Alfred A. Knopf, 1976), pp. 236–77.
11. Newton, p. 73, 80–5.
12. Bettelheim, p. 275.
13. Poovey, p. 200.
14. Michele Barnet (ed.), *Virginia Woolf: Women and Writing* (New York: Harcourt, Brace, Jovanovich, 1979), p. 156.
15. See Harding, 'Regulated Hatred' in Watt (ed.), *Jane Austen: A Collection of Critical Essays*, pp. 176–7.
16. Duckworth, pp. 4–5.
17. Janice Simpson, 'Folk and Fairy Tale in *Mansfield Park*', *Persuasions*, 9 (1987) 26.
18. See Fleishman on the movements, arrivals and departures in *Mansfield Park*, pp. 60–1.
19. See Halperin, *Life*, pp. 237–8.
20. See, for example, Huang Mei, p. 103.
21. Fleishman, p. 60.
22. Wiesenfarth, 'Austen and Apollo' in Weinsheimer (ed.), *Jane Austen Today*, p. 51.
23. Halperin, *Life*, p. 243.
24. A. Walton Litz, for example, claims that *Persuasion* reveals 'a new

allegiance to feeling rather than prudence'. See *'Persuasion*: Forms of Estrangement' in Halperin (ed.), *Bicentenary Essays*, p. 221.
25.   Litz in Halperin (ed.), *Bicentenary Essays*, p. 223.

CHAPTER 6   PATRIMONIAL ISSUE: DUTIFUL AND PRODIGAL BROTHERS

1.   See Trumbach on relations between the eldest and younger sons, *The Rise of the Egalitarian Family*, pp. 77–97. See also Stone on fraternal and sororal relationships, *The Family, Sex, and Marriage*, pp. 115–16, 244, 652.
2.   Trumbach, pp. 87, 96.
3.   Smith-Rosenberg, 'The Female World of Love and Ritual', p. 20.
4.   Of her own six brothers, Austen was most fond in her early years of her youngest brother, Charles, to whom she referred as her 'own particular little brother'. In later years, Henry was her favourite, and he also became her literary advisor. See Halperin, *Life*, pp. 22, 64, 219–20.

Index

The manufacturer's authorised representative in the EU is Springer
Nature Customer Service Centre GmbH, Europaplatz 3, 69115 Heidelberg,
Germany. If you have any concerns regarding our products, please
contact ProductSafety@springernature.com

Printed and bound by CPI Group (UK) Ltd, Croydon, CR0 4YY
23/04/2026
02095595-0014